ROAD KILL

ROAD
KILL

❖

A Dido Hoare Mystery

Marianne Macdonald

THOMAS DUNNE BOOKS
St. Martin's Minotaur
New York

THOMAS DUNNE BOOKS.
An imprint of St. Martin's Press.

ROAD KILL. Copyright © 2000 by Marianne Macdonald.
All rights reserved. Printed in the United States of America.
No part of this book may be used or reproduced in any manner
whatsoever without written permission except in the case of brief
quotations embodied in critical articles or reviews. For information,
address St. Martin's Press, 175 Fifth Avenue, New York, N.Y. 10010.

www.minotaurbooks.com

ISBN 0-312-24234-4

First published in Great Britain by Hodder and Stoughton,
a division of Hodder Headline PLC

First U.S. Edition: September 2000

10 9 8 7 6 5 4 3 2 1

This book is for the masters of the learning curve

David and Andrew Korn

with love

ACKNOWLEDGEMENTS

Thanks are due, as Dido goes from one crisis to another, to all the usual suspects who have given me practical and critical help and support: the readers in both the UK and North America who have advised on earlier drafts (Alex, Andrew, Eric, Hope – you know who you are!); my agent, Jacqueline Korn; the editors at Hodder/NEL, St Martins and HarperCollins, who seem to like my writing even though I know I sometimes try their patience; and all the people who have answered technical questions when I badly needed help, including the fellow-writer who stopped the family's Jeep Cherokee in the car park of a California shopping-mall and dangled herself from the steering wheel, just so we knew it could be done.

CONTENTS

1	After Dark	1
2	Jigsaw Pieces	7
3	Old Spice	13
4	Hard Drive	25
5	Kinds of Message	31
6	Old Acquaintance	43
7	Loyalty Checks	51
8	Looking	65
9	Three Bears	75
10	Contact	83
11	And Goldilocks	89
12	A Nice Place in the Suburbs	93
13	Connections	105
14	Scene of Some Crimes	113
15	Red Light	121
16	Histories	125
17	'★ ★ ★ ★ ★'	133
18	Paperwork	137
19	Skeletons	141
20	Saraband	147
21	Message Delivered	159
22	Jam Tomorrow	165
23	Fishing Trip	175
24	A Window of Opportunity	179
25	Still Running	183

26 Where We Are   189
27 Lal's   195
28 Wrong Tack   203
29 Cold Reality   209
30 Moving Out   219
31 Illusion   225
32 You Make Your Own Luck   233
33 On Balance   241

CHAPTER ONE

After Dark

When I try to remember what happened that night, most of it's a blur. Maybe I was sleepwalking, at the beginning, anyway, because my mental warning buzzer was certainly switched off for a few hours. Then it was simply too late to pull back.

I'd spent most of Monday evening down in the shop, unloading the boxes that I'd brought back from the weekend book fair and starting to reshelve the contents. Book fairs are hard work. I fell into bed at about ten o'clock, too sleepy to bother with the hot bath that my aching muscles wanted, too tired even to close the curtains. I certainly can't remember anything between the time I rolled myself into the duvet and the moment I opened my eyes with an echo telling me that something had just happened or just stopped happening. I focused a bleary eye on the bedside clock. The illuminated numbers claimed that it was just after three, so it was obvious that I ought to be sound asleep. Ben, my baby son, was breathing regularly in the cot across the room. Whatever had woken me hadn't disturbed him.

The room was dim, not dark. The sky in central London never has the real blackness of night-time: not with the city's miles of streetlights, neon signs and headlamps that build up in an orange glow hanging in the polluted air and bouncing off low cloud layers. The gleam from outside my window was bright enough to let me identify the shapes of the big Victorian wardrobe, the chest of drawers, the mound of folded laundry on the little table: everything normal. I told myself I'd only heard some kind of noise in the street. That's normal, too. London doesn't sleep at night.

Then the thought trickled into my mind that I might have forgotten to set the security alarm in the shop before I came upstairs. Perhaps I'd been wakened by the sound of a thief breaking in. Or just some drunk smashing the glass in my display window again. I stiffened, listening. Across the room, Ben stirred.

Something else was moving. The door creaked. I watched it open an inch and heard the footsteps on the carpet, so I was ready for the weight that landed abruptly on the foot of my bed. Mr Spock, my ginger cat, plodded heavily towards the pillow and examined my face with care. I whispered, 'Settle down, cat,' and waited for him to retreat and make himself a nest in the bend of my knees so I could get on with the business of sleeping.

When I'd been lying there stiffly for ten minutes or so, I gave up.

I crept past the cot and down the icy carpet in the hall. In the kitchen, I ran a glass of water and sipped it as I crept into the living room. The curtains here were open, too, with light from the streetlamp shining in brightly enough to let me sidestep the toys scattered on the floor. I slid past the settee to the nearest window and looked out on the silent street where nothing moved.

When I turned around I saw the red light blinking on the answering machine. Somebody had been phoning: that was the noise which had pulled me out of a deep sleep.

Barnabas!

I swooped at the machine, fumbled for the 'play' button. My father is seventy-four, and he has already survived a heart attack. The machine beeped and whirred. I hung over it, my own heart thumping in my throat, and listened to it rewind.

'Dido?'

The voice confused me for a moment. It certainly wasn't my father's.

'Dido, please wake up . . .'

Phyllis! Phyllis Digby, my rock-solid, calm, practical nanny, had spoken in a voice so small and high-pitched that I couldn't mistake panic. It had to be a problem with Frank — Phyllis's middle-aged, invalidish husband. I'd only met him a few times, but he too had health problems, weak lungs. I started to jump to conclusions. The second message was simply, 'It's Phyllis.' The third one was, 'Phyllis again . . .' Her voice was rising.

I switched the machine off and punched her number. The phone was answered on the first ring.

'Phyllis, what's wrong? What is it?'

But she was already speaking. 'Dido, I need help. Can you come?'

My foggy brain was struggling. 'Ben and I can be there in ten minutes. It's all right, Phyllis, don't . . .'

I meant to say, *Don't worry*, but she was talking again: 'I'm sure they've gone, but Dido — just in case, be careful when you come in.'

I blinked, slowly adjusting my ideas. 'Phyllis, what *is* this? I'll phone for the police, or do you need . . . ?'

'No! Please . . .'

No? I opened my mouth. And forced myself to shut it again. Whatever had happened, I'd better go. Eventually I said, 'All right . . . I'll be right over. It's going to be all right,' and hung up. What made me say that?

My clothes were on the floor beside the bed where I'd dumped them a few hours ago. I felt my way into them, laced on my trainers, pulled the old jacket off the hook in the hall, grabbed my keys, then went back and picked Ben up, rolled in his blankets. He was getting heavy. He stirred, and in the light from the hallway I could see his eyelashes flutter. I whispered, 'We're just going for a ride in the car.'

The Digbys' flat was on the top floor of a twelve-unit building about five minutes' drive eastward through these empty, early-morning streets. Power Street is an obscure side road lined with identical, twenty-year-old, brick-built, double-glazed, three-storey blocks, each encircled by patches of litter-strewn grass. I pulled the Citroën up just short of the one I wanted and parked under the dripping branches of an ornamental cherry at the corner of its rain-sodden lawn. From there, by craning, I could look up through the top of the windscreen at my destination. The Digbys' place occupied the right-hand corner on the top floor. The living-room curtains were open, but it was dark inside. I could still hear the odd sound in her voice, though, and I suddenly pictured Phyllis up there, crouching in an armchair, silent, hiding in the dark.

In the baby seat, Ben dozed. 'The question is,' I muttered to him, 'what are we going to do with you? I certainly can't leave you alone in the car. And I certainly can't take you in with me.' On balance, the car option felt safer than the darkened flat. I'd be back in a minute. Feeling guilty anyway, I slid out, set the alarm and locked up. When I looked back through the window he was still sleeping.

Halfway up the front path, I realised exactly what was bothering me: whenever I'd dropped Phyllis off at home after dark, there had always been lights in the entrance hall and up the stairs. Not tonight. Probably there was a time switch? For saving on electricity bills? Would you need to light the stairs all night?

Well, in fact I thought that in a block of flats you would.

My finger was poised over the row of intercom buttons beside the door before I noticed that I had no need to use them to get myself into the building; somebody had left the door wedged slightly open with a rolled-up newspaper. I slid inside and pushed the roll with my toe, letting the door click behind me.

The foot of the stairwell was a rectangle of blackness straight ahead, flanked by the silhouettes of two leggy Swiss cheese plants that were supposed to lend a little distinction to the cramped lobby. I stepped forward. Something crunched. It took me a moment to understand. There should have been a wall light above my head and instead there was broken glass under my shoes. My mind struggled to accept that whatever had frightened Phyllis was real. I pressed my arm against the comforting lump in my coat pocket that was my mobile phone. All I had to do was make sure not to be taken by surprise by anything. Or anybody. If I heard so much as a pin drop, I'd just ring 999 and start yelling for a police car, never mind what Phyllis had said.

On the first landing, another of the wall lights was reduced to its naked metal fixture, but my eyes had adjusted enough to see that the flight ahead was deserted. Presumably Phyllis was right and 'they' were gone. ('*They?*') I pulled my mind away from that and told myself that probably it was safe, as Phyllis had said . . . Oh yes. I crept onwards, wishing I had a weapon. A golf club would be nice, I thought dreamily. Or a double-barrelled shotgun? *Get a grip, Dido!*

The Digbys' door was one of four on the top landing – the one that was standing wide open.

I'd wait here for a bit. *Unless something happens.*

My watch said it was nearly four o'clock. I gave it two minutes. One hundred and twenty seconds. It was so quiet that I could hear the faint rush of water in the central-heating pipes. When my watch eventually confirmed that the time had passed I reminded myself deliberately that the whole building was full of ordinary, kind, sleeping, concerned citizens, and if somebody respectable like me just screamed, they'd all come running. Or I hoped that they would. Anyway, nothing could possibly be going to happen: that was the important thing to hold on to. Since I obviously couldn't turn and leave, it was time to go in.

There was a car moving in the road in front of the building. It didn't stop, and nothing else made any noise except the soles of my trainers squeaking faintly on vinyl tiles. I felt for the wall switch inside the door of the flat, flipped it, and blinked in the brightness.

CHAPTER TWO

Jigsaw Pieces

The Digbys' entrance hall was a narrow, L-shaped passage. It turned the corner a few steps from where I stood. Aside from the empty hall table, the door I'd just walked through, and the doors in the opposite wall, there was nothing to see. The door across and to the left was open, and the light from the hall shone inside across the empty tiles, a washbasin and a rail with towels folded neatly. The other doors were closed.

Somehow, this silence wasn't as reassuring as it might have been.

The sitting-room door was around to the right. I crept up to the bend in the passage and peered around. That door was open, too, with a faint blue light inside. Nothing was moving among the shadows and the shapes of furniture. I slid across and turned on another light.

I'd been half expecting some kind of disaster, so the reality was almost shocking. The Digbys' small living room with its maroon three-piece suite arranged around the big television, and the dining alcove with its little table-chairs-and-sideboard set, all looked perfectly normal. Normal for Phyllis, that is, though by my own standards the place was unnaturally tidy. The only things that would have been out of place in a department-store display were the half-empty cup of something brown – cocoa? – on the lamp table beside one of the armchairs, and a piece of knitting that had been dropped on to a footstool halfway through a row of stitches. The blue light had been coming from the television, which was on but muted, an all-night news announcer mouthing silently. Phyllis had been sitting here when something happened. I crept over. There was a skin on top of the cocoa, and the cup felt cold. And if she was here somewhere, why hadn't she put in an appearance when I'd started turning on the lights? She must realise I'd arrived. I opened my mouth. Then I decided not to call out, because I'd just noticed the telephone. It was a cordless model, and the receiver was missing. I pulled my mobile out of my pocket, checked that it was on stand-by, and held it in my hand as I went exploring.

I opened the kitchen door slowly. When I flipped the wall switch, a double fluorescent ceiling fixture flickered and lit the room harshly. Nothing wrong here . . . except for the fridge door standing open a crack. I crossed the room and pushed it, but it banged against the salad drawer, and I had to push that in before I could shut it. Careless of somebody. I dragged my mind away from *Who?* and *Why?* I just had to find Phyllis.

Next was the open bathroom door. (No bodies in the bath, or anywhere else for that matter.) I left the light on there. The two rooms beyond it would be bedrooms. I'd never been in either, but it took no previous experience to know that I was getting warm when I stood in the first of the doorways. This was a tiny room, obviously Frank Digby's office. Or had been. I switched on the ceiling light. Frank supplemented some kind of invalidity pension by doing freelance bookkeeping, but he wasn't going to be working in this rubbish tip for a while. Someone had dragged his desk and filing cabinet into the middle of the floor, removed the drawers, tipped the furniture over, and left a snowstorm of paper and files everywhere. A small bookcase stood with empty shelves behind a hillock of papers and filing boxes. A computer had been deposited on top of the mess. Correction: part of a computer – I could see the keyboard, monitor and printer. The body of the machine might be hidden under something, but for the moment I couldn't find it. For the moment, it seemed unimportant.

The master bedroom was almost as bad: mattress stripped and pulled off the bed, chest of drawers and dressing table hauled away from the walls and upturned, empty drawers lying higgledy-piggledy on top of it all. For a panicky instant I thought I saw a body on the floor by the bed, but it was only a quilt.

I slid through the doorway and whispered, 'Phyllis?'

'Dido? Is that Dido? . . . Can you get me out?'

The voice was coming from the closed door of a built-in closet. I slithered over the mattress, turned the key sticking out of the lock, and jerked the door open. Phyllis looked up, blinking in the light. The closet had been emptied of everything except a few wire hangers, and she was sitting on the floor in her flowered dressing gown with her back against the wall, her knees drawn up defensively in front of her body and the phone on the floor at her feet. I was relieved when a smile started to inch across her pale face, but when I reached down and helped her up, she staggered.

'No, no, I'm all right, just stiff. I've been sitting in there . . . I don't know how long. What time is it?'

'Phyllis, what's happened? Is Frank all right?'

She shook her head slowly, as though my question puzzled her. 'He's not here. He's away. I was just getting ready for bed when they knocked at the door, and you see I thought it was one of the students from across the landing; they're always coming over for something. But when I opened the door . . . One of the other flats must've buzzed them in.'

'Did they take much?' I asked. But I knew as soon as I'd opened my mouth that this was stupid. Why would burglars come all the way up to the top floor of this particularly ordinary building, carefully and presumably silently destroying the light bulbs as they climbed the stairs, then ignore the few things like the television set and video that were worth a little money? For that matter, why would a thief – or several thieves, because she'd said 'they' – raid the Digbys at all, and choose to do it at a time when they knew that somebody was at home, when the lights were on? I rephrased my question almost without thinking: 'Who were they?'

'I couldn't see. The landing light was out when I opened the door, and one of them pushed in and grabbed me before I knew what was happening. He threw something, a coat, over my head. I . . . I didn't even have time to think. I couldn't . . . he was holding me. There were three of them. Three voices, whispering. They pulled the clothes out of this cupboard and pushed me inside, but the funny thing is, one of them came back after a while and opened the door; he didn't say anything, just threw the phone inside and locked it again.'

I stared. 'Then why didn't you call the police?'

Phyllis said wearily, 'When I switched it on, the line was dead. They must have unplugged the base unit.'

'But you just rang me!'

She seemed to sag. 'I know, so they must have stopped and plugged it in again just before they left – but I didn't think to try it until after they'd gone. They were moving around for a long time, moving things in here and . . .' I watched her take in the state of the room. It silenced her.

I said, 'The study is worse, but everything else seems all right. What happened after that?'

She shook her head helplessly. 'Well, after a while I couldn't hear anybody. I told myself that they must have had some reason for chucking this in to me, so I tried phoning you, and it worked. What time is it?'

This time I told her, and all the while my mind was saying, sarcastically, *Plugged it in so she could call for help? How kind.* If I were Mr Spock, every hair on my body would have been standing on end.

Leave that now. I tried to think what to say, and came out with, 'I've left Ben downstairs in the car.' My voice sounded strangely normal. 'I'll go and get him, and then we'll make a cup of tea and wait until the police get here.'

Phyllis looked at me, and I saw the colour beginning to return to her face, and also something hardening in her eyes. She was getting back her self-control. She said, 'No! Wait. Frank . . .' and stopped again.

When I'd waited long enough I asked, '*What?*'

'Just before he left, Frank said that if anything happened

while he was away, I shouldn't contact the police. Not until I'd had a chance to speak to him about it.'

I looked at her. She was avoiding my eyes. 'If *what* kind of thing happened, Phyllis? Are you saying that he was *expecting* this? And he left you here *alone*?' I could hear my voice rising.

Phyllis looked down at her hands and shook her head. 'I don't know, I didn't say anything at the time. I'm sure he couldn't have guessed . . . Anyway, I think he meant it. I mean, that's clear now, isn't it?'

I woke up. At last. No, nothing was clear to me. A man who had left such curious instructions must have his reasons, and it would be nice to know what they could possibly be. It would also be nice to know how much Phyllis wasn't telling me. I chose my questions very carefully: 'Where is he?'

'Well . . .' Phyllis stuck again, but I'd heard something in her voice. I stared at her. 'It was some kind of business trip. Something came up suddenly Saturday night. He came in and took the phone into the study. He was on the phone for a long time. In the morning he said he'd be back as soon as possible, and not to worry if it was a day or so. He didn't take a bag, though, so he can't have meant to be away long. I haven't heard from him, but the thing is, I think he might have tried to phone me this evening. When I got back from doing my shopping, there'd been three calls to the answering machine. No message. It must have been him.'

It was becoming blindingly obvious that the more questions I asked, the less satisfactory the answers I got. I sat down on what remained of the bed. Possibly it would all make more sense in daylight, when I'd had some sleep, when we'd both had some sleep. But I doubted it.

Very carefully, I said, 'What are you going to do?'

Phyllis looked at the mess around us in a way that seemed eloquent. 'Could I sleep on your couch?'

I looked around too and decided to shut up about it. 'Of course. But can you get ready? You know I hate leaving Ben in the car like this. Grab anything you need.'

She hesitated. 'I won't get dressed. I'll just put my coat on over. I'll take something for the morning, and my keys.'

I wasn't arguing. She dipped into the confusion and extracted underwear, a skirt and some kind of top to stuff into her big blue shopping bag. I tried not to notice that her wallet was inside. They hadn't even taken her money. I wrenched my thoughts away because it wasn't doing any good.

We shut the front door, double-locked it, hurried silently down the stairs, made sure that the main door had also shut and locked itself behind us, ran to the car and opened the doors.

A voice spoke in the darkness. From the child seat, Ben said something that sounded like 'Sweetie!' in the reasonable tones of somebody who was wide awake and wished to make it clear that he was being very good.

I said hysterically, 'I'll take that as a compliment. Phyllis, this is all crazy.'

'Dido,' she said, 'you're a brick. Ben, my poppet, we're going home.'

CHAPTER THREE

Old Spice

Sidling into the kitchen five hours later, I was sharply reminded of my personal problem. The current state of the room was just a symptom: my whole flat is barely able to hold one and a half human beings and a cat, never mind the occasional emergency house guest.

Ben and I live on the upper floor of an early-nineteenth-century cottage in north London which has been both my home and place of business for the past six or seven years.

The ground floor contains my shop: *Dido Hoare ~ Antiquarian Books and Prints*, as the elegant gilt-lettered sign above the display window informs the world. Or any part of the world that happens to walk down my obscure back street in North London. Above the sign is the sitting room with its high Georgian sash windows stretching across the front of the house; and at the back, overlooking a patchwork of high brick walls and little yards, the tiny kitchen, midget bathroom, and bedroom which I share with Ben. What was delightfully intimate when I was newly married to Ben's father, and then just right for myself and my loud-mouthed ginger cat, Mr Spock, was bursting at the seams now that I had a toddler. With a house guest, the whole thing had gone far beyond a joke.

Phyllis and Ben had settled at my postage-stamp kitchen table, sharing toast and boiled eggs. I looked hard and saw that, whatever had been going on last night, my visitor had pulled herself together now. Phyllis Digby is a tall, tough, stringy

Australian nurse with sandy-coloured hair, observant blue eyes, and a forthright manner: I always picture her wading through billabongs and taming kangaroos without so much as turning a hair.

Mr Spock sat on the windowsill shoulder to shoulder with the little radio that was pouring out the morning's depressing news bulletin: a grotesque massacre in a village outside Algiers, another Cabinet minister discovered taking freebies from a dubious millionaire, an unidentified corpse in a London suburb, the financial triumph of some titanic disaster movie. My cat was eyeing the breakfast table, not quite daring to intervene because even he respects Phyllis's kangaroo-taming abilities. I breathed in, sidled over to the work counter to pour myself a mug of fresh coffee from the machine, switched off the radio, and leaned against the fridge. 'Your turn now, if you'd like a bath,' I said to her. 'There's lots of hot water.'

She hesitated. 'Dido, I think I'd better go back. I have to be there when Frank phones. I have to tell him.'

'Not by yourself,' I said quickly, because it wouldn't be much fun walking into that mess in the grey light of the winter morning. Friendly encouragement is what I would have needed if I'd been in her place: a handkerchief, a shoulder to cry on, and certainly a helping hand.

Besides, something was going on; and even ignoring my notorious bump of curiosity, I didn't want to take my eye off events because Phyllis and I had become more friends than employer and employee in the previous months. Well, back me into a corner and I'd probably confess that my motives were also partly selfish: Ben and I needed Phyllis, and anything that affected her was going to upset the delicate arrangements that allow a single parent to earn a living. So I'd gone to sleep a few hours ago, and wakened again, worrying about the fact that something I didn't understand was happening and Phyllis needed my support.

We exchanged places at the table and a moment later I heard the water running. Ben and I spent some time drinking coffee and discussing how funny it is when you crunch empty eggshells flat with your hand, and how disappointing that you can only do it once. While our attention was on that, Mr Spock grabbed a buttered crust and hid in the corner behind the pedal bin. I apologised to him for taking my eye off events and went to look for the cat food.

It was a mild morning in late February, with a high wind blowing the thin clouds from west to east and sending patches of weak sunshine sliding across the brick walls and slate roofs. The kind of day that makes you think that spring might perhaps arrive sooner rather than later. We were in the Citroën, zigzagging eastwards through the side streets. In my rear-view mirror I could see Phyllis, quiet beside Ben in the back seat, a V-shaped furrow between her sandy-coloured eyebrows, staring at nothing. It was a silent journey except for Ben's running commentary in a language that was starting to be English.

Somebody had already swept up the broken glass from the stairs. Phyllis unlocked the door of number 9, said, 'Well . . .', marched in, and turned towards the living room. I put Ben down on his feet and we watched her check the room and relax when she realised that the damage had been limited. She crossed and picked up her abandoned cocoa cup.

I heard myself saying stupidly, 'Are you sure that you shouldn't report this? It's not too late.'

'Frankly, Dido, I can't see the point. They can't have taken anything.' This time, she didn't mention Frank's instructions.

'Are you saying you think this was a prank?'

She looked away. 'Or a mistake. Somebody broke into the wrong flat. Or maybe, yes, it was just a joke that went wrong.'

I chose not to remark on the fact that she was obviously squirming after an excuse and just asked her, 'What about the mess?'

'All right. I'll make sure there's no real damage. But I don't think the police would even bother to investigate something like this. Oh, they'd probably file a report, but nothing would happen. Waste of everybody's time.'

'That's it?'

'I think so. I'll see what Frank thinks. Maybe I'll get a new chain for the door, though, a locking chain. From now on, I'll keep it on when I'm alone here.'

'Are you expecting them to come back, then?' I asked. I hadn't said that I didn't take her excuses seriously, but I could hear my voice rising. That was when I realised that Phyllis wasn't the only one who was feeling edgy about this.

A shadow crossed her face. 'Dido, I wasn't expecting them in the first place. But we ought to have a chain on the door.'

I counted to five, made my voice calm and asked, 'Who were they?'

'If it wasn't just some kind of mistake, then I think they must have been some . . . people Frank once knew.'

Ben wriggled and pulled his hand away while I was still thinking. He set off unsteadily to explore.

Phyllis said quickly, 'Don't worry, he can't do any harm. I'll keep an eye on him.' She picked up the knitting needles and put them out of reach on top of the television set.

I gave up. 'Why don't we start by getting the bedroom sorted out, then?'

All three of us headed down the hallway. As I'd expected, daylight somehow made the room look worse.

'If you lend a hand,' Phyllis said gruffly, 'we can hoick the chests of drawers up and shove them back against the wall. Then we'll have space to move.'

We manhandled the bigger one upright and pushed it back against the wall with a crash, exchanging guilty looks. Though it did strike me that as the neighbours downstairs had managed to ignore the noise someone had made tearing the place apart, they were probably stone deaf. The second was lighter. We edged it more quietly into place.

'But why would anybody . . . ?' I was beginning, contrary to my intention of keeping quiet, when the buzzer sounded. Phyllis turned white.

'The downstairs door? Ignore it,' I suggested.

She nodded, and we waited unhappily. There was no further

warning, but we realised that some carefree resident had let yet another unexpected visitor in when we heard the feet on the stairs. I picked Ben up quickly and cuddled him, whispering 'Ssshhhhhh' into his ear. He squirmed. The doorbell rang sharply. Out on the landing there was a mumble, and a mumbled reply. Ben kicked, and I knew he was going to announce our presence; the bell rang again, followed by a thump on the door.

'Mrs Digby? – police! Are you all right, Mrs Digby?'

Phyllis exhaled sharply and went to open up. Ben and I followed her.

On the landing outside stood two men who were wearing suits under black leather coats. The only people who wear suits nowadays are bankers, Members of Parliament, the royal family, and policemen, and I would have guessed which these were even before one of them flashed his warrant card.

'Mrs Digby, I'm DI Moore, this is DS Andrew. We were told there was a disturbance here last night.' He spoke through his nose with the remains of a Birmingham accent. Looking from Phyllis to Ben and me and back, he added, 'Are you all right?'

They entered when she stepped back, wiping their shoes on the doormat, looking alert. Moore was a solid man, middle-aged, middle height, mid-brown hair turning grey mouse around the edges. Somebody had broken his nose for him at some time in the past. He moved clumsily, like an old athlete with bad knees, but there was still power in his shoulders and hands. His sergeant was a taller man, with watery blue eyes in a yellowish, heavily lined face under a shock of white hair. They both inspected us.

'Neighbour?' Moore asked the air between Phyllis and me.

She was silent, so I introduced myself as a friend, and we all smiled carefully at one another. 'Nice little chap,' Moore said to Ben, who had lost interest in them suddenly and was wandering off towards the living room. We tagged after him and formed a circle.

'How did you know about the break-in?' I asked.

Moore cocked his head and looked at me without any

expression. 'There was a report. Not you? Must have been the neighbours.'

Perhaps they hadn't been quite deaf after all.

Phyllis was saying quietly, 'I don't want to lay a complaint. I don't think anything was stolen. I don't need police here.' Her voice sounded funny.

'Mind if we take a look?' Moore said. 'I'll check your parlour.' He gestured at Andrew, who turned towards the rear of the flat; Phyllis, Ben and I followed Moore and watched him casting a comprehensive eye over the tidy room. When Andrew reappeared, they exchanged grimaces.

'You say nothing's missing?' Andrew asked. Unlike Moore, his accent was native East End. ''Ave you checked your valuables?' He looked at his boss. 'There's a mess back there, sir.'

Phyllis was silent, so I said, 'We just got back. She was just starting to clear up.'

'Well, madam,' Moore said impartially to that space between Phyllis and me, 'you should do that now. We'll wait. If you can tell us what's missing, we'll put in a report.'

Andrew shoved in his contribution: 'Your insurance company will want to know we've been notified.'

Phyllis was looking at me, not at the detectives. 'Dido, I'll be fine now. I think you and Ben should go home or you'll be late opening the shop.'

I managed to bite my tongue. It was Tuesday. Tuesday is my day for catching up. On Tuesdays I open the shop by appointment only, and Phyllis knows that as well as I do.

I said as casually as I could that I'd give her a hand for a little while longer. I was looking for the chance to ask her what was wrong, but the two detectives followed us down the hallway and positioned themselves like Tweedledum and Tweedledee on either side of the bedroom door to give us their silent and unblinking attention. Something about them discouraged talk. They watched us picking up the drawers and laying them out in a row, empty. Phyllis wasn't stopping to sort things. She seemed absorbed, like somebody struggling with a problem in mental arithmetic, scarcely aware of what her own hands were doing. We retrieved a mixture of underwear, shirts, sweaters, bed-linen and single socks and tossed them at random into the drawers, slotting each one back on to its runners when it was full. That left the clothes from the hangers in the wardrobe, and the sheets and covers from the bed.

'Still nothing missing?' Moore said into the silence. 'Are you sure?'

Phyllis shook herself. 'These are just clothes. Nobody in their right mind would steal them. There's nothing.' But I'd watched her put away quite a nice camera in the top drawer of one of the chests, and my feeling of unease about last night's raid was growing.

I managed a wide smile and started to chatter. 'You must think all this is pretty stupid. Why ever d'you suppose they didn't take the television set? Or the video? I'm sure I read in the paper that those are the things that burglars always take?'

Moore returned a smile that seemed to be about as meaningful as mine and said that perhaps they had been interrupted. I decided I was getting indigestion.

But my questions had made him impatient. 'Don't you have any valuables in here?' he asked Phyllis. 'Jewellery, maybe? Documents? Money? Could you check, please?'

The three of us watched Phyllis locate a red plastic case and look inside. A glance, when she snapped open the lid, showed that it was full of costume jewellery and that this wasn't going anywhere. She closed the lid and tossed the box on to the dressing table.

'What about the other bedroom?' Andrew suggested. 'That's been turned over too. Would you take a look in there, Missus Digby? Miss, er' (he had forgotten my name but I didn't mind), 'will you come and help her? Bring the kiddie. We don't want him getting into mischief.'

We trailed into the study, and the men watched us hoist the desk and the filing cabinet to their feet, which left us with a room that was ankle deep in rubbish. I was getting the edge, because obviously this was all wrong. I've learned something about police procedures the hard way, and nothing that I knew could explain why an inspector and a sergeant from the CID had arrived to investigate some vague second-hand report of a twelve-hour-old disturbance. If they had arrived hotfoot last night hoping to make an arrest, I might just have swallowed it. Also, why were they standing around watching us tidy up instead of sending for forensic back-up? Phyllis's burglars seemed likely to have some kind of record, so a little bit of fingerprinting before we destroyed every piece of evidence couldn't have come amiss. Besides, these detectives had been acting pushy, and yet they hadn't even asked about the raid. Sat Phyllis down and asked her to describe what had happened. Taken notes. That was how they should have started this visit. I glanced at my wrist-watch. They had been in the flat for half an hour now, hadn't asked Phyllis to tell them what had happened, hadn't asked any questions at all. They were wasting a lot of time. Nobody but me seemed to have noticed.

I tried an experiment. 'If you can manage,' I said directly to Phyllis, 'I guess I will get back and open up. Will you be all right now?'

I didn't see Andrew move, but he was blocking the doorway. Moore said, 'If you don't mind, I'm going to have to ask you to stay a little longer, miss. We'll need a statement from you.'

'But I don't know anything about it!' I told him. I tried to make my voice express dimwitted astonishment. 'I wasn't here – I didn't even get here last night until it was all over!'

'We'll be as quick as we can,' he assured me.

I definitely had a stomach ache. I asked myself why I assumed that they would stop me if I tried to reach the front door.

My eyes fell on Ben, tunnelling happily into the mess that was still lying on the floor. 'All right,' I said brightly, 'but I'd better change the baby right now. Phyllis, do you mind if I use your bathroom? Sergeant, er . . . ?' If he could forget my name, I'd forget his. 'Would you mind passing me the nappy bag? I think I left it on the hall table when I came in.' I threw the man a dazzling smile, followed him as he retrieved my property for me, and retreated into the privacy of the bathroom.

There was a bolt on the door. It was flimsy, but it would

keep them from walking in without warning. I edged it silently into position, turned on the taps in the basin, and sat on the edge of the bath at the far end of the room, with the water running noisily between me and the door. I'd dumped my mobile phone in among the spare nappies as I was leaving home. One of the numbers programmed into it belonged to Paul Grant, a police detective I've known for a while. He answered on the second ring.

'Paul, this is Dido. There are two CID men – Inspector Moore and Sergeant Andrew: they're here in Phyllis Digby's flat.' I was gabbling with haste. 'They claim they're answering some report of a break-in here last—'

'Can you speak up?' Paul asked. 'How've you been? What's wrong? Do I hear water running?'

Louder? I took a deep breath, curved my hands around my mouth and the phone, and tried *clearer and slower*, instead. 'Paul, listen to me: I'm locked in the bathroom. I turned the taps on so they won't hear me talking. These two detectives, Moore and Andrew . . .'

'They're not ours,' Paul interrupted.

I sat down slowly on the floor and leaned against the bath; why wasn't I surprised? 'Then what are they doing here in Phyllis Digby's flat? They claim they're responding to a report of an incident here last night.'

'Good question. What do they say? You're sure they're real?'

'I saw a warrant card.'

'Moore and Andrew?'

'Paul!'

I caught an echo of amusement. 'Maybe you've run up against Special Branch again? What have you done this time? Look, I'll pop over, just in case. What's the address?'

I told him. Before I'd finished speaking, Ben had got bored and decided to rejoin the others. I was watching him toddle over to the door, ready to grab him, so I happened to notice the handle turning before he got to it.

'Miss? Everything all right?' Andrew's voice.

I dumped the phone back into the nappy bag, jumped to my

feet and flushed the toilet. Then I grabbed one of the clean disposables, held it under the running tap for a moment, and doubled it over. I slung the nappy bag over one shoulder, hoisted Ben over the other, unbolted the door and emerged, holding the soggy nappy out in front of me between a finger and thumb. 'Just finished,' I said brightly. 'I'd better find a bin for this thing.'

Andrew was silent, but he followed me to the kitchen and watched me dispose of my excuse in the pedal bin under the sink.

The others were in the bedroom. Phyllis looked up as the three of us returned. She was methodically rehanging clothes in the cupboard, and I clocked Moore making himself useful at last, picking up Frank Digby's things from the floor and passing them to her. I also couldn't help noticing him run his hand over a pocket as he passed her a jacket. It was a small, casual gesture that might have been accidental.

Policemen make me nervous. It's not as though I often do things that are actually illegal, or no more than most people. But policemen always make me feel as though I might be. I had no idea what this pair were after, which perhaps explained why I found them about the most nerve-racking specimens I'd ever come across.

I deposited Ben and his nappy bag on the floor beside the bed, handed him the make-up mirror from the dresser to keep him amused for the moment, and made myself uselessly useful by remaking the bed, tucking in sheets busily and straightening the spread, just killing time. It took a lot of killing. A week or two passed while I plumped up the pillows and took exquisite care positioning them absolutely straight along the headboard.

'That's it?' Moore said suddenly. 'Nothing missing in here? We'd better finish the other room, then.'

We left obediently in single file, the two women and child under guard. Phyllis still wasn't speaking. That worried me. They would notice something, sooner or later.

Buzzer.

I dodged Andrew, trying to look as casual as possible, and hit the intercom button. 'Hello? Yes?

'Detective Inspector Grant, Islington CID, here in response to your call.'

As I touched the button that unlocked the main door, I couldn't keep myself from glancing back at the two men. They weren't even looking at each other.

Moore said, 'Right, then. Inspector Grant is going to take over from here, Mrs Digby. We'll be in touch.'

Andrew opened the door of the flat, said, 'See you later,' and stepped into the hallway. Moore followed, and I went out on the landing to watch them descending the stairs briskly in single file. Paul was climbing two steps at a time. Nobody spoke. Though they all gave each other a careful glance as they passed.

Behind my back, Phyllis said in a harsh, low voice, 'Moore – he was one of them last night. The one who grabbed me.'

I whirled around. '*What?* How can he be? I thought you said you didn't get a look at them.'

'I didn't.' Her face suddenly looked drawn. 'I smelled him. I guess it's aftershave. You couldn't mistake it. Funny.'

With aftershave – well, you probably could mistake it if he was wearing a popular brand. But it would have been a coincidence.

'Those were the ones?' a familiar voice said behind me. I turned around and looked up at Paul Grant's wedge-shaped face and brown eyes. The face looked tired, and so did the character-istically elegant grey suit, but in present circumstances I didn't feel ready to quibble. He was looking down at me thoughtfully, one eyebrow raised. 'I've never seen those two before. Funny they didn't stop to have a word.'

CHAPTER FOUR

Hard Drive

'What's going on?'

I went on strapping Ben into his padded car seat while Paul watched with such cold attention that you would have thought he'd never seen a child seat before, or even a child, perhaps. I asked him, 'What do you mean?'

He rewarded my show of ignorance with the growl it probably deserved. 'Do you two expect me to swallow this story about three burglars breaking in and not taking anything except a home computer? And two of them coming back this morning pretending to be police officers? And she doesn't want us to investigate? *Any* of it?'

I straightened up and countered, 'You're the policeman – aren't you supposed to understand these things? What do *you* think?'

He laid an arm across the car's roof, narrowed his big brown eyes at me and said, 'You're looking good.'

I told him that he was looking good too in what attempted to be a tone that suggested we should stick to the subject. I do try not to be too obviously pathetic about the fact that Paul Grant remains the hottest thing in my life, even though we agreed some time ago that the two of us weren't going anywhere. We are unfinished business, and I'd more or less decided that it was going to stay that way.

'Paul, believe me: she hasn't told me any more than she said to you a minute ago. Those men frightened me stiff without even trying. They frightened Phyllis too. Couldn't you see that?'

'I'll tell you four things for free,' Paul offered, shifting suddenly into a forthcoming mood. 'One is that they came here for something specific. Unless you can believe they were collecting second-hand clothing for a jumble sale? Obviously they came back to have another look at the place. It was a stupid risk. Not that burglars aren't dim, but they usually aren't dim enough to come back in the morning to a place where they hadn't found anything worth taking the night before. What if our people had been here when they arrived? So I guess it was important to them. Two: your Mrs Digby guesses, or more likely knows, what they want. Three: that old computer probably has a street value of about twenty quid, so they wanted the hard drive, but not to sell.' He came to an abrupt halt.

I said, 'What was the fourth thing?'

When he was silent, I looked up and found him staring at nothing. I waited until he said, 'Fourth is the warrant card. Are you sure? Burglars shouldn't have police ID.'

I gave Ben a meaningless pat and closed his door carefully. I couldn't meet Paul's eyes, because I was busy putting two and two together and wondering whether the sum I was thinking of mightn't be a bit over the top. I reminded myself that this wasn't the moment to give in to my natural dislike of authority and began, 'Actually . . .' and had to stop to try to put my thoughts in some kind of order that would persuade him I wasn't dreaming.

'Are you going to tell me, or do I have to arrest you?'

I looked up quickly and found him grinning. I said, 'Don't beat me up, I'll confess. Last night, when she was too upset to be on her guard, Phyllis let it slip that Frank had told her not to call in the police if anything "happened" while he was away. And now you say that those must have been real policemen all the time?'

Paul's expression soured sharply. 'The husband? Did I see a row of accountancy books in that little office of his?'

I noticed that he was avoiding answering my question, but I told him what I knew about Frank Digby, which wasn't much.

26

He had been a quiet man, withdrawn; we had met by chance a few times and found very little to say to each other.

'Then what's missing, with the computer,' Paul announced confidently, 'is his clients' accounts. At a guess, the real ones, the ones that the Inland Revenue would like to see. Maybe this makes sense after all. I wonder what he'll say when he gets back and finds out?'

I told him that he was a nasty, suspicious cop, but my heart wasn't in it because I was trying to remember just where I'd picked up the impression that Frank Digby had a criminal record. 'He's just a freelance bookkeeper,' I protested faintly. 'He works part time for tiny businesses.'

'VAT fraud,' Paul said promptly. 'Income tax evasion. He hasn't done your books, has he?'

He hadn't.

'Ben's getting fed up,' I observed into the awkward pause. This wasn't hard to guess, given that my son had just started kicking out with both feet in time to a monotonous chant. His meaning was perfectly clear: time for me to get into the car and make something happen. 'Would you like to come back for a coffee?'

He shook his head. 'We've got a minor drugs dealer back at the station, and I'm supposed to be there urging him to name his supplier. I only ducked out for half an hour while the duty solicitor talks to him. Listen, perhaps we could have a drink some time soon?'

'About Phyllis,' I said . . .

'All right, I know. There's nothing much I can do if she doesn't want help, but I'll ask around about Andrew and Moore. I didn't recognise them, but somebody must know where they popped up from. Your friend doesn't have to make a complaint but I wish she would, because then I could ask her what she's keeping quiet about. You persuade her if you can, but I'm betting that you won't manage. I have to get back. You'll be all right?'

I said I would, and he said goodbye and took off in his battered old car. I watched him drive off southwards until he made a right turn into the next street in a little, illegal cloud of blue exhaust smoke.

'Want,' Ben remarked thoughtfully as I climbed into the driver's seat. At least, it sounded like that.

'Don't try the mind-reading act,' I snarled.

The sky had darkened since our arrival, and a thin rain had started again. I switched on the engine and the wipers, signalled, and pulled out into the traffic, feeling for the moment as though things were rushing away from me out of control.

Perhaps that was why my concentration faltered, and we arrived at the junction with Essex Road and were signalling a left turn before I got around to noticing that somebody had decided to have a southbound traffic jam this morning. I checked the rear-view mirror. A grey car was just drawing up behind me, its indicator also flashing, but there was nobody beside us in the right-hand lane. I changed the indicator to signal a right and edged diagonally across to show that I really meant it. A woman driving a little Fiesta slowed to let me slide through a gap in the traffic, and then I was heading north, looking for a way to circle back through the side streets. Behind me there was a sudden blaring of horns. Glancing into the mirror, I realised that the car that had been behind me had decided to follow my lead and pulled out across the traffic so abruptly that various cars had been forced to brake.

There were two men in the front seat.

I swung the Citroën abruptly into the next turning and pulled over to the kerb. Then I turned around. The grey car passed the end of the road and vanished behind the corner building. At that point I realised I was still holding my breath. I gave myself a mental slap for letting my imagination play tricks and then contradicted that by waiting for a minute and checking very carefully both ahead and behind before I took off again.

Without even thinking about it, I made my way home indirectly. I turned north again, away from George Street, then circled around the council estate, slid down a service road between two of the big blocks there, and made a loop that took in a section of Upper Street. The roads were packed with grey cars that morning. I made a second detour to the east of St Mary's churchyard, pausing for three or four minutes with my engine running in the street at the back of the church, and then back-tracked into my own street to look for a space in the residents' bay, feeling silly. But not too silly. Something about Moore and Andrew had spooked me.

Safely parked, I disentangled Ben from his straps, zapped the central locking, and trotted towards my front door carrying him, though he squirmed and wanted to walk. Two more grey cars passed the end of my road one after the other, and I found myself wishing I'd at least noticed the make of the one that had worried me. But I hadn't.

It would appear that I'd panicked. I got hold of myself, put Ben on his feet, took his hand, and made myself slow to his amble. Maybe I should get a little more sleep and try to calm down.

CHAPTER FIVE

Kinds of Message

When Barnabas arrived I was pretending to work.

I'd called into the shop to retrieve the morning's post from the floor in front of the letter slot and check my answering machine. Having arranged to do my duty, I carried both the mail and Ben up the narrow stairs and into the quiet of our flat.

Ben had agreed to go into his playpen to unpack all the toys from the red plastic storage box he keeps there. He was tossing them over the top rail, one by one, on the understanding that this would sooner or later make me stop whatever I was doing and toss them back. Mr Spock had stalked in to investigate the noise and taken refuge on the shelf over the fireplace. Hard-hearted, I was ignoring both of them. I'd located a pencil and settled to some serious reading of postal catalogues, which is something that booksellers have to do. As I reminded myself. Literally minding my own business. At some point I'd managed to concentrate long enough to phone in an order for the Stacpoole *Pierrot* with Beardsley illustrations that one of my regular customers had asked me to locate a couple of months ago; but when the downstairs bell gave a blip and I heard the key in the street door and the footsteps on the stairs, I realised that it was some time since I'd taken in anything from the lists I was pretending to read.

My father appeared in the doorway, examined my face sharply, and said, 'What is it?' Ben greeted his arrival with a squeal which distracted him long enough for me to decide that

I really did need some input. I waited for him to settle into the armchair beside the playpen and enter into Ben's other game of passing toys back and forth before I said, 'I have a problem.'

'The mind boggles. Could you be more specific?'

I warned him that it was a long story and started to tell it. I was watching the two of them as I talked: my blond son, big for his age, confidently sunny, with his father's eyes as I keep being reminded (but hopefully not Davey's morals as well), and his grandfather – the tall, thin, white-haired old academic with the alert grey eyes and the sharply focused, logical mind. It took Barnabas quite a long time to run out of questions, and by the time I'd gone through events repeatedly and in detail, I'd reached the gloomy belief that Paul Grant had been correct on all counts, and probably in his conclusion, too.

My father interpreted: 'You're worrying about Mrs Digby's motives, I assume?'

'I think I'm worrying about everything. I can't imagine what's going on. I don't really know Frank Digby at all – we've never spoken, beyond polite chitchat. Maybe Paul's right and he is some kind of crook. If so, how much does Phyllis know about it, and should that bother me?'

Barnabas grunted enigmatically and frowned on Ben's game. After a while, he announced, 'I would have thought that, if worse came to worst, she would be unlikely to induct my grandson into a life of crime, not for a few years yet. I believe you've found her entirely honest in your dealings to date?'

I had, but that wasn't my point. There was the question of trust. Barnabas nodded almost imperceptibly, as though he were reading my thoughts. Sometimes I wonder.

'Therefore,' he continued with barely a pause, 'you have the luxury of being able to wait and see. And she has the right to demand it of you, I think.'

'What?'

'I merely suggest that Mrs Digby has the right to keep her own counsel. She will make up her mind to confide in you if she wishes to do so, though you should remember that she is a self-reliant woman nearly twenty years older than yourself.

Possibly you may need to exercise patience and an entirely uncharacteristic tact. However, if it's any consolation to you, I could point out that when she found herself in trouble, it was you whom she chose to contact.'

I said, 'What if Moore and Andrew come back?'

Barnabas said he thought that wouldn't arise. He was about to explain when the phone rang and we both jumped.

I grabbed the receiver and opened my mouth.

'Dido, I'm really sorry to ask . . .'

Panic. I gabbled, 'Phyllis? What's happened?'

My voice must have told her what I was thinking, because I heard a sound that was almost a laugh. 'No, no, it's just . . . Dido, do you mind if I come around? The post has been delivered, and there's something I need to talk to you about. Also . . . well, I guess this place is getting to me. I keep hearing noises. I want to get out a bit.'

I said, 'I'll drive over and pick you up. Give me two minutes. Barnabas is here; he can keep an eye on Ben for a while.'

I hung up, looked everywhere for the car keys, and found them on the hook by the front door where I always intend to hang them and almost never remember to. Barnabas watched the flurry with such interest that I stopped long enough to say, 'She's had a letter of some kind. She sounds funny. I won't be long.' Then I headed for the car.

I was crossing the lights on the Essex Road when my mobile burbled, and I slowed and switched it on.

'Dido?' For the second time in five minutes, the mere tone in a voice was a warning that something was very wrong.

'Paul?'

'Listen carefully: you might want to go back to Mrs Digby's place – don't interrupt, I've only got a second and there's no time to explain, but get there as fast as you can; she'll need your company.'

I breathed deliberately into my diaphragm and found enough voice to say, 'As it happens, I'm on my way there now. What's wrong? They haven't come back?'

'Don't be crazy, I wouldn't send you if it was that. Look . . .'

I waited, listening to the hiss on the open line. My eye fell on the speedometer, and I realised that I was doing over forty miles an hour down a narrow residential street lined on both sides with parked cars. At this rate I was going to kill somebody, possibly me. I had time to slow gently to twenty-five before he said, 'Dido, if you ever tell anybody I made this phone call, I could be in trouble. All right?'

I said slowly, 'All right, but—' and realised that I was talking to a dead line. I screamed. 'This is *stupid!*', and since there was nobody to hear me went on to the flat.

The door buzzed at me before I reached the top of the path, which meant that Phyllis had been standing at the window, watching for the car. As a result I galloped up the stairs a little faster than was comfortable and gasped, 'Phyllis, it's me' at the closed door. When she opened up, I noticed that each of us looked cautiously over the other's shoulder. I slid inside, and she slammed the door behind me and snibbed the catch. I decided to pretend I hadn't noticed and said, 'What about this letter?'

'There's no letter,' she said, 'that's the problem. Just this,' and thrust a long envelope at me. Her voice shook. So did her hand. The address was written, not typed; the name on the envelope was 'Phyllis Kingsley'.

'"Kingsley"?'

'That's my maiden name; it's Frank's handwriting.'

'What is it?'

She said, 'You look.'

She had slit the envelope neatly along the top edge. I extracted two things: an airline ticket and a greetings card. The ticket was in the correct name of Phyllis Digby: an open, one-way ticket to Sydney, Australia. My heart sank a few inches. The card said 'HAPPY BIRTHDAY!' and was decorated with watercolour blue violets and forget-me-nots; inside it there was a printed verse that began 'Down your happy birthday years . . .' and a scrawl which said, *Remembering your birthday*. It wasn't signed. The postmark was clear enough: the envelope had been mailed yesterday in 'North London', whatever that meant.

Phyllis said quietly, 'I don't think he's coming back.'

Sitting in the kitchen, with our conventional cups of hot, strong tea that neither of us really wanted and the envelope on the table between us, I tried again. 'Talk to me. Where do you think he's gone? Why did he send you the ticket? Isn't your birthday in October?'

Phyllis fixed her eyes on her cup. 'If you want my guess, he thinks something bad is going to happen and he wants me out of the way. Maybe I didn't mention it, but he was edgy when he left. He told me something had come up and he had to go and talk to somebody. He wouldn't say anything else, except that it was business and he wasn't sure when he'd get back . . . He said he'd phone me.'

'He hasn't . . .' I could hear my voice trail away, but I found it again to ask, 'Has he left you?'

'No, of course not! But something's wrong.'

I tried to think of how to sidle politely around what I wanted to say, and failed. 'Phyllis, Paul Grant noticed that Frank's computer is missing. He thinks that Frank was keeping illegal accounts for some of his clients, and that's what the men were looking for last night.'

I waited for her angry denial, but it didn't come. She scowled. 'He may have done that sort of thing in the past, but not now, not any more. I never told you that he was in an open prison when I met him. I was doing agency nursing in a hospital down in Kent when they brought him in for a lung operation. Cancer. It was pretty serious, and he was in for nearly a month. They had him on his own, in a private room, and he didn't get any visitors except prison staff, and they were around all the time. At first I thought Frank was somebody dangerous, but – well, he seemed so down, and so grateful for anything that I did, that I started to try to cheer him up. When I had a bit of time I'd go in with a cuppa, and we'd just sit and talk about silly things. He's a friendly man, when he gets to know you, but he never talked about himself. He got bored with the television, and he's not the reading type. He liked me to tell him about growing up in Melbourne, you know? He has a big family, too, but he said they'd lost touch. I thought that maybe they didn't want to know, after he was arrested.'

'What was he convicted of?'

Phyllis hesitated. Eventually, she said, 'Something called "false accounting". And I think there was some kind of fraud charge too.' She looked at me quickly. We both recognised that it wasn't much of an answer, and that she didn't intend it to be. 'I didn't ask because I could see he didn't want to talk about it, it was something he'd finished with; but I thought it was something to do with embezzlement, maybe. He told me before he left hospital that he was going straight, and asked if he could write to me. He got out a month or two later, and he turned up, and we took it from there. He's always been straight with me. I hope you don't mind that I never told you about it.'

I said, honestly, 'I don't see that it was my business. But the question is whether those men last night were people he knew before . . . before he was convicted, or whether they really were the police.'

Phyllis nodded for me to go on.

'They got his computer – his records – last night, so why did they come back this morning?'

Phyllis got to her feet and stood looking down at me. 'I might know the answer: Frank always says if you have something to hide, a computer is the worst place because that's the first thing anybody looks at these days. He had a little . . . trick, he called it: he wouldn't keep any files on his hard drive, just the programs; he had all his data files on disks. And I honestly don't see why anybody would be interested in what he's doing now, but if this *does* have something to do with the old days, old records, they would've found out they hadn't got them as soon as they looked.'

'And come back to find them? Then where are they?'

Phyllis frowned. 'If they were old accounts, then I have no idea except that they aren't here. When we moved in and unpacked, I saw everything, and that's why I know that he owned nothing from before about three years ago. He kept all the recent spreadsheets on disks.'

'So they looked,' I speculated, 'and decided it was so important that they'd risk coming back to find the rest?'

I noticed another hesitation, but all she said was, 'Perhaps they didn't think there was much danger. They might have thought I'd be on my own.'

I protested, 'Or the police might have been here investigating your burglary!'

The hesitation was even longer this time. Eventually she said slowly, 'Frank and I never talk about what he did before I knew him. He never wanted me involved, he said. Dido, what if it's something so serious that if I knew about it I'd be scared to call in the police, no matter what happened? That bothers me. I thought I didn't want to know, you know? I thought it was all old news and didn't matter. Maybe I was wrong.'

'And when they got here they found me with you, not the police. Maybe that threw them.'

Phyllis shuddered. 'I don't know what would have happened if I'd let them in when I was alone.'

I decided to focus on this line for the moment, because it suggested a danger that had to be considered. Next time, I wouldn't be with her. Next time, Paul Grant wouldn't turn up just in the nick of time, which was probably what had happened today.

She'd been lucky today. Me too, probably.

Assuming it was information that Moore and Andrew had wanted, the missing computer would be the key. Assuming they had already taken the hard drive to an IT expert who found it didn't contain the files they wanted, then obviously they'd rushed straight back to get the information some other way. From Frank himself? Only Frank had scarpered: I was inclined to think that was the reason for the arrival of the air ticket. A hint to Phyllis that she should get out of here? Perhaps that he was intending to join her in Australia?

I explained what I was thinking. We drank our tea.

I said, 'You'd better get out of this place, hadn't you?'

'I guess. If you're right. Only why hasn't he phoned to tell me? Why do I have to guess? It's not like Frank.'

I was thinking aloud: 'The trouble is, since they've got the computer, there doesn't seem to be any way we can even find out the point of it all.'

'There are the disks.'

She had said that already. Theoretically, Andrew might have pocketed Frank's back-up disks when he had gone to 'check' the study while Moore talked to Phyllis and me in the living room. No, because if he had, he would have tipped the wink to Moore and they'd have vanished, not hung around making Phyllis search the rest of the place for 'valuables'. Later, I'd been out of the way, locked in the bathroom, for a few minutes; but the same objection could be made that the two phoney detectives had shown no sign of leaving until Paul's arrival. So they still hadn't got what they wanted.

I was getting to my feet. 'We'd better see if we can find them. They must be in the mess somewhere.'

Phyllis shook her head. 'Not in his office: that's what I'm telling you. He installed a fireproof safe. Look, I'll show you.'

Absurdly, she headed into the bathroom. Somebody had boxed the bathtub in with a cover made of narrow, varnished pine boards screwed vertically on to a frame. I stood in the doorway and watched her dig her fingernails into a crack between two of the boards and yank out a section that had been held in place by a couple of snap-catches. The opening had obviously been made originally to give access to the plumbing, and it revealed the usual slightly damp and dusty under-bath space, in this case filled with an enamelled steel box about fourteen inches wide and nine or ten inches high. I could see the numerical pad of a combination lock.

'Can we get it out?'

Phyllis looked at me. 'It's bolted to the floor.'

'Then do you know the combination?'

She shook her head.

We stood and looked at it for a while, but no inspiration came. In the end, Phyllis snapped the cover back and we drifted into the sitting room.

A sound – a series of faint sounds – gradually intruded into the silence . . . distinct, repeated ringing noises, not all in the same key and not in this flat but near by and clearly audible in the morning silence of the empty building. We noticed them simultaneously and exchanged a silent question.

Phyllis understood first. 'The downstairs door. Somebody's ringing around, trying to get in.'

I said doubtfully, 'The postman?'

'More likely somebody trying to get in to deliver leaflets . . . or something.'

Neither of us believed that.

I mumbled. 'They aren't even trying this flat,' and we went over to the window.

A marked police car was parked across the road. Phyllis started to speak, stopped, hesitated, and slid the double windows open so we could both lean out. The person at the main door was a uniformed police officer.

Phyllis grabbed my elbow hard, and we both jerked back out of sight. Then I remembered Paul's telephone call. 'It's probably all right,' I said, carefully. 'They wouldn't try the same trick twice. Anyway, there's only one man. Look – I'll find out what he wants.'

She nodded and made way for me, and I leaned out. 'Can I help you?'

The face that turned up to me belonged to a tall, blue-eyed young redhead who removed his cap and looked up. 'I'm looking for a Mrs Digby.'

'I'm a friend of hers,' I said, and watched a look of relief flicker across his face. 'It's flat nine,' I said slowly. 'I'll let you in. Wait a minute.'

I went and buzzed to unlock the main door, and then opened the door of the flat. We listened to the sound of footsteps climbing briskly. He appeared promptly, stepped slowly over the threshold and tucked his cap politely under one arm. His face was flushed, probably from the cold wind, and it made him look about eighteen. His eyes flickered around the corridor before they settled on Phyllis's face. That was the moment when I knew that something was wrong.

'Mrs Digby?'

Phyllis stiffened.

He shifted his cap to his other arm. 'PC Mathews, Mrs Digby, from Palmers Green. I'm afraid I have some bad news. You should prepare yourself for a shock. Your husband is Mr Francis James Digby?'

We stood there for a moment in a bubble of silence. I was the one who finally broke it by growling, 'Yes.'

He said, 'I'm very sorry,' sounding as though he meant it. 'I don't know whether you might have heard an item on the news, but the body of a man was found last night up at Cockfosters. He had no identification on him, but his fingerprints identify him as a Mr Francis Digby, of this address. Would you like to sit down, Mrs Digby?'

Phyllis said almost inaudibly, 'He didn't like to be called "Francis". He was called "Frank". No . . . no, I'm all right.' But she obviously wasn't.

The constable put a hand under her elbow. 'Let's just go into your parlour. Miss? Take her other arm.'

Between us, we supported Phyllis into her living room and settled her into one of the armchairs. She moved between us like a baby learning to walk. I crouched and took her hand.

'Wait a minute,' Mathews said abruptly.

He vanished, and in a few seconds I heard the click of one cupboard door in the kitchen, and then a second. In a moment he was back holding out one of Phyllis's little tumblers with an inch of brown liquid in it. I took it, smelled brandy, pushed it into her hand, stared hard into her eyes and whispered, 'Sip it. Come on.' I raised her hand for her and watched her drink. Her face was pasty and expressionless, but her eyes were on the constable.

Suddenly it seemed as though we had been waiting for this all morning, and I whispered. 'Was it an accident?'

He avoided answering me. 'I've been sent to ask Mrs Digby if she'd be willing to talk to somebody about what's happened. I can drive her to the station. But take your time. Would you like a cup of tea or something?'

Phyllis made a gesture of refusal and said, 'Where is Frank?' in a flat voice.

'At the mortuary up in Wood Green, Mrs Digby.'

She said coldly, 'I want to see him.'

Mathews looked embarrassed. 'It isn't really necessary, Mrs Digby. He has been formally identified.'

Phyllis looked up. 'I heard you. I want to see him. Where is he?'

'Up in Tottenham,' the constable repeated. 'Well, I . . . of course I can take you there. I'd better make a phone call.'

'You do that,' Phyllis said in her new, hard voice.

I said, 'I'm coming too.' Nobody contradicted me.

CHAPTER SIX

Old Acquaintance

There was an empty chair at the side of the room and I tucked myself in beside the filing cabinet, trying to make it clear that I was small and harmless. Just a responsible friend of the bereaved. Part of the background.

The body had been Frank Digby's, of course, since fingerprints don't lie. I had watched Phyllis stand for a long time staring at his face under the harsh lighting in a basement room. She looked as though she was making sure that he really was dead, as though she couldn't accept the evidence of the fingerprints, or of anything else except her own eyes. It had taken her a long time to turn away.

He had not looked as though he was sleeping. They don't. His face was empty. Frank Digby had looked like a badly coloured wax dummy.

A short drive had brought us on to this police station near the North Circular, where Constable Mathews had ushered us down a narrow corridor between rows of glass partitions and knocked briskly at one of the doors. There was time to examine the name-plate before Superintendent Charles D. Paige called something unintelligible from the other side, and Mathews opened the door for Phyllis and stood back.

Paige was a uniformed policeman in his late forties who rose to greet us and ushered Phyllis to a chair by the desk with a solemn air that made me think of undertakers. He was a neat man with a neatly trimmed, sparse little beard. It looked newish, and gave him a slightly naval air. Mathews had stood stiffly in the open doorway, looking as though he was waiting to salute, and remained there until Paige gave him a fatherly smile and told him to stay. He was sitting opposite me now with an open note-book, looking bright, keen and somehow satisfied. Presumably uniformed constables in surburban police stations don't often get the chance to be involved in anything more interestingly bloody than a drunken driving case. We listened to Paige's brisk condolences, though Phyllis hadn't come for condolences. I settled back trying to look blank and, like Mathews, waited for something to begin.

Paige abandoned the preliminaries by clearing his throat. 'Mrs Digby, I need to ask a few questions, if you feel up to it now.'

Phyllis said, 'Go ahead' in a voice that had become quieter and developed a more Australian twang during the last hour.

'When did you last see your husband?'

She repeated the things that she had already told me about Frank's movements. Mathews made himself useful by scribbling notes.

When she stopped, Paige scratched his chin. Something seemed to be bothering him. Perhaps the beard itched. 'Mrs Digby, I'm sorry I have to ask about this just now, but I understand you haven't been married for very long? I wonder just how much you know about your husband's life before you met him. You were aware that he had a criminal conviction dating from 1992?'

Phyllis said deliberately, 'I met him nearly three years ago. I was working as an agency nurse then, and he was serving a prison sentence at the time.'

Paige seemed to relax, and I understood that he'd been wondering how to approach the real problem. He confirmed my impression by asking, 'Then you know that wasn't his real name? That his name was Francis Brunton, and that he has been helping the Metropolitan Police with certain investigations?'

Phyllis nodded curtly, and I breathed 'Ahhh' but just managed to avoid doing it loudly enough to be heard.

'And presumably you know that we – the Met, that is, not this division specifically – were involved in setting him up with a new identity when he left prison?'

'I knew that he was hiding,' Phyllis said bluntly. 'He changed his name. He never told me why he was hiding, or being protected, but I guessed it was something to do with organised crime, I'm not a fool. He asked me to stay out of it completely, to trust him; and I did. He said the less that I knew the better it'd be. He made a joke of it. He used to say, "In this case ignorance is bliss, Phyll."' She threw a look in my direction, and I pulled myself together enough to return a reassuring nod.

'The question we have to ask,' Paige was saying softly, 'is whether somebody from the old days finally located him last night. It seems possible. I was hoping that you could tell us something that would help us to understand what happened.' The words dropped into a silence.

Making connections, I had to ask, 'Who are Moore and Andrew?'

Paige said flatly, 'Moore and Andrew.' If he thought it sounded like a question, I could have told him that he didn't make the grade. I could see that he'd known the names.

Well, patience has never been my strong point. I thought I might just try to move this conversation on a bit. I said, 'I think you already know that some men broke into the Digbys' flat last night, and that Phyllis phoned me after they'd gone. It was reported to Islington.' And Paul Grant's warning phone call only made sense if he and Paige had been in communication this morning, because Paul had certainly known that Mathews was on his way. Therefore it followed . . . I was thinking hard. 'And you also know that two men who claimed they were police officers turned up at the flat this morning, and Phyllis realised that one of them – Moore, or whatever his name really is – was one of the three who attacked her last night.'

Paige said smoothly, 'Before you leave, perhaps you'd see if you can identify them.'

Phyllis asked, 'Are they the ones who killed Frank?' Her voice was cold.

Paige said just as quietly, 'I don't know; but their appearance at your home this morning can't be a coincidence.'

Exactly. 'When was Frank killed?' I asked, since that seemed relevant. 'And where?'

I saw Paige hesitate. What he said was, 'Constable Mathews says you're Mrs Digby's employer?'

I opened my mouth, but Phyllis said, 'Dido's right: I want to know everything.'

Paige twitched one shoulder in a half-disguised shrug. 'The doctor believes that he was killed some time yesterday evening.' I watched him glance at a paper on his desk. 'He thinks that Mr Digby may have been hit by a car – I'm sorry, Mrs Digby – more than once, or beaten up, probably both, and then driven to a lay-by on the Potters Bar Road and dragged through a break in the chain-link fence at the edge of a country park up there. A police patrol noticed a big off-road vehicle there briefly after ten o'clock, but of course we don't know whether that was actually involved.'

I saw Phyllis shiver. She asked, 'Did he – was he . . . ?'

Paige knew what she wanted and wouldn't quite give it to her. 'He must at least have been deeply unconscious before he was taken there. His injuries were severe. He probably wasn't aware of much after the . . . the initial attack. I'm sorry that I can't be more reassuring. He had probably been dead for several hours when he was found by a security patrol making their rounds in Trent Park. I'm afraid that's all I can say right now. Unfortunately, his pockets were empty except for his car keys, so identification took a little while.'

Phyllis looked up and said flatly. 'We don't have a car.'

Paige glanced at Mathews. 'Hire car? We'd better find it.'

Mathews said brightly. 'There was no hire-company tag on them, sir. No identification at all.'

'Ask them to look at the keys for make or serial numbers – anything.' Paige turned his attention back to Phyllis. 'Mrs Digby, I'd like to send a forensic team into your flat. I'm sorry to have to bother you at a time like this, but as your break-in and the murder are almost certainly connected, we need to examine your premises. I'll get the constable to run you back shortly, and some people will meet you there.'

Phyllis shrugged and nodded and glanced at me again. 'I've done some clearing up,' she said. 'That was while Moore and Andrew were there.'

Paige frowned. 'That's too bad, but our people might still be able to find something useful.'

It was a shame, as I almost remarked, that nobody had given Phyllis advance warning, say in writing, say about a week ago, of what was going to happen and what we were supposed to do when a couple of large men who were presumably not real policemen, although at least one of them had a warrant card, turned up making demands on her time.

I was also starting to wonder something else. I couldn't get over the fact that those two had been taking quite a risk. Even if they'd counted on Phyllis not recognising them, they must have known that she would report their visit as soon as Frank's murder was discovered, describe them, present them as the prime suspects. Frank's murder made their actions almost insanely reckless.

Alternatively, what if they'd believed that Phyllis would keep her mouth shut? That sounded crazy; and yet I'd been convinced all morning that there were things she wasn't telling anybody – evasions, half-truths . . . If these men had some reason to think she wouldn't complain, then they would only have to be careful about leaving any physical traces that would incriminate them. The more I considered it, the more I thought I was starting to make some sense of their behaviour that morning. Had either of them actually done anything but watch us? I tried to recall whether I'd seen them touch anything that would take finger-prints. They had watched us manhandling heavy furniture without offering to help. Moore had handled Frank's clothing, but I couldn't remember anything else.

We manoeuvred for a little longer without making any progress, then Phyllis and I spent half an hour in front of a computer screen while an operator cut and pasted portions of face, adding and altering the shapes and colours of chins, mouths, noses and hair on the screen to our instructions, until at last he produced portraits of our two visitors that, thanks to our joint efforts, really did look surprisingly like them. Constable Mathews hovered encouragingly.

It was while he was taking us back to the car that we saw the Superintendent again. He was standing by the desk in the entrance area, greeting a visitor: a woman in her early forties, dressed unremarkably in a dark tailored suit, with neat mid-brown hair, mid-blue eyes, and a face that you wouldn't pick out in any crowd. You might put her down as somebody's highly competent secretary, unless you saw her in action, as I once had. When I'd known her, Inspector Diane Lyon had been working for Scotland Yard's Special Branch. I stopped to ask myself whether I believed in coincidences and heard the end of her sentence: '. . . been over to Islington and sorted it out.' That was the moment when she glanced up. I was pretty sure that I saw a flash of annoyance when she noticed me eavesdropping.

'Miss Hoare,' she said flatly. She smiled with her mouth. 'How nice to meet you again.'

I said, 'You too. How are you? Are you stationed here now?'

'No, just visiting.' She looked from me to Phyllis. 'Mrs Digby, isn't it? We met once. My condolences on your loss.'

Then she and Paige nodded impartially at us both, and moved off towards the offices.

Diane Lyon had just recognised Phyllis, whom she had seen once for a couple of minutes about a year before. A good detective certainly has a memory for faces, but I didn't think hers could be that good; so she had to be here about Frank's death.

The constable edged forward. 'If you don't mind, they'll be waiting for us.'

We walked out into the rain. I knew now: there had been no coincidences today. Scotland Yard already had their fingers in our pie.

There was an unmarked white van sitting at the kerb outside the flats when we got back. 'Those are our people,' Mathews said to Phyllis. 'Would you like me to . . . ?'

'As a matter of fact,' Phyllis said dryly, 'yes, I would like you to check that they're who they're supposed to be. I'm not letting strangers into my flat again. Dido . . .'

I said, 'If you don't mind I'd better get back and make sure Ben and Barnabas are all right.'

She smiled faintly. 'I suppose your father will have something to say about all this.'

I supposed so, too.

There was something else. 'About Frank: there were some things I probably should have told you a long time ago.'

I looked her straight in the eye and said, 'It wasn't necessary. Phyllis, are you sure you'll be all right?'

She smiled. It was a small, tight smile. 'I expect so. I guess I'm old enough and ugly enough to deal with this.'

As I got into the Citroën, I made a silent promise that I wouldn't leave her to deal with it alone. Then the image of a door handle popped into my head. I jumped out of the car and sprinted over to the group that was gathering outside the van.

'The handle on the outside of the bathroom door,' I said to them all equally. 'Andrew turned the handle. That's where you'll find his prints.'

And then I waltzed off with the smug feeling that I'd contributed something real at last.

CHAPTER SEVEN

Loyalty Checks

I was fitting my key into the door when I noticed the scrap of paper stuck to the fanlight with an inch of clear tape. It was well above my eye level, though obviously not my father's, and the scrawl on it said, 'Gone around the corner for lunch – join us'.

I grappled with the news. There were several corners for them to have gone around at each end of my short street, but the nearer one was the more likely. I made my way curiously to the end of the street and peered up and down without catching sight of any familiar figures. Trusting to luck, I turned towards the main road.

They were sharing the window table in the little shopfront greasy spoon across the street, the old-fashioned, chips-with-everything café that must have been there for decades, certainly since long before Islington had grown fashionable – there still isn't an aubergine in sight. The pushchair had been dismantled, its seat clamped firmly to the back of the chair at my father's side. Judging by the state of the table top, they'd been there for a while. Somebody had tied a tea towel around Ben and brought him a small bowl of apple sauce with a dab of ice cream on top. He was making determined but inaccurate use of a large spoon. Barnabas looked stiff, alert and a little apprehensive. I delved into my shoulder bag for a handful of tissues and went to join them.

'He has also had two fish fingers,' Barnabas was saying reproachfully as I came into earshot, 'and a spoonful of mashed potato. And much of a cup of milk. He is a little wet – all over, I believe. We were not expecting your continued absence.'

I said quietly, 'Frank Digby's been killed.'

It took him a moment to ask: 'How?'

I told him that Frank had been hit by a car – several times. My father formed a word that might have turned into 'why' or 'when' but instead became, 'You must explain. I'll just pay.'

'Ben hasn't finished,' I pointed out, 'and I'm starving, so I'll have a toasted ham and cheese sandwich while we're waiting, please. And a tea. And I don't want to talk here, partly because there are too many ears, and most of all because I have a feeling you're going to hit the roof.'

Barnabas looked at me hard and demonstrated his decency by giving the owner my order and watching me eat with the most gentlemanly, and pointed, tolerance of this unfortunate delay.

'How is Phyllis taking it?' my father asked eventually. 'And, most importantly, where does she stand in all this?'

We had returned to my chaotic living room and were sitting there in comparative peace. I delayed my answer for a moment by pretending to listen for noises from the bedroom, where Ben was now taking his afternoon rest. The silence suggested that he had fallen asleep after the excitement of dining out. The thought of it produced a jaw-cracking yawn; my interrupted night was catching up with me, and I didn't feel sharp enough to deal with the questions my father had been asking, especially this last one. Because as I'd been telling my story my own uneasiness had grown, if anything. There were too many of his questions I couldn't even begin to answer.

I tried even harder, reviewing my impressions of the morning. 'She was,' I said slowly, 'bowled over at first. Then brave. Tight-lipped. She didn't cry. She didn't actually say much. I can't say why, but the more I think about it, the more I wonder whether she wasn't . . . "expecting it" is a bit strong. But not quite surprised when the constable turned up. Almost as though this was something she'd been afraid of.'

Barnabas closed his eyes. I watched him thinking about that.

I added hastily, 'I don't suppose the marriage was a grand romance, but I know she really was fond of him. And loyal.'

'Meaning?'

'Meaning that she wouldn't do anything against his interests.'

'But what were his interests,' Barnabas persisted; 'and does that mean she might be lying to everybody, including you, in defence of them? Why, for example, was he in jail when she met him? In what type of criminal activity had he engaged? "False accounting" could mean anything or nothing very serious. It could even have been some kind of compromise patched together because he had agreed to co-operate with the prosecution. I believe the Americans call it "plea bargaining", and it is not supposed to happen here. The question is, what was the actual crime? Something serious enough to lead to murder? That is not impossible, although I would be more inclined to imagine fraud or embezzlement, considering his profession.'

I'd thought of that already and dismissed it because I assumed that a man who had a record for embezzlement would find it hard to get work as a bookkeeper. But Barnabas maintained that I was wrong to ignore the possibility, and lectured: 'It is a principle of British law that when a criminal has served his sentence, he has "paid his debt" and has the right to pick up his life, if he can. Consider also the point that this superintendent let drop. He *did* say that Digby had been "co-operating" with them, if I remember you. If he was getting help from a grateful police force, they would undoubtedly have pulled strings, provided references, got him contracts . . .'

'Paige said something about helping him to set up a new identity when he left prison.'

'There!' Barnabas snapped. 'He co-operated and they were protecting him. Inadequately, it would seem. I have heard of something called a "witness protection programme" – unless that is another American invention? Clearly we are in that territory. Presumably your Inspector Lyon is involved because

Scotland Yard were running the operation. Now, everything suggests that he was still of measurable value to them and a continuing danger to somebody else. Therefore, the police will delve into it and uncover a sordid tale of revenge. The nub of the matter remains: whatever had he been mixed up in? Deliberately and repeatedly running the man down with a car strikes me as unpleasantly gangster-like.'

He was probably right. It made some sense of what Paige had been saying. Though not of everything. I ought to make a list of the questions that kept popping in and out of my mind. There was the matter of the stolen computer in particular. Something Phyllis had said that I couldn't recall for the moment, though I remembered wondering about it. Something in Paige's manner that had even suggested . . .

'For goodness' sake go and take a nap!' Barnabas snapped. 'I shall be downstairs. In all likelihood, I shall even write a few catalogue entries. I'll wake you up when it's time for you to make a pot of tea, if Ben hasn't already done so. Go!'

I yawned myself to my feet and tottered down the hallway. In the darkened bedroom, Ben was lying on his back in the cot with his eyes closed. I staggered over to the bed, fell down and closed my own eyes . . . opened them, rolled on to my elbow, and was wide awake. It took me a few minutes to work out what had started to buzz around in my head. When I knew what I'd remembered and what I'd decided to do about it, I crept back into the living room and picked up the phone.

Phyllis's number was answered by the machine. I said, 'It's Dido,' and hung up. Then I perched on the arm of the settee, stared out at the empty street where the rain was falling with a kind of languid determination, and considered the possibilities. When the forensic team had finished, she might have gone out. Or she might not feel like answering the phone. Or there was a problem.

I padded into the bedroom where Ben was still sleeping off his lunch, switched on the baby alarm and retrieved my shoes. Then I pulled my raincoat off the hook, transferred my wallet, mobile and car keys to my shoulder bag, and closed the front door behind me as quietly as I could, because although I didn't mean to be gone for long, it would be convenient if Ben went on sleeping.

At that point the phone in the sitting room rang. I unlocked the door and ran to catch it.

Phyllis's voice said without preliminaries, 'I was lying down.'

'I'm just on my way over. I take it they've finished?'

'They left half an hour ago. They weren't looking too happy until they got round to that bathroom handle. That cheered them up.'

'At least they're out of your hair,' I said weakly.

'Yes . . .' Her tone suggested she thought this was a little doubtful.

I said impatiently, 'Look, don't worry. We're going to work it out. I'll be there in ten minutes.'

Letting myself into the shop, I paused for a second just inside the door. I have a nice shop, with high oak shelves that stretch along the walls and form an island in the middle of the room, all packed with desirable books. I wanted to wander up and down the aisles for half an hour, taking volumes down and opening them up, checking that the prices were up to date, smelling the dust, looking at the illustrations. I'd even have enjoyed getting down to the boring round of invoicing and wrapping orders to post, instead of rushing around north London on private rescue missions. I could think of quite a lot of little tasks that were overdue.

In the back room, Barnabas was speaking. At first I thought he'd let an unexpected customer into the shop, but then I heard him hang up the phone and went to join him.

'I couldn't sleep.'

'So you're going out instead,' he observed, eyeing my coat. 'Shopping at Harrods? Assignation? Skiing holiday in Austria?'

I flipped the switch on the baby alarm that sat on top of the filing cabinet. 'I'm going back to Power Street. I think I'd better bring Phyllis here to stay for a few days.'

Barnabas grunted approval.

'I might be gone for a while. She may need convincing,

and she'll have to pack a case. Ben is still asleep, but . . .'

'It doesn't matter,' Barnabas said briskly. 'I might as well be upstairs, for all the good I'm doing here. When he wakes up, I shall read aloud from Sir Philip Sidney's *Sonnets*. But in the morning, let me warn you, you're on your own. It's too late now for me to get to Colindale before they close, but I've decided to run up to the newspaper library first thing tomorrow. It will save time if you can find out from Phyllis the date of her husband's trial.'

'There's no reason to think it would be reported in the newspapers, is there?' I asked vaguely.

Barnabas snorted. 'Of course it was! If Frank Digby had been prosecuted for, say, disorderly conduct, or travelling on the tube without a ticket, do you really think that superintendents and ladies from Scotland Yard would be running about after him?'

I apologised and pointed out again that I was short of sleep. However, my memory was working now. 'Paige mentioned that the conviction was in 1992. And don't forget that you're looking for somebody called "Francis Brunton". I'd better go – she's waiting.'

The baby alarm had started to broadcast the sounds of somebody stirring. Barnabas sighed elaborately, though we both knew that this was just an act, and I turned to go.

'There is another thing,' he said to my retreating back. 'Who was the one who was there last night but didn't return this morning with the others? The third man?'

I called back smartly, 'Orson Welles.'

Barnabas growled.

The last of the afternoon light was fading as I got out of the car once more in front of the flats and pulled my collar up against the rain. Somebody had already fitted new bulbs into the light sockets, but the broken shades hadn't been replaced, and all the corners of the stairwell were bright. Standing at the glass door waiting to be buzzed in, I felt conspicuous and vulnerable. Anybody could be waiting in the road, looking through the big windows in the front wall, watching me climb up to the top. It would be like that all the time now for Phyllis.

When she opened the door of the flat, I said, 'You can't stop here.'

She looked at me bleakly. 'No.'

'What are you going to do? Will you use the air ticket?'

Her answer came so quickly that I knew she'd been asking herself the same thing. 'I can't leave now. Not until it's finished. I have to know . . .' She stopped.

I took a breath. 'Then I've come to invite you to stay with us. It'll be the settee in the living room, I'm afraid.'

She nodded slowly. 'It might be a risk, you know.'

I couldn't believe that, unless . . . I said, 'I don't see that, unless Frank was doing something illegal and you were mixed up in it.'

She stiffened and said, 'If I was some sort of criminal . . .'

Damn! I interrupted very carefully, 'That isn't what I was saying. It just sounded that way. I'm sorry. What I mean is that if Andrew and Moore were looking for something Frank had, they must know by now that it isn't here. So unless they thought that *you* know about it, or that you'd been involved, I don't understand why you think it would be dangerous for you to stay with me. All right?'

Her face softened. 'That's just the trouble. Dido . . . look, will you go and play the message tape in the answering machine? You know where it is. I'll just pack a few things.'

Phyllis had replaced the machine on one shelf of the little bookcase in the living room. I pressed 'playback', the machine clicked and whirred, and I listened until I understood. No message, just a click as the connection was broken. Silence. After about twenty seconds there was another click because somebody had phoned and hung up for a second time without speaking. The same thing happened with the third call. And the fourth. Each time, the message they left was silence, not even heavy breathing. Then my own voice, sounding like a stranger, was saying, 'It's Dido.' I switched off and wandered back to the bedroom.

'You didn't use dial-back to find out the number of the person who was phoning?'

'Of course I did. The message said that the number of the caller was "withheld", whatever that means.'

It couldn't be helped. My impulse was to leave the machine turned off, let them ring until they got bored. The problem was that Phyllis needed to pick up messages over the next few days because there would be people trying to get in touch with her: police, family, friends . . . and the silent caller. I was starting to wonder what else had been left on this tape recently.

I went back, opened up the machine, and saw that the message tape was only a standard audio cassette. There were others like it beside the music system, and I located a new tape and unwrapped it. Then I pocketed the old one. I'd return it after I'd run it through my own system and made sure I hadn't missed anything, but there was no reason why Phyllis should be forced to listen to a series of phone calls that were nothing but silent threats.

By the time I returned, she was closing the top of a small case.

'When did that start?'

'I told you about the ones I thought were from Frank? Maybe they weren't, after all. There was another when we got back from the police station this morning. The next came half an hour after. He's phoning every hour or so. If I pick up the receiver, they hang up. If I leave it, then they hang up after six rings exactly.'

I'd been right that it was a threat. 'But there's no reason for them to know you're at my place, or even that I exist. I've left the machine turned on, so you'll be able to pick up your messages any time you want to, but if it goes on you ought to report it. The police can probably trace the number. What did they find this morning – those people?'

'I heard one of them say there were three different lots of fingerprints on the handle of the bathroom door. When did Sergeant Andrew touch it?'

I described what had happened while Ben and I were locked in the bathroom. 'So they'll be able to identify him, assuming he has a record. Phyllis . . . did you tell them about the air ticket?'

Phyllis shook her head. 'It's not as if I'll be using it. Anyway, not yet.'

'Did you tell them about the safe?'

She looked away. 'No. Maybe I should've, but that safe was Frank's, and I want to know what's inside before I tell them about it.'

It was time to say what had popped into my mind when I was supposed to be napping. 'You know that card from Frank?'

'Do you want to see it again? It's in my bag.'

I said I did, and she found the envelope and handed it to me. I pulled out the blue flowers and opened the card. I'd remembered correctly.

'When's your birthday?'

'October fourteenth.'

'This isn't a birthday present. He's just reminding you about it.'

Phyllis frowned. 'What does that mean?'

At last I knew. 'He was sending you a message – privately, in case somebody else read it. He's reminding you of a date. It must be important. Is it the combination of his safe?'

For the first time that day she smiled slowly. 'Of course. He likes – liked – number tricks. Do you mind staying a little longer?'

We pulled the panel away from the side of the bath and I sat on the floor in front of the hole. The electronic lock had an ordinary numerical keypad. It didn't look particularly sturdy, and I wondered whether brute force wouldn't work, if the birth date didn't.

'Ten, fourteen?' Phyllis suggested over my shoulder.

I pushed one-oh-one-four and it didn't work. Then I tried fourteen-ten, because I was sure that we had the right idea and the combination wouldn't be difficult to find. That wasn't it, though. All right.

'Year?'

'1952.'

I played with eight digits, and then tried six, using date, month, and then '52. It was right. Something clicked under my fingers. Phyllis reached past me and pulled the door open.

We had got into a small box with thick, cemented wall linings. I'd been expecting to see a few computer disks, but the small space was half full. Phyllis pulled cautiously at a transparent plastic sleeve and tipped out three passports. The first one was in the name of 'Francis John Digby'. Then 'Frank Brunton'. Also 'Laurence Elliot'. The photos were all Polaroid shots of Frank which had obviously been taken at the same time.

Beneath the collection of passports was a large brown envelope. Phyllis pulled it out and emptied the contents on to the tiles: cash cards in the names of Frank Digby and L. Elliot, National Insurance cards in the names of Brunton and Digby; birth certificates for Digby and Elliot: Digby had been born in Sheffield in 1948 and Elliot in Clapham the following year. A savings deposit book with the name of a building society on the cover, and the signature of Laurence F. Elliot inside. It all looked genuine. So did the stack of fifty-pound notes held together with a thin rubber band, thirty-five in all.

'It looks like he was ready to scarper,' Phyllis said unnecessarily. Her face was stiff. Nothing we'd found had surprised her.

'Maybe that's what the air ticket is about: so you could join him in Australia if he had to make a run for it. Didn't you have any idea at all?'

She seemed unable to take her eyes off the documents that we had scattered across the tiles. 'Oh, I knew something was wrong, all right. But he was going to tell me about it when he got back. I'm sure he would've told me when . . . We better pick this stuff up.'

The last item was another brown envelope, unsealed. I could feel the hard slab of a computer disk inside it. I put it aside and thought fast.

'I think we'd better put all these documents back and shut the door. This must be what Moore and Andrew were looking for. I think the best thing is to lock the safe again, but if you leave the cover off then anybody who breaks in here for a look will see it right away. They should assume that the disk or whatever they want must be inside. With luck they'll concentrate on getting the door open, and if all these things are here, they might even decide that there's nothing else, so they'll leave without taking the place apart – or waiting for you to come back.'

Phyllis laughed explosively. 'Right now, I don't give a monkey's. All right, you're right – of course you are. I can't stand this, I don't even want to touch the bloody stuff . . . Dido, what am I going to do?'

My heart sank, but I said, 'Just give yourself time. Maybe we can find out what's going on. Look, we're going to need some information. If you don't mind, I'm going to phone Paul Grant again.'

For the second time that day I sat on the bathroom floor and rang his number, but this time there was no answer. I knew the number of the Islington station switchboard and dialled that. After the usual delay, it was answered by a man's voice. I asked for DI Grant.

A silence lasted just long enough to tell me that something was wrong. When the voice finally spoke, it said, 'Inspector Grant is on leave. Can I put you through to somebody else?'

I searched my memory. Nearly two years ago I'd met Paul's superintendent, a man called . . . called . . .

'Superintendent Colley, please.'

'I'll try him,' the voice said. 'Your name is . . . ?'

I told him and waited.

The voice returned after another interval. 'I'm sorry, miss, but the superintendent isn't available at the moment. Would you like to leave a message?'

I switched off.

'What is it?'

'They're trying to tell me that Paul's on leave, but he didn't say anything about that when I was talking to him this morning. In fact, he said he was busy. I hope it's all right.' I could still hear his voice in my ear saying rapidly, *if you ever tell anybody I made this phone call, I could be in trouble.* I certainly hadn't told anybody. I tried his personal number again and let it ring until an electronic voice invited me to record a message. I didn't.

I said, 'I need a phone book. The business directory,' and handed Phyllis the brown envelope and the banknotes before I stuffed the rest of the things back where we'd found them and pushed the door shut.

'I'll get it,' Phyllis said abruptly. She left, and came back in a minute with the directory I wanted. I found Scotland Yard's number, dialled it, asked to be put through to Diane Lyon. This time there were no funny pauses: the voice merely said, 'Inspector Lyon is in a meeting. Who is this? I'll put you through to another . . .'

I interrupted. 'Thanks, no. Thanks, I'll try again,' and hung up. *No names, no come-back.*

Watching Phyllis reopen her case and push the disk and Frank's bundle of money down under the rest, I urged myself to do some lateral thinking. Diane Lyon probably wouldn't have told me anything anyway. But there was somebody else who might help, within the limits of correctness. I returned to the bedroom for my shoulder bag and leafed through the names in the back of my organiser. I'd had dealings with Oxford CID some months ago, and one of the detectives I'd met then hadn't been unfriendly: Jen Lassalle. I found a number and tried it, and this time reached my target.

We exchanged greetings and I explained, 'I need a favour. To make a long story short, I have a friend who's having some problems, and a detective in Islington CID whom I've known for a long time was helping her. I've just phoned him, and they say he's on leave. But he was at work when I saw him earlier today – he certainly wasn't about to go off on leave. I'm worried about him. Could you find out what's happened? It might just be some kind of communications problem, but it could be something serious. Can you possibly . . . ?'

'I could phone Islington and ask for him.' Her voice was cautious. 'Do you want to hold the line? Or shall I get back to you?'

I said I'd hold, and lay flat across the bed with my legs dangling, listening to faint sounds at the other end and trying to keep from jumping to conclusions. I passed more time by worrying about my phone bill. A few pounds ticked away before she returned.

'I've spoken to them. I can tell you he's been suspended.'

'*Suspended?* What does that mean?'

'I didn't ask for any details.' Her tone was stiff, which told me as clearly as anything could that I was pushing my luck. I thanked her for her help and switched off, presumably to our mutual relief.

Phyllis was trying to force her overfilled bag shut. She leaned on it until it surrendered and asked, 'What happened?'

I said, 'Let's go. Let's just get out of here so I can think. They claim that he's been suspended. Something's wrong.'

CHAPTER EIGHT

Looking

As I swung the car into the Essex Road, the rain that had been falling over London all evening turned to sleet. It was the middle of the evening; it had been dark for nearly four hours already under the heavy overcast, and it felt like the middle of the night. The pavements were empty; most people were probably sensible enough to be at home watching television, and the traffic was sparse and moved cautiously. I turned the wipers to their high setting, nudged the heater up a notch, and watched the slush collecting at the bottom of the windscreen.

My thoughts kept scattering. The image of Frank Digby's empty, waxy face intruded. Sooner or later I was going to have to go to bed. I opened my window so that the raw air would blow into my face and remind me to concentrate on my driving.

We'd spent the past hour in my sitting room trying not to stare too much at the brown envelope on my coffee table. Staring didn't help. The multiple passports and identity documents had told their story clearly enough, but the disk seemed useless. It was visibly bigger and thicker than standard floppy disks, bright blue, with two corners chopped off. Whatever the thing was, my computer wouldn't cope with it.

Well, I could do something about that.

Ernie Weekes had been my part-time employee for more than a year. He was by now in the final months of a business course at a college in Kilburn. An old friend of mine who taught him there had originally introduced us in response to my whingeing about computers in general and my own pathetic attempts to use one in particular. In theory, Ernie works at the shop two half-days a week. He enters acquisitions into the stock database, helps Barnabas to get the next catalogue set up for printing, and, since Christmas, has run the website he persuaded me to put up and from which I have actually started to sell books. From time to time in the past he has been helpful in less technical ways. A twenty-year-old from a family of Sierra Leone refugees, he is short, tough, optimistic and very strong. He would be at the head of any sensible person's shortlist for a computer-genius bodyguard.

In the circumstances, I rang his mother's house. Ernie himself answered the phone, listened to my apologies and explanations, cut to the point, and made me describe the disks.

'Zip disks.' His tone rang with authority. 'You gotta have a special drive. Listen, I could get you one tomorrow. Cost you, but they're good f' backing stuff up fast. Now we're running website operations, an' the whole stock is on a database, you really need one.'

I thought rapidly. 'They're extras? I mean, a zip drive wouldn't be an internal drive?'

'Not likely,' Ernie said decisively. 'Not 'n a *old* computer like you said it is. You're prob'ly lookin' at a little box with a cable and a transformer. Bit like your old modem except it'll have a little window on top.'

I came to a quick decision and announced, 'Ernie, it'll be quicker for me to go and get the one that belonged to the person who owned these disks. You *are* coming in tomorrow afternoon as usual?'

He was. We arranged that unless I phoned back within half an hour to tell him it was missing, Ernie would arrive as early as he could, bringing a program from college to install Frank's drive on my machine. His bright tone made me suspect that he was planning to skip a class or two so he could arrive early and find out what I was really up to. I gritted my teeth, borrowed Phyllis's keys, left her putting Ben to bed, and set off in the rain.

You must be doolally. As Barnabas would assure me if he knew what I was up to. *It could have waited until morning.* It couldn't wait until morning, because I was supposed to be opening the shop in the morning. *You must be doolally!* I sang, 'Do-o-olally', mostly to drown out the silly feeling that I might not want to go into the Digby flat alone, and pulled up outside the block once again. After I'd killed the engine and the lights and set the central locking, I stood beside the car until the sleet on my face woke me up enough to move.

I tried to assess the situation. Cars were parked tightly on both sides of the road, but I couldn't see any lurker. There were lights on everywhere in the block except at Phyllis's windows. It looked all right. Of course it was all right. *In and out,* I urged myself. *No hanging about!*

I let myself in with Phyllis's key and climbed the stairs one more time, past closed doors with the ordinary sounds of living behind them – the beginning of the BBC news on a television set, a voice calling, vaguely familiar theme music playing . . . I stepped through the Digbys' front door and shut myself into a deadened silence. The air already smelled stale. I had to check the sitting room first. From the doorway I could see the red blink on the answering machine in the darkness. Somebody had been phoning her. I could guess who. I pressed the button on the machine, listened to the tape whirring and the click of the speaker. Silence. Click. Then again.

The third time, though, there was a voice. A woman.

'Frankie?' She hesitated. There was something odd in that voice. I felt a shiver run down my spine. 'Frankie, it's Lal. Listen, about my car, I told Andy it'd been towed away, and I'd get it back myself. If it don't turn up soon he'll want to know. You better get it back 'ere. If there's a problem, you phone me in the morning just after nine-thirty an' we'll figure something. After nine-thirty. Orright?' There was a silence before the connection was broken. Then the machine clicked and rewound.

That was the last of the messages, so I flung myself on the telephone, dialled 1471, and listened to the measured, artificial tones of the digital voice say, *The number of the last person who called, was: zero, one, eight, one, eight, eight, three . . .* I lost track of the digits while I was looking for something to write with, got them on the second try, and finally went back to the collection of cassettes for another replacement. Phyllis might know who Lal was if she heard the voice, and Lal certainly knew something about Frank's actions that we didn't. It had been a strong, mature voice, but hesitant. Anxious. Middle-aged, maybe? Something about the way she had spoken suggested an old friend. Or family, even. Who else would Frank have borrowed a car from? Phyllis had never told me anything about family, though she had talked sometimes about her own younger brother and his family at home. But Frank's accent had marked him as a native Londoner. So had Lal's. Phyllis had to know who she was.

In Frank's office I flipped the light switch. The drive I was looking for was sitting on top of the filing cabinet. I might even have seen it there earlier. I wound the cables around the box and its black transformer, turned out the lights again, and let myself out on to the landing. Meatloaf was playing loudly behind one of the other doors. I ran down the stairs, pushed by the driving music, and out again into the sleet.

Back in George Street, I left the car on the yellow line outside the shop, stumbled yawning past its door, and let myself in the second door, leading on to the stairs. At the top of those I let myself in silently. There was a light in the sitting room, but the only occupant was Mr Spock, who half opened his eyes at my arrival, twitched an ear, and remained curled up on the settee. Phyllis must have remembered to feed him, or he would be telling me about it. I crept back to the bedroom and pushed its door open slightly. The light from the lamp on the bedside table fell across the cot, where Ben slept with a thumb in his mouth. Phyllis was lying sideways across my bed, on top of the duvet, fully dressed and snoring. She must have been sitting there, telling Ben a story, when they both fell asleep. I pulled the door to and retreated into the other room, budged Spock into a corner, and sat on the spot he had been warming. He yawned delicately, curling his tongue, and settled again.

After a few minutes I found I'd been asleep and the telephone was ringing. I levered myself to my feet and staggered over to pick it up.

'Dido?'

I found my voice with difficulty. 'Paul! What's happened and where are you?'

'Listen, will you turn off your lights and then come downstairs and let me in?'

'Where are you?'

'Just outside. I don't have long.'

I was trying to think, frustrated by the questions pouring into my mind and the slowness of being three-quarters asleep. 'Are you in your car? Where is it? Should I come out? Phyllis is here, asleep, so . . .'

'All right, maybe you'd better.' He sounded impatient. 'We need to talk.'

'Where?'

'Just across the road, two cars up. Will you come?'

'I'm there,' I said and hung up. With the light off, I went to the window to check the street. I could make out the familiar shape of Paul's Ford just where he had said it was. The interior was dark. It had stopped sleeting, and nothing was moving out there. I took my house keys and slipped out of the silent flat. Across the street, the passenger door opened for me; I slid inside and closed it.

'Paul, I've been trying to contact you all day . . .'

'I know. That's why I'm here, damn it!' There was an edge to his voice. 'You've got to stop it. I've been suspended. You have no reason to contact me, to get people to try to find me, or ask questions. The more you go on, the worse you make it. If I know you, you'll stick at it until everything goes down. You can't do this to me!'

I was abruptly reminded how Paul hacks me off sometimes. When he does this kind of thing. Most of the time.

I took a deep breath and started, 'Can't? You know, I haven't even begun yet! Frank Digby's been murdered. He must have been killed by those two policemen you saw, the ones who visited Phyllis this morning. What do you know about it? You more or less told me that Frank was dead when you phoned, so you obviously knew what had happened. What does it have to do with you? You phoned me, and then the next thing I hear you've been *suspended*. Nobody can even *speak* to you! *Why?*'

I could hear him shifting in the driver's seat. 'Will you shut up for a minute?' I looked at his profile. He was staring straight ahead over the wheel at the road, not looking at me. 'It's simple: I've been ordered not to talk to you. If I disobey, that's a disciplinary matter, as Colley kept saying this morning. It's something you've never been able to accept.'

I copied his stance. Now we were both staring coldly ahead. All right, I understood what he was saying. 'Then why are you talking to me now?'

'I'm trying to persuade you to stop what you're doing. I'm not giving you information or discussing the case. I'm telling you to keep out of Frank Digby's affairs. You're well out of order. You are endangering an investigation, and you don't have any idea what you're getting into.'

A little knot of anger was growing in the middle of my chest. I said stiffly, 'If I tell you what I think I'm getting into, will you tell me how it affects you? Frank was some kind of police informer. I haven't found out what he was doing, but he must have been killed because of it, and there are corrupt policemen involved in his murder, aren't there? Moore and Andrew, or whatever their real names are. They raided the Digbys' place last night because of something of his they were looking for: it had to be financial records, since they took his computer. The records they wanted weren't in the computer, so they came back this morning looking for them.' I turned my head and looked at his profile, silhouetted against the dim light beyond his window. 'Your turn. You've been suspended. Why are you involved, then?'

There was a long silence, then a little snort. Laughter? I waited. A car turned into the road at the northern end. Paul stiffened and grabbed my arm; but the car slid to the kerb, the headlights blinked off, and we watched a man and a woman get out, slamming the doors and heading towards one of the

Victorian houses thirty yards away. His grip relaxed, at which point I wondered whether he'd been frightened. The anger I was feeling faded abruptly. If I shivered, it wasn't really because of the cold.

'It was your fault, you know.'

'What was?'

'When I got back, I asked Colley if he knew anything about a couple of CID men from another division wandering into our patch. He said he'd ask around, and I think he made a couple of phone calls. Half an hour later, he called me into his office and got me to give him a blow-by-blow description of what'd happened. When I told him about Moore's warrant card, he nearly flipped. He asked me whether I thought your two men had any idea who I was.'

I remembered. 'They gave you a funny look when you passed each other on the stairs. And . . . yes, you gave your name and station when you spoke to me on the Entryphone. Andrew was standing right beside me at the time.'

He sighed. 'That's what I thought. What I told Colley. He left me sitting there in his office while he went out to make another phone call or two, I suppose. Half an hour later the Chief Inspector called me in and told me I'm suspended until further notice. Go home. About two minutes later, as I'm walking out of the building feeling pissed off, I hear a rumour that I've been caught taking kickbacks from that dealer I'd arrested, and I'd handed him in to try to get the ACS off my back.'

'Oh,' I said.

He echoed, 'Oh.' He didn't sound happy.

'Then you aren't really suspended?'

'The whole station believes that I am.'

I asked, 'But what are you really doing? Paul, do you remember Diane Lyon?'

'No!'

I was thrown for a moment. 'What do you mean, "no"? She—'

'Leave it alone.'

'What?'

Paul stirred. 'I've said everything to you that I can, and more. No, not exactly. One more thing: this is dangerous.'

That was obvious. Frank had been killed. I waited silently.

'You said you thought that bent cops are involved.'

'Yes.'

'Well, if you're right about that – use your head! You can't just call the station, the way you called me this morning, if you know that whoever comes running might be on the other side, and that he knows all about you: where you live, what you're doing, how much of a danger you are to him and his mates.'

I said, 'Oh,' and sat back thinking, as recommended. Putting it that way suggested not just two stray crooked detectives, but something more like a conspiracy. Of course, Paul was quite likely to be exaggerating, trying to frighten me off, but it made sense in.the light of his story about the 'suspension' that something was going on. I had some more questions about that. The knot of anger and anxiety tightened.

Paul continued relentlessly. 'So the only thing you can do is just keep out of it. You say Phyllis Digby is upstairs with you? Could she go right away somewhere in the morning? Take a holiday until things are sorted out? No forwarding address? They wouldn't like it, but it would be a good move from her point of view, believe me.'

I said I'd suggest it.

'And set that intruder alarm tonight before you go to sleep. And every night.' I heard his voice falter, then harden again. 'Don't try to contact me, because you'll just put us both in the wrong. Keep out of it from now on. You'd better go back. Sleep well.'

Sleep well. I stood inside the door of the flat, thinking about it, nursing a rush of anger. I keep being roughly reminded just why, about half the time, I find Paul Grant intolerable. I could feel my hands shaking, but I wasn't sure whether that was anger or fear.

I drew the heavy curtains on the sitting-room windows before I switched on the table lamp again and, by the dim light seeping halfway down the hall, slipped into the bathroom and used the mouthwash. On the way back I stopped at the control box and set the alarm; it was the first time in months that I'd bothered, but it covered the area of the downstairs door and the staircase, and was linked to the police, which I counted a plus despite the way Paul had tried to frighten me; and with bars on the kitchen window it made the flat effectively safe from any intruder who was too big to get down the chimney. After that I panicked because I couldn't remember double-locking the street door, and my head wasn't working, and there was no way I could just leave it at that and still manage to get to sleep. I did remember to disarm the alarm system again before I crept out and began my furtive descent to the street door.

This time I checked the chain and snibbed the catch too.

I was aching for sleep: stupid with sleep. I counted myself grimly back into the flat, trying to do everything properly this time: one, re-re-check the downstairs door; two, climb the stairs; three, snap the catch on the upstairs door; four, reset the alarm. Five, slump on to the settee wrapped in the sleeping bag . . . But ideas were still running around my mind like ants. The idea that Paul had been got out of the way by suspending him. Was that for his safety? Or was it because somebody thought they could make use of a detective like him, somebody with a brand-new black reputation as a crooked cop?

Something heavy landed on my chest, attempted to force a bony head under my chin, and began a deafening purr. I growled, 'Geddoff,' and slid helplessly into darkness.

CHAPTER NINE

Three Bears

Bad temper filled my living room like smoke. We were all there together, trying to wait it out. Phyllis and Ben had sprawled on the settee with my sleeping bag as a bolster. Only fifteen minutes ago I'd been rolled up inside that with my head well down, as warm and comfortable as the yolk of an egg, listening to the gusts of wind against the windowpanes and trying not to think about the fact that I needed to have difficult conversations with two people as soon as I could, and even though I wasn't in the mood: Lal Whoever and Phyllis Digby herself.

This morning, Ben had woken up bad-tempered and grizzling, probably coming down with a cold. So had Mr Spock, who had eaten his breakfast with a haughty air and now was sitting on the back of the settee lashing his tail at the wet street. They both had as much of my sympathy as I could spare. I'd slumped into the armchair, watching Phyllis trying to distract Ben by reading aloud from his book, a brightly coloured *Goldilocks and the Three Bears* presented by Barnabas for his first birthday. I was wondering whether this was likely to give Ben a jaundiced view of women and some overly optimistic expectations of bears. I also wondered about last night. At least the coffee I was drinking was fresh, and somebody else had made it before I'd even managed to fall out of bed.

I tried to pull myself together.

'Who is this "Lal" person?' I asked. 'Don't you want to hear the message? It sounds odd.'

Phyllis threw me a sardonic glance. 'I'll take your word for it.' She waited until Goldilocks had been dealt with – pushy brat – then closed the book and finally said, 'That's Lal Fisher.'

'Who?'

'Frank's sister. She's stuck by him, and she was his witness when Frank and I got married. She came to London for our wedding. She was the only one in his family that Frank invited.'

'So they kept in touch. So why did Frank—?'

'As far as I know,' she interrupted, 'they didn't really, not regularly. I know that she phoned Frank sometimes – his birthday, Christmas morning, that kind of thing: but he didn't mention her very often. He never talked much about his past, even if I asked him some question. It's funny: there were times, especially the first five or six months that I knew him, when he seemed like a person who'd turned up out of nowhere when he came in for his operation.'

The thought popped out at me: *Like Goldilocks, opening the door and walking in from nowhere to take over your life.* Was that really how Frank had been with Phyllis? I dragged myself back to the current question. 'Did you see her much after the wedding?'

'Never. She went home to Spain and for a while I more or less thought they'd lost touch. But like I said, she started to ring Frank every couple of months.' She hesitated and frowned. 'Come to think of it . . .'

I waited.

She blinked and shook her head slightly. 'It just came to me: I don't think he ever phoned her, not that I noticed. We'd be doing something, and the phone would ring. Frank would pick it up and after a while he'd call to me, "It's Lal – got any message for her, luv?" and I'd say, "Give her my love . . ."' Her voice cracked. Ben covered the moment by sneezing vigorously, and we got in each other's way looking for the tissues and urging him to blow.

'And yet she's back in London now, because he borrowed her car,' I pointed out when things had settled again.

Phyllis said opaquely, 'Those two were close from the time they were kids.'

I was considering that, but it didn't explain much. 'All right, now we know those were her car keys that they found in Frank's pocket. I think we have to tell the police: they'll want to know what kind of car it is. And you know that they need to find it. The other thing is, I don't suppose she knows he's dead.'

We watched Ben come to a decision. He croaked, 'More!', and I sat back thinking about how he was really beginning to talk while I watched them leaf backwards ceremoniously to the first picture. When I'd thought some more about Frank's sister I said, 'I think we ought to break the news to her. It'll be a chance to find out what she knows about . . . anything. Why he had her car, at least.'

'Well, you speak to her; I don't mind.'

'She doesn't know me.'

'Nor me. Met me once.'

Yes. Well, that would leave me breaking the news of her beloved brother's death to a woman I'd never met at all: not an opportunity I felt particularly qualified to grasp. I dropped the topic for the moment and went back to brooding on the other unpleasantness – Paul's behaviour, which was beginning to seem, in retrospect, melodramatic. I'd passed on his warning to Phyllis, who seemed noncommittal.

I left her and Ben still admiring Goldilocks' appetite for porridge and went to pull myself together.

It was quiet in the bathroom with the door shut. I opened the taps and leaned against the basin, watching it fill with hot water, and recognising that there was a kind of impatient sizzle in the pit of my stomach which wouldn't let me relax. I stared at the face in the mirror. The eyes that looked out at me appeared bloodshot and shifty, and my hair, which on good days is dark and curly, looked limp, greyish and matted this morning. Also, I seemed to be getting a pimple on my chin. Some feeble character in there was feeling sorry for herself. I switched my thoughts off, found the cloth lying sodden in the bottom of the bathtub and began to apply hot water to my face.

By the time I was dry again the mirror over the basin had steamed up. (I hunted around until I found my toothbrush hiding on top of the medicine cabinet.) If I could just decide what my next steps should be, then I'd get on with taking them. I printed 'Lal F' with my index finger in the steam that had condensed on the glass. That was first: when she phoned Frank last night she had asked him to ring her after nine-thirty this morning, and it was nearly that now. So I would speak to her first. What happened after that would depend partly on what she said. I persuaded the tube to disgorge the last hardening slug of toothpaste on to my brush and printed 'Paul' in the steam to look at while I brushed my teeth. There were things Paul obviously should explain, but I didn't think there was much chance of that, even assuming I could locate him. Cancel. I drew a line through him. Better to assume we were on our own for the time being.

I wrote 'Frank – trial?' third on the list, and added 'B'. Barnabas would be on his way right now to find out what kind of criminal Frank Digby had been. Or, to be more accurate, Francis Brunton. The law reports, if he found them, should give us an angle on the truth. Well, at least a place to start looking.

I finished my notes by printing 'Phyllis???' That was the most questionable item. I added a couple more question marks and flourishes to it. Paul had insisted that there was danger for both of us in what was going on, though he hadn't deigned to give his reasons. In fact, I wasn't quite sure why I'd even put her name on the list, unless Paul had started me wondering just how well I knew Phyllis. If his main purpose had been to put me off, he hadn't succeeded. But this morning it seemed that nothing in this whole mess made much sense. Maybe when I'd spoken to Lal and my father I'd be more able to work out what was happening and decide what if anything had to be done.

After consideration, I wiped out Phyllis's name with a swipe of the face-cloth. Like Paul, she was somebody to worry about, not really a line of investigation.

In practical terms that left Lal, exactly as I'd thought at the beginning.

Of course, you could behave sensibly for once, my internal voice remarked in the confident tones of my older sister, Pat – as it tends to – *for instance by phoning Superintendent Paige and telling him about the silent phone calls and Lal Fisher and everything.* There was something attractive in the idea that I might roll up all my questions into a little bundle and plonk them down on the desk of a chief superintendent. Let *him* deal with it. Good old Paige. I stared at what I'd written in the condensation. It would be a relief to get rid of all the problems with one more wipe. I shivered as I rubbed the words off the mirror. Paul Grant was daft. What had possessed him to turn up in the middle of the night bearing melodramatic warnings, trying to frighten me into what he would certainly call 'minding my own business', and generally acting like something out of a bad movie? I gave the mirror a grumpy last polish with the hand towel and went to find some clean clothes.

At about nine-thirty I drifted into the sitting room washed, dressed, in a state of mind that verged on the normal, and with a strategy. Ben and Phyllis looked as though they had settled in for the day.

'Phyllis, would you mind listening to the tapes now? I'm wondering whether there's anything else on them that might help us.'

She sighed mildly and told me to go ahead, but I noticed that she was listening carefully when I fitted the first of them into the cassette deck in my music centre and pushed the 'play' button. I'd put in the new reel, and we were treated to the same pattern of silences and clicks that we'd already heard, followed by Lal Fisher's voice. At the end of her message, we listened to the faint hiss of clean tape.

'Why did he borrow her car?' It had popped out. 'He could have hired one.'

This time, Phyllis's hesitation was obvious. 'Well, he didn't have a driving licence.'

All right, obviously you have to show a licence when you're hiring a car. 'But if he couldn't drive . . .'

'Oh, he could drive,' she interrupted quickly. 'He'd lost his licence. That's what he told me: he hadn't got round to sending away for a replacement. I thought it'd probably got lost when he was arrested. We never needed a car.'

I realised in time what it was going to sound like if I remarked that a man who had three passports and an assortment of other ID in various names would scarcely need to go without a driving licence when he needed one. In a way, it was lucky; it suggested that his need had been both urgent and unexpected, and that his sister should be able to give us some idea what had happened. Good! One step forward.

I changed tapes, rewound, and set the second one playing. Frank and Phyllis must have had this in their machine for a long time; the sound quality was poor and sometimes almost inaudible, presumably because it had been reused for too long. I heard my own voice near the beginning and identified a message I'd left for Phyllis in the middle of last week. There were lots of clicks and short bursts of message. Most were from people that Frank had worked for: from a 'Tom Laurence' about a VAT inspection, from a firm of chartered accountants in west London about a set of books that were overdue – dozens of similar fragments, largely obliterated by subsequent voices. Then we were in the patch of the silent phone calls, and my voice from yesterday suddenly said, 'It's Dido.' That brought us up to date. It was followed by an older message that seemed to go on for ever – Laurence again, worrying about his VAT returns – and a few fragments.

'There!'

I jumped. 'What? What was it?'

'Didn't you hear? That was Lal's voice, too: I'm sure of it.'

I rewound to the end of Laurence's fussing, and we listened again. A woman's voice started in mid-word, and was interrupted almost at once by a later message, but I thought that Phyllis had been right. I played that second or two of tape for the third time. She was saying something like '—Frank, you got to he—'. That was all. The tape itself ran out a moment later after a man's voice said, 'Please ring Smith and Howard as soon as possible.' There was no way of telling when any of these messages had been left.

'"Frank, you got to help me"?' I suggested.

Phyllis took a breath and said, 'Right.'

'So *she* phoned *him* in the first place?'

'Sounds like it. That was normal, anyway.'

'Is it just my imagination, or was she upset?'

'Worse,' Phyllis said, thinking about it. 'I mean, you can't be sure from a few words, but . . .'

'Frantic?' I offered. We looked at each other. 'So,' I re-capped, 'she is back in London now. Frank didn't tell you that? And it sounds as though something unpleasant happened.'

'She was upset,' Phyllis said slowly. 'I know it was just a second, but I thought she sounded really upset, much worse than yesterday.'

'"Fisher" – she's married?'

Phyllis nodded.

'So there was something she couldn't ask her husband to help with? Something *about* him?'

Phyllis found a tissue and held it to Ben's nose. 'Blow,' she said evasively, and then, 'I guess we ought to tell the police, eh? Unless we check with her first.'

I knew I'd won my point. My wristwatch said that it was time to phone.

But the telephone rang as I was reaching for it, and a male voice with an edge of authority in it said, 'Miss Dido Hoare?' I agreed that I was; the voice said, 'Please hold.'

I held, and simmered. It makes me want to spit when I'm interrupted in the middle of something and then told to cool my heels and wait for the arrival at his telephone of somebody who thinks his time is too important to spend any of it making his own phone calls. But it was only a second before the voice returned and said, 'Putting you through.'

'Miss Hoare?' A man. Not a familiar voice.

I said 'Yes?' unenthusiastically.

'Miss Hoare, I don't suppose you remember me, but we met a while back. Colley, Islington CID.'

I sat up. Paul Grant's boss was quite wrong. I did remember him very clearly. Once, a couple of years ago, he had demanded my attendance at a minor crime scene, asphyxiated me with his chain-smoking, and treated me like a schoolgirl. Perhaps my memory was exaggerating the event, but I certainly hadn't forgotten that yesterday he'd refused to talk to me when I phoned him, but now presumably something had come up and it had suited him to change his mind.

I said that I did remember him.

'Well, I was wondering if we could have a word. I don't suppose you could drop by the station? Some time this morning? As soon as possible? Just for a chat. I won't keep you long.'

I snarled silently at the receiver and said, 'I have a business to run.'

'It won't take ten minutes,' Colley informed me blandly. 'I'll send a car for you, if you like.'

I realised that he was not intending to enlighten me about the topic of our proposed chat, told him I would provide my own transport, and graciously agreed I would be with him as soon as I found it convenient. If my tone said that I begrudged wasting the time, I couldn't care less.

'What was that?'

I ungritted my teeth and explained to Phyllis.

She thought about it. 'Is it about Frank?'

Or Paul, more likely. A little chat might be interesting, after all. That was when I knew for sure that I was hooked by my own fatal curiosity. Again.

'Dido, I'm so sorry about all this trouble.'

I looked at Phyllis hard, and told her that nobody blamed her for anything – anything at all.

It was nearly twenty to ten. I smoothed out the crumpled sheet of paper on which I'd written down Lal's phone number, and dialled.

CHAPTER TEN

Contact

The phone rang. And rang. I was just deciding to try again later when a woman's voice spoke in my ear.

'Mrs Fisher?'

'Yes?'

I caught my breath and plunged in: 'My name is Dido Hoare; I'm a friend of Phyllis Digby. She . . .'

The voice said, 'You better wait.' The receiver clattered on a hard surface. Somewhere in the background I heard a door close and then footsteps returning.

'Yes?'

'Phyllis asked me to contact you about Frank. And your car.'

'*Phyllis* did?' There was alarm in the voice.

Enough. 'Mrs Fisher, something serious has happened and I need to talk to you. Can we meet? It's urgent. I'll gladly come to your house . . .'

'That's not possible. No.'

'Then would you like to come here? I run a bookshop in Islington – I don't know whether that's convenient for you, but this is really urgent.'

'A bookshop?' The voice sounded startled. 'What did you say your name is? You say you're a friend of Phyllis?'

Impatiently I repeated myself and added, 'She looks after Ben, my little boy.' There was a silence, but I could hear that the line was still open. After a moment I said cautiously, 'Phyllis and I really need to talk to you. Something very serious has happened . . . I know you're worried about your car.' That was idiotic, but I couldn't blurt out the news about Frank's death over the phone.

'I could meet you both somewhere,' the voice conceded slowly.

'We'll meet anywhere you like,' I said for Phyllis's benefit, raising my eyebrows at her. 'This morning, please? Where?'

'You say you live in Islington? Do you know 'Ampstead 'Eath? 'Ighgate Road?'

I said, reasonably accurately, that I did.

'Well, you know at the bottom end, Parliament 'Ill, there's two schools? There's where I can meet you, just by the tennis courts inside the gate to the park. At eleven? Say a quarter to, that's better.'

I'd have to be satisfied, because our whole conversation felt so tenuous that I was afraid of frightening her off. 'How will we recognise you?'

'I'll know Phyll,' she answered promptly. 'Look, you be sure she's with you.'

'She wants to see you,' I was telling Phyllis as I hung up.

She nodded slowly. 'We'd better wrap his lordship up warm, but a bit of fresh air will do us all good. If it doesn't rain.'

'If it rains,' I said, 'we'll persuade her to come and sit in the car while we talk.' I was working it out. 'Phyllis – that was weird. She wouldn't come here and wouldn't let us go to her. I think she wants to meet us in a public place. I think she only agreed because I said you'd come. She's still frightened of something. I hope she turns up. Anyway, if we leave now, I can call in on the way and find out what the police want.'

Phyllis just said, 'Well, it's a funny family.' She and Ben were already moving towards their coats. 'We'll find out,' she added, though (it struck me even then) without much enthusiasm. This was going to be a really difficult day.

Islington police station stands in a bleak street beyond the Green. Its only advantage is the large walled carpark, which meant that we wouldn't have to look for parking. I negotiated the traffic that was heading slowly south towards the chronic roadworks at the Angel and turned into the first available side street, after which it was only a short zigzag down to the big yellow-brick building. I left Phyllis and Ben blowing noses in the car and trudged around to the front door and the desk, where a receptionist passed me through the inner door so fast that I knew Colley had left his instructions. I edged around the uniformed men waiting in front of the lift and arrived at the superintendent's office, where the door sprang open in front of my face just as I was raising my hand to knock.

It was nearly two years since I'd last seen him, but he hadn't changed. Colley was a detective of the old school: rumpled, middle-aged, balding, pudgy. He waved me inside; and once again as I walked around the edge of the door I found a familiar face waiting for me. Diane Lyon was sitting at the head of the small conference table which filled one side of Colley's office, with a little stack of papers in front of her and an unreadable expression on her face.

Was I supposed to believe that this was a coincidence?

I made an effort not to let either of them see that her presence surprised me, nodded at her coolly. 'We keep bumping into each other.'

'Not exactly.' She smiled briefly. Naturally, there were things on her mind. 'I asked the superintendent if he could arrange a meeting while I was here. He thinks that you might be able to help us.'

Colley was emptying his overloaded glass ashtray into the wastepaper basket, sending a smelly cloudlet of ash into the overheated room. I watched him reach automatically for the cigarettes on his desk and rejected his offer of one. He coughed. 'Miss Hoare, good of you to come over.'

I said, 'Not at all, but I have my baby and his nanny waiting for me in the car, so I can't stay long. What's this about?'

The superintendent had put a disposable lighter and a cigarette together and was inhaling with enthusiasm. He exhaled a cloud and said into it, 'Hope you can help with a problem. You know DI Grant.' I looked at him carefully, suspecting sarcasm, but his face was noncommittal. 'I'm sorry to have to tell you there's been a complaint laid against him. We're trying to straighten it out. I hope you can confirm some of the things he told us.'

Liar. I looked at the two of them: obviously the story of Paul's suspension was still live, and my presence had something to do with that. I smiled warmly at Diane Lyon and said, 'Are you still at Special Branch, then? Or is it the Police Complaints Authority now?'

She looked at me coldly. 'Actually, it's a department called International and Organised Crime.'

I told her that I hoped it was a promotion and added, 'Drugs?'

'Among other things. Superintendent?'

Colley coughed again, looked at his cigarette and stubbed it out. 'Miss Hoare, DI Grant claims you phoned him here yesterday morning.'

It seemed safe to confirm that.

'Can you tell us what time you phoned, and what it was about?'

I estimated the time of my call and launched into an account of the visit to the Digby flat of two suspicious characters claiming to be CID officers, and then explained perfectly truthfully that I had called Paul to check on their identity and credentials. I explained that the two had removed themselves as soon as he had arrived. It was exactly the same story that I'd told Paige yesterday, and I was sure that none of it was news to my audience.

Diane Lyon extracted two sheets of paper abruptly from the top file and slid them down the table in my direction. 'Those are the two men that you and Mrs Digby saw yesterday?'

I nodded. 'Those are the computer pictures they did when we were up at Palmers Green.'

'Do you feel these are the best you can give us? Is there anything you'd like to change, now you've had time to think about it?'

I told her that although they might not be as accurate as photographs, I certainly couldn't improve on them. Actually, I was still marvelling at the system they had used to produce these things.

'Exactly what happened when DI Grant arrived at the Digby flat?' Colley put in. 'Did he exchange any words with them?'

'No. I saw them all look at each other as they passed on the stairs, but nobody said anything.'

'Are you sure of that?' Lyon snapped.

I raised my eyebrows and told her that I certainly was.

'So would you say that DI Grant would be able to identify those two?'

'I think so. Probably.'

Colley mumbled something that wasn't quite audible. His face was grim.

'They gave him a pretty close look too, so I suppose they'd all know one another again.'

Colley winced. 'Did DI Grant follow the men out of the building?'

I explained that Paul had remained upstairs with us for some minutes. 'He and I left together, maybe five minutes later, and there was no sign of them by then.' Or no evidence of it, anyway. My mind flickered back to the question of whether I'd been followed when I left Power Street. I added hastily, 'Where exactly is this leading? He must have told you all this himself.'

'You've corroborated aspects of his statement, thank you,' Colley said pompously. 'Very helpful . . . Have you seen DI Grant since yesterday morning?'

'I've been trying to get hold of him,' I murmured accurately and virtuously, 'but the switchboard here says he's on leave, and he isn't answering his mobile.'

'But you telephoned a contact who told you that he's been suspended from duty,' Lyon said softly.

It was one of those moments when it's hard not to say too much. I thought *Damn!* and decided just to say, 'I was worried when I couldn't reach him.'

'This is a disciplinary matter,' Colley growled after a pause. The words echoed Paul's to me the night before. So we were still playing that game. 'I'd be obliged if you wouldn't try to make contact, it's just going to cause him unnecessary trouble.'

I said that I understood, although I was lying about that. 'Is there anything else you'd like to know?'

'If there is,' Lyon said, 'we'll get in touch with you. By the way, about Mrs Digby . . .'

I told her, 'I'm keeping an eye on her. She was shocked by her husband's death, but I'll make sure she's all right.'

Diane Lyon said, 'That's good of you.' She thought about it for a moment. 'We'll be in touch.' I envied the way she was able to keep her face absolutely unreadable. Perhaps you take some kind of special training course at the Hendon Police College.

CHAPTER ELEVEN

And Goldilocks

We drove straight up to the big roundabout at Archway, cut through the side streets of Tufnell Park, and arrived at the bottom of the Highgate Road just before ten-thirty. The rain was still holding off as I turned up the hill and identified the schools on the west side, sheltered from the main road by tall hedges that made it impossible to see anything.

'There.'

I avoided a bus and threw a quick glance to my left. Through an opening in the hedge I could see a broad path and a high chain-link fence, and I pulled the Citroën in just past the entrance. Phyllis clambered out without comment and retrieved the pushchair from the back of the car. I unstrapped Ben, locked up, and staggered on to the pavement with him. He was getting heavier by the day, or maybe I was getting older. At that point he made it known that he was going to walk, so the three of us proceeded hand in hand through the entrance behind the empty pushchair and stopped just inside.

The park was busier than I had expected for a bleak February morning. Then I realised what it was: the two schools had both begun their morning break, and most of the pupils seemed to have opted for a breath of fresh air. Or an illicit smoke – I noticed a bunch of girls who looked about thirteen huddling in a corner of the hedge passing a cigarette around. They looked half frozen. The path towards the school was a confusion of sauntering, running, posing, talking teenagers. I almost laughed. Lal Fisher was making sure that whoever wanted to meet her would find it impractical to cause any trouble. An argument or scuffle would attract the interested attention of about fifty enthusiastic teenagers.

Phyllis said quietly, 'That's her.'

'Where?' I followed the direction of her gaze, and at first glance I thought she was mistaken. A woman was standing motionless by the corner of the tennis courts, watching us. She wore shoes with very high heels and a brown fur coat that looked like real mink, and her uncovered head shone with an elaborate confection of ash-blonde curls. At this distance she looked about thirty. We strolled ahead, going at Ben's most enthusiastic pace, and as we approached I realised that first impressions were mistaken, and that behind a full layer of make-up, skilfully applied, was indeed the face of a woman older than Phyllis. Her blue eyes flickered from me to Ben to Phyllis, where they stayed. We arrived at the fence.

Phyllis said, 'Lal. You're looking well.'

Lal said, 'Phyll, you're . . . are you all right?' She looked at me then, and I suddenly thought of an animal with sharp teeth and eyes. Maybe it was the coat.

I said, 'I'm Dido, and this is Ben. We need to talk to you about Frank. Do you want to stay here, or shall we go somewhere?'

I watched her look around at the park and the people in it. After a second she said, 'I don't think there's anywhere to go. We could sit down over there.' I was going to say that the empty bench she had indicated was probably wet, but she turned and moved towards it and we followed her. I'd been right about the slatted seat, but she sat down anyway in her expensive fur and watched us join her gingerly. Ben clambered on to my lap, and Phyllis sat silently between us. I edged forward on the bench so that I could look at Lal directly. She was still sizing us up. When her gaze flickered over Ben, I saw the shadow of a smile.

'How old is he?'

'Nearly fifteen months.'

'He's a good walker for his age.'

'Just started.'

'Does he talk?'

'Some words,' I said. 'Do you have any children?'

'One son. Thirty now. Married, doing very well. They 'ave this nice 'ouse in 'Ampstead. Look, what about Frank? I know that somethink's wrong, isn't it? Phyll . . . ?'

Phyllis said harshly. 'Somebody killed him.'

I opened my mouth to protest at the harshness of her words, but was silenced by the way Lal's face froze suddenly into deep lines. Now she looked fifty. Older. Without any warning, tears started to slide down her cheeks. She didn't move at all, made no attempt to wipe them away. Half of me wanted to pull out a tissue, dab at her face and urge her to blow. The other, nastier half was noticing with hard-hearted admiration that her eyeliner was barely smudged.

I pulled myself together, put my arms around Ben and said, 'This is no good. Won't you come back to my car? We could go somewhere warmer and get a cup of tea, or a drink. In fact I think I saw a pub across the road . . .'

She got to her feet with a stagger, and at first I thought she was agreeing to my suggestion. Then she drew herself up. 'No. No, I don't 'ave time.'

Phyllis and I were also scrambling to our feet, but she had already started towards the gate. She made remarkable speed on her stilettos. After a moment I ran around her and stood between her and the exit, and she stopped in front of me with the tears still pouring down.

'What do you mean, you don't have time? You can't go like that!' I shouted. 'We have to talk. You're in no state . . . Don't you want to know . . . ?'

'I don't need to know about it,' she interrupted. Her voice was hoarse. 'It's my fault. You people will be better off if you just go away and leave me alone. Tell Phyll I'm sorry, but I don't want to talk to you . . . sorry. There's something I got to do.' Then Phyllis arrived with the pushchair. Lal looked at her and then away. 'I'm very sorry for you, Phyll, I really am.'

I wanted to reach out and hold her, but she stepped around me, and I was still carrying Ben. I think my jaw dropped. Lal kept on going.

Phyllis was taking Ben out of my arms. Her face was strained, but intent.

I said, '*What's going on?*'

'I guess . . .' She stopped, and I looked at her. 'It isn't just about Frank: she's scared; something's wrong.'

'But,' I said, 'but . . .'

'Dido, something awful is happening to us all. You know?'

I did. I knew something else, too: that Frank's death had been news to Lal, but not a surprise. We had told her something she might almost have been waiting for, though the news had hit her like a hammer blow when it came. Her reaction reminded me of Phyllis's – of how Phyllis had been yesterday; and the first thing Lal had said was that it was *her* fault. I definitely had to talk to her, whether or not she was willing.

'I have to go after her. I need to know what she meant.'

Phyllis looked at Ben. So did I. She said, 'There's a bus. If we catch it across the road, it will take us to Kentish Town, and then the Tube will get us home all right.'

I nodded. 'You're sure? I'll get back as soon as I can.'

Phyllis hugged Ben and said, 'Dido, just hurry!'

Something had changed during our short meeting with Lal. Perhaps Phyllis had decided to make a stand. I popped a kiss on Ben's damp red nose and trotted after the mink coat that had already vanished around the end of the hedge.

CHAPTER TWELVE

A Nice Place in the Suburbs

———◆———

I tucked my car in behind a small white delivery van, trying to stay hidden from the big German car I'd watched Lal Fisher climb into. I had no difficulty keeping up with her. In fact, my problem was not to get too close. She was driving uphill erratically towards Highgate Village. The row of cars parked at the kerb had narrowed the northbound lane to half its width, and she was driving well over the centre line, trying to give them a wide berth and being forced to brake and swerve repeatedly for the traffic coming downhill. She kept braking sharply for the speed bumps too, like somebody who was having trouble judging distances. I started to worry. She might be too upset about Frank to be safe at the wheel. The driver of the van pulled up close behind her and then fell back. I slowed a little more. We were all holding up the traffic. After a minute the van made an impatient left turn. I let the Citroën fall back even farther. My big blue estate car was an unusual model, conspicuous; on the other hand, I doubted that she had even noticed me, because it looked as though she was having too much trouble manoeuvring her own vehicle to spare much attention to her rear-view mirror.

But of course her own car was missing. Perhaps that was the problem. The silver-coloured car she was driving today might be unfamiliar, and it was a big, heavy vehicle, almost a limousine. Either that, or she was too shocked to be paying enough attention to her driving. Either way, I hung back.

At the top of the hill she took the left-hand fork. I hesitated, encouraging a black taxi that was waiting to enter from a side road. It took up position between us. In the centre of the village she turned on to a mini-roundabout without stopping, and a car entering from the right braked hard and sounded its horn. By the time I could insert myself into this new stream of traffic, half a dozen cars and a bus had driven in between us. I followed her hopefully up the main road.

Past the next little roundabout the roadway widened, and I edged out into the right-hand lane and picked up a little speed. I could see the rear of Lal's car more clearly at this angle and would have some warning if she decided to pull over, or manoeuvred to turn. Where the Great North Road crossed our route, she moved out in front of me and headed up towards Finchley. I cut between a lorry and a bus to slide through the lights just as they were changing. We proceeded northwards. If she knew I was still there she gave no sign.

A mile later, she signalled a right turn and swerved into a broad suburban avenue lined with large trees and substantial houses. The sign on the railings at the corner called it Verwood Avenue. It was almost traffic-free, and if Lal was ever going to notice she had been followed, it would be here. I sat in the middle of the main road for as long as I dared, signalling and waiting overcautiously for the oncoming traffic to pass. My tactics gave her the chance to get a few hundred yards ahead. She was driving faster now. I followed, past rows of big houses and the iron railings of what looked like a patch of ancient woodland to my left. She was still well ahead of me when a side street opened up; the silver car swerved across the road and vanished. I put my foot down, and by the time I arrived at that point it was sitting at the top of the driveway of one of the big corner houses. The driver's door was opening, and I caught a flash of brown fur as I drove past.

When I was hidden by the tall garden fence belonging to the next property, I also veered across the road, stopped the Citroën far enough along to be unseen from the Fishers' drive, switched off the engine, and wondered what to do next. Was there any choice? A light rain was just beginning as I got out, locked up and trotted back. The door of the house was closed, but she hadn't bothered to run the car into the garage. Perhaps she meant to go out again. I hesitated on the pavement, trying to decide what I was going to say to her. A trickle of cold water ran under my collar, and I decided not to bother with a story: I plodded up the slope to the door, rang the bell and waited.

After a while I rang again. I could hear the bell inside, so obviously she'd heard it too. Having left a second polite interval I leaned on the button. When I got tired of that I backed away and looked around.

The house where Lal Fisher had gone to ground was a bulky, two-storey brick place built in the neo-Tudor fairytale style, with a sloping roof of red tiles and windows with phoney leaded panes. The front garden was a neat stretch of shorn lawn between tidy rose beds, all pruned for the winter. The single-storey garage attached to one end of the building looked large enough to hold at least two cars the size of the one that she had abandoned in front of its door. Frank Digby's sister must have made a good marriage, because there was money in this place.

There also had to be a person in this place, because she'd had no time to go anywhere in the seconds before I'd arrived on the spot. I rang the bell again sharply and listened to the echo. Then I listened harder. I could hear the faint sound of a motor running somewhere and began to imagine Lal taking refuge from her sorrows by doing some hoovering, in which case it was just possible that she really couldn't hear the doorbell. I tried to look in through the big window. It was double-glazed, with that imitation lead on both the inner and outer windows. This was like trying to peer through a double security grille, and there were no lights on. I could make out that it was a large room and could just see the shapes of some furniture, but I couldn't be sure that Lal wasn't inside, peering back and waiting for me to go away.

I would have liked to try the other windows, especially at the back of the house, but the garage abutted the thick hedge of roses bordering the western edge of the lawn, full of the kind of thorns that guarantee an intruder won't push through without losing most of her clothes and too much of her skin. At the other end of the frontage, beyond two small windows that were even more obscured with vertical slatted blinds as well as the heavy ornamental leading, a solid, seven-foot garden gate led to a side passage between the house and the fence at the eastern boundary. A determined burglar could climb it. Which, I realised at that moment, was probably why they had fitted the security camera to the wall overhead.

I retreated for another look at the situation. A second camera had been fitted to the side wall of the house above the garage and security lights decorated the front and sides of the building. Either the Fishers were operating a small private museum full of Picassos, or they were very nervous people. I accepted the fact that the only way in, for me at least, was going to be the front door.

This time when I rang the bell I leaned against the door, put my mouth to the letter flap, and shouted, 'Lal? It's Dido Hoare. I need to talk to you!'

The door moved away from me so abruptly that I would have fallen inside, except that Lal stood there in her coat blocking the way. She was only about my height, but the three-inch heels gave her the advantage, and she managed to stare down at me forbiddingly despite the fact that she was still crying. 'You can't come in.' Her voice caught in a hiccup.

'I'm sorry,' I told her. I searched for inspiration. 'I know that I gave you a shock, and I apologise, but we had to tell you. We were afraid you'd hear about Frank somewhere, or read it in a newspaper. Isn't there anybody else here? Can I come in and make you a cup of tea or something? Is your husband here?'

'No.' Suddenly she reached out a hand and pulled me roughly inside, slamming the door at my back. She still gave no sign of inviting me farther than the entrance hall. 'No, Andy had to go out this morning. There was some kind of problem at the depot. That's why I was able to get away for a while. He could be back any time, though, and I don't want him to know you've been here.' She must have seen the puzzlement on my face, because she moved back. 'All right, let's go into the kitchen, just for a minute. D'you want a coffee, Dido? That's a funny name – "Die-Doh". Is it English? How do you spell it?'

It was a start. I told her that my father had chosen the name from a Latin epic poem in which a Queen Dido and a Prince Aeneas had a brief fling, while I followed her across the wide entrance hall into a huge country-style kitchen, complete with solid oak cupboards, chintz frills at the windows (the ornamental double glazing was repeated here at the back), an Aga range, and big French doors, protected by a folding metal grille. It was like being inside a birdcage. Outside, a wintry patio dotted with shrubs in pottery tubs overlooked a big sweep of grass and flower-beds.

I said, 'What a lovely garden,' since it seemed wise to find another neutral topic.

She dumped the mink over the back of one of the kitchen chairs, switched on the electric kettle, hesitated, and nodded. 'It's nice up here. It's a nice house. We have six bedrooms. I'd like to show you around, only . . .' She had spoken in an absent-minded voice that faded away.

I sat down quickly at the heavy wooden table and said. 'Do you and your husband live alone?'

'Yes, it's just us.' She had turned away from me, getting the cups and saucers and a tall china coffee pot out of a cupboard. There was a catering pack of instant coffee in the cupboard beside the Aga.

'Do you take sugar?'

I said I didn't. I watched her hesitate, then pull a bowl off the shelf. 'I shouldn't either,' she said. 'At my age you 'ave to watch your hips. But I like it sweet. You only live once.' I saw her wince. She rushed on: 'You want milk?'

I said, 'Thanks,' and watched her pour a dollop from a carton into a small saucepan and set it on top of the stove to warm. I let the silence grow while she waited for the kettle to boil, made coffee in the pot and then placed everything carefully on the table. She filled our cups and poured the hot milk in from the saucepan, her little finger elegantly raised. She added two good spoonfuls of sugar to one of the cups and sat down with it in the chair opposite me. It was so quiet that I could hear a fridge humming somewhere. It could have been any neighbourly coffee morning in any suburban kitchen. Only it wasn't.

I pulled myself together. 'Phyllis and I need help with something. Information. And you probably want to know what happened.'

She went on stirring her coffee until the gesture wore itself out. I watched her attention drift somewhere else. Then she got to her feet with a little whimper of exasperation, tore a square of paper towelling off a roll fixed to the wall above the sink, and turned back, dabbing at her eyes.

I took a breath and tried again. 'I'm sorry to upset you this way, but I really can't help it. We need to know exactly when it was that you phoned Frank. And why you said you needed help. And what happened when he contacted you. Did you see him on Sunday?'

For a moment she looked puzzled; then she flushed. ''E didn't say nothing to Phyll, did he? No, 'e wouldn't. It must've been that answer machine. I knew I shouldn'ta left a message as soon as I opened my mouth, but 'e never answered when I rang 'im.'

'That doesn't matter now. You told him you needed help. He agreed. Phyllis says the two of you were always close, so of course he'd help you if you asked. Was that why somebody killed him?'

'It wasn't like that!' She batted her eyelashes at me sweetly, and I knew she was lying. I leaned my elbows on the table, clasped my hands and waited. She tried to laugh. 'It was just this old family stuff. Rubbish. Something I was keeping for him, a coupla boxes. Frank asked me to keep it safe a few years ago, just before 'e . . .'

She looked at me and hesitated. Light dawned. 'You mean when he was arrested – in 'ninety-two, or whenever it was?'

'Summer of 'ninety-one,' she corrected me automatically. 'No, before then. Me and Andy moved to Spain the year before, and Frank 'ad this stuff he wanted to put somewhere, didn't want anybody to know, even Andy; so I put it in with our stuff, some things we stored at the depot. Nobody'd notice a coupla extra boxes, Frank said.'

This made no sense. 'Why did you suddenly want him to take them away?' I demanded.

'Well . . . See, we've come back for good. Andy bought this 'ouse last year and we moved in just before Christmas, and Andy said we should get all our old stuff out of store now, so they brought it round. So I shoved the stuff, Frankie's, in a corner in the basement, but I thought, well, Andy's going to see it there sooner or later and look, so I phoned. Frank got 'ere Sunday, but 'e needed a car to move the stuff and I lent him mine, just for overnight, just to get the boxes somewheres. Only 'e didn't come back. So when Andy asked me where my car was, I said I was shopping down the West End and it'd been towed away from a meter, and I said I'd go get it this afternoon or maybe tomorrow, as soon as I wasn't too busy. That's Andy's car I was driving just now. 'E doesn't really like me driving it, so you won't mention it if you meet 'im?'

I'd been half listening to her babble. She was lying. I could still hear the sound of panic in the voice on the tape. I examined the possibility that she had merely been asking Frank to come along and pick up some old clothes. It was ridiculous.

'You didn't see him again? He didn't phone?'

She shook her head slowly.

'What did he mean to do? Where was he going to take the boxes?'

'Take them away,' she said blankly. 'Take them to their flat, I thought. No? Maybe 'e dumped them. I don't know what it was, but it couldn'ta been nothing much.'

I shook my head at her. Then I suddenly wondered whether the flat in Power Street might have some kind of storage locker that Phyllis hadn't mentioned. Stupid of me not to have thought of that before! On the other hand, Phyllis hadn't seen Frank again, and if he'd returned home with some cartons, surely she would have known? I gave up.

'That was Sunday?'

She hesitated only slightly before she nodded.

'Then where was he on Monday?'

She blinked. 'Not at 'ome?'

No, not at home. With a car and twenty-four hours, he could have moved his 'stuff' almost anywhere in the country. The story was full of holes but I couldn't seem to get hold of anything.

'Frank's conviction.' That at least was something she could tell me. 'What had he done?'

She shook her head. 'We was away during the trial. Andy was building up the Spanish end of the business, and we moved there for a coupla years while it got sorted. There was no point coming back. We couldn't of done nothing.'

'But you must know what he was accused of!'

'Something to do with business. People he worked for then. There was other people in it, but they got off, I think, I'm not sure, we didn't see much except if we got a English paper sometimes. Andy was busy with business, very busy, and Frankie wrote and said I shouldn't come back, it wouldn't do any good.'

'What kind of business is your husband in there?' I was trying to feel my way.

'Time share,' she said promptly. 'Andy and my dad set up a company, years ago, for time share, down the coast from Marbella. Andy went down and built a kind of estate there for old English people, retired. Then they branched out into 'aulage. There's a lot of Brits retiring to Marbella, you'd be surprised, so Andy started this business moving their stuff back and forth, and it's really grown. Clever. There's a big depot off the Lea Valley, over Walthamstow way. Maybe you seen it? Black Cat 'Aulage? Black cat for luck. Lorries all over north London, too – you must of seen them. Andy's doing really well.'

'Is it his own business?' I asked politely. If I could just keep her talking about family matters, she might wind up telling me something I didn't yet know that I needed to know.

'Runs it all on 'is own now. The family started the time share a while back. 'Course they used to live in 'Oxton then.' The idea made her laugh. 'We've come up in the world!'

'Lal, when I told you about Frank why did you say it was your fault?'

Her face changed suddenly. 'What time is it?' She was pulling up the sleeve of her cardigan to look at her watch. 'Dido, it's after twelve! Andy'll be back for his dinner any minute, and I 'aven't made anything. Look, you got to go now.'

But I hadn't even started. I hadn't had a chance to lead the talk back to her phone call to Frank and push her about why she had been so anxious about a couple of cardboard boxes. (*Frank, you got to help* . . . She was lying through her teeth. She hadn't just been talking about a few knick-knacks.) But there was someone childish and anxious looking at me from out of the reddened eyes; and I'd seen the blue bruises, like thumb and fingerprints, just above her watch bracelet. I got slowly to my feet, wondering what to do but knowing that I didn't want to bump into her husband here.

'What about your car?' I asked her. 'When they found Frank, he had the keys in his pocket. The police need to find it, but they have no idea where it is now, or even what make they're looking for.'

'Gold,' she said. 'Gold Toyota saloon, new last year, with real leather seats, black leather.' Suddenly she simpered and gave me a little shrug, and her little-girl-fibbing voice came back. 'Andy gave it to me when we got back. I guess it'll turn up, won't it? I better tell Andy it wasn't towed off like I thought, it was stolen.'

Wrong, all wrong. 'If you'll tell me the registration number,' I said, letting myself be led towards the door, 'I'll let the police know.'

She mimed the act of thinking hard. 'Oh, God! I'm that stupid, I can never even remember my own phone number.' She giggled apologetically. 'Well, I mean, you don't phone yourself, do you! Go on, now, there's a good girl. I want to start cooking. Don't worry about my car, the police will find it, and when they get in touch I'll tell them Frank borrowed it, I guess.' A sour look flitted briefly across her face and was smoothed away. We were at the door; she opened it and stood so close that I was almost forced to back outside. 'Please, don't say anything about this to anybody — 'cept Phyll, of course. Andy won't like it. Put off the evil day, eh? Tell Phyll I'm sorry about Frankie. And you take care of yourselves. It'll all work out, right?'

I opened my mouth to say something, to protest, to ask her . . . and stared into her face and again gave up.

'I'll see you later, then. Will you be—?'

She interrupted with 'See you later', and banged the door in my face.

A lorry passed, driving too fast. I listened to the sound fade, to the flock of crows having a shouting match in the woods across the road. It seemed there was nothing I could do here for the moment.

I'd almost reached the main road before I started to wonder whether I knew any more now than I had at the beginning of the day when I'd written a list in the steam on my own bathroom mirror. I braked, pulled in to the side of the road, and sat with the engine running, going back over my visit.

I knew the Fishers' address. I'd confirmed my assumption that Frank had gone off on Sunday to complete some family business and that his sister probably knew all about it. Though she wasn't going to tell. I had a description of a car. That seemed to be about it.

Perhaps not quite . . .

I pictured the bruises on Lal's wrist. Those, and the little-girl act, along with her repeated insistence that her husband mustn't be told about anything, suggested to me that she was frightened of Andy Fisher and probably with good cause. Then there were the 'couple of boxes' she claimed Frank had removed in her car, but I wasn't sure how seriously I ought to take that story. Her car certainly seemed to be missing, I'd believe that much.

If you could accept that some boxes Frank Brunton had handed over to his sister for safe-keeping years ago were still important to somebody, then what did they hold? Assuming that the police found the car, would the boxes still be in it? Not if Frank had been killed because he had come to Lal's house and taken them away . . .

Damn it, because of *what*?

That was when I saw I'd been taken for a ride. Lal had spent the morning presenting herself as some kind of loopy stereotype, a caricature dizzy blonde out of some working-class soap opera.

It was a very wide road and I came close to swinging the car around in a big circle and heading back, but I didn't. I wish I had. Instead, I headed home to talk to Phyllis again, to see whether we could make any sense of the little I had learned. I was also thinking that the late Frank Digby had a sister who was a lot cleverer than she pretended. And terrified of something: that's what I thought.

CHAPTER THIRTEEN

Connections

Driving slowly past the front of the shop, I caught a glimpse of the desk lamp burning in the back room. There are only two keys that fit the high-security lock on the shop: mine, which was definitely there on my ring, and my father's, which was supposed to be in his pocket at the newspaper library. Logically, this meant I had an intruder. There were five or six feet of empty space at the far end of the residents' parking bay; I backed as much of the Citroën into it as possible, so to show willing in case a traffic warden came past, before I jumped out and dashed across the road.

Then I remembered the arrangements I'd so carefully made. The door was unlocked when I pushed through it calling, 'Ernie? I'm sorry, I forgot all about you! How did you manage to get in . . . ?' At the door to the inner office I stopped short.

Ernie sat at my desk, where an unfamiliar tangle of wires showed that he had managed to hook up Frank's zip drive to my computer. Ben looked up from the floor beside him, flat on his back on a surface that had been covered with old newspapers, surrounded by a litter of what looked like chewed bread crusts dipped in ketchup. He had a lump of something unidentifiable in his fist and was sucking it.

'What's happened? Is he all right? Where's Phyllis?'

'Hey, Dido!' Ernie bounced to his feet with a grin and stretched up slightly to give me a smacking kiss. 'Mrs Digby said she needed t' go home for a bit and get some clothes an' stuff.

So I said I'd look after him. Only I guess she's been held up, an' he wanted his dinner, so Ben and me phoned out and got a pizza delivery.'

I looked at the mess. '*Pizza?*'

'Sure. Babies love pizza,' Ernie assured me with all the confidence of an experienced older brother. 'Jus' bread, tomato an' cheese, nothin' hot. We bought some milk round the corner, but he wanted a taste of my milk-shake, an' then he liked that, so I let him have most of it. That's all good stuff for babies. He's been fine, only I couldn't change him because your flat's locked, and I think maybe . . .'

I sniffed at Ben and thought that I thought so, too.

'How long has Phyllis been gone, and how did you get into the shop?'

Ernie snapped his fingers. 'Nearly forgot! I was standing around out front, talking to Mrs Digby, and th' Professor turned up in a taxi an' unlocked the door. He couldn't stay, but he left somethink for you to look at, and a message.' He hesitated. 'I know it sounds crazy, but I did get it right. He said to tell you, "Dido, this business may be serious. You might take Ben upstairs and lock the door and go to bed or somethink; don't budge until I get back." So will you do that? Because it sounded like he meant it. I been worrying when you didn't turn up.'

'Don't budge until he gets *back*?'

Ernie assured me he had reproduced Barnabas's words accurately.

I may have grunted, 'Very funny.'

He eyed my face anxiously, and added, 'He left this.'

'This' was a big brown envelope. I dumped it on to the desk as I edged around to look at the computer screen. It showed a jumble of gibberish: numbers, letters, symbols.

'Ernie, have we got some kind of bug?'

'Encrypted file,' Ernie announced. 'They aren't all like that. There's some ordinary stuff. Wait a sec, I'll show you.'

He flung himself back into the chair, tapped a few keys, and brought up a screen full of boxes and figures. 'That's accounts,' he announced. 'Spreadsheets. Ordinary stuff. I do this sort of stuff at college. There's some letters to businesses he's working for, I can show you them, it's all boring stuff. There's lots of self-assessment tax files. There's files that's just columns of numbers, and there's this stuff. It's "encryption"; they showed us about it. You gotta have the program to turn it back into words, and a password.'

'Where do you get them?' I demanded.

He pointed. 'See? That bit at the end of the file name where it says ".xpt"? That'll give us a clue to what program. I can hunt it down on the Net, but the password – that's the tricky bit.'

'How long will it take?' I could hear my voice rising.

'I'm gonna back up this disk just to be safe,' Ernie announced. 'I pinched another one from school. Then I can play around.' He frowned. 'Might take time, 'specially wiv your computer. Dido, you really gotta get some more memory. D'you think I . . . ?'

I interrupted sternly, 'How much more time? Hours? Days?'

Ernie grinned enigmatically. 'Maybe.'

It was beyond me for the moment, and I thought that it might turn out to be beyond Ernie, too, good though he is. I abandoned it briefly. 'Where's my father?'

'He didn't stop. He said he was going to Fleet Street to listen to some tapes.'

Barnabas? In Fleet Street? At a music shop? Clearly everybody had gone mad in my absence. Or else Ernie had misunderstood. He seemed edgy.

'Dido, the Professor said look at that stuff right away.'

I gave in. With one eye on Ben, whose snuffle seemed to have dried up and who showed no immediate sign of being sick, even though bloated with pizza and chocolate shake, I tore the envelope open and fished out the single sheet of paper inside. It was a photocopy of part of what looked like a news page from one of the tabloid newspapers. The contrast left something to be desired, and Barnabas had made it without paying any attention to the text, which was cut off annoyingly in the middle of all possible lines so that it was difficult to read anything meaningful. The thing that had interested him so much was a large photograph of a street scene. I held the sheet close to the reading light and stared at a medium-range shot of six or seven men striding up the steps of a large building. One was in police uniform. The two figures in the middle were obviously prisoners. One had turned his face away from the camera; the other had hurriedly flung up a hand, palm out and fingers spread, between himself and the lens, but I could see just enough of the face to recognise him: this was clearly what had worried Barnabas. The caption read: *Defendants being escorted into the Old Bailey at the beginning of today's hearing.* No names, and he looked younger, but Frank Digby hadn't changed that much in five years. I wondered who the other defendant was, but the caption gave no help. All right, so my father had found his evidence that Frank Digby had been tried for some major crime. But that was years ago, and I couldn't see that it was any real cause for panic. I was about to look away when I noticed someone else I knew. Trailing behind the uniformed escort, his eyes fixed stonily on the prisoners, was DI Moore. Oh.

'What's wrong? . . . Dido?'

I caught my breath. 'I don't know, exactly. Maybe nothing.' No – there *was* something wrong about this. I glanced at the smaller picture and caught my breath for the second time. The caption read *'Big Andy' Fisher believed to have fled the country.* It was a poor reproduction, and the original had probably been a family snapshot, but I had no difficulty in recognising the deeply lined face of the man who had turned up at the Digbys' flat to be introduced as 'Sergeant Andrew'. *Lal's husband.* If she told him I'd been in touch . . .

'Trouble?' Ernie asked.

I found that I was still capable of speech if I tried really hard, and whispered. 'That's putting it mildly. Look, when Phyllis gets back, she'll probably call in here for Ben. Tell her that I've taken him upstairs. Ask her to ring the doorbell twice before she uses her key, so I'll know who it is. I think after all that Ben and I might go to bed and hide under the covers, the way Barnabas suggested.'

Ernie was staring at me in alarm. 'You want me to do something? You just gotta ask, Dido.'

'Yes,' I said. 'Almost certainly. At the moment I'd just be grateful if you'll stay as late as you possibly can today, to keep an eye on things.' I stopped for a second, trying to think of everything that I needed to arrange. 'I'm going to lock the shop door as I'm leaving. I'll stick up our "Back in an Hour" sign. Have we had any customers so far?'

Ernie shook his head. It wasn't book-buying weather. I might worry about that later, but the book fair at the weekend had helped with the week's turnover, and my attention was too crowded with other things to bother. Because the fact was that, adding Andy Fisher and Barnabas's mysterious caution to Paul Grant's warning, I was beginning to wonder whether I wasn't out of my depth.

Frank Digby. DI Moore. Andy Fisher. Lal. *Connections.*

'See if you can get anywhere with the stuff on that disk,' I said slowly. 'It's important. And if anyone turns up here or phones here for me, will you say that you don't know where I am? Take a name and phone number and say that I'll call them.'

Ernie's grin had grown wider. 'Sounds like trouble,' he said.

I picked up my sticky, sleepy son and told them both, equally, that it certainly did. 'And when you do see Phyllis, when she gets back, ask her to come straight up, because I have to go out again. And, Ernie, now I think about it, can you stay until either Barnabas or I come back? No matter how late it is? I'll try to be quick, but I definitely don't want Phyllis and Ben to be left alone.'

Ernie looked ecstatic. He loves trouble. I tried to take some reassurance from the knowledge that I can always count on him in a tight spot, but it was modified by knowing that Barnabas would be horrified that I'd got myself into a position where I needed to. No! It was too late to think about being careful, because I'd just worked out what I was going to do.

First of all, I'd have another word with Lal Fisher just as soon as I could get up there again. She was my only route into this muddle, and this time I was going to ask her all the right questions about her husband and her brother and what they'd been up to together, back in 1991 or 1992, to say nothing of why Andy had really left the country and what had brought him back, just for starters. I hadn't forgotten what she'd said about Frank's death being *her fault*: it was perfectly clear that she knew more than she pretended about that, and she certainly owed her brother's widow some answers. I meant to offer her a choice: she could answer all the questions I would have worked out by the time that Phyllis got back, or I was going to call the police and sit on her head until they arrived. All this might take some time, because I was going to have to get her away from her gangster husband before we could talk, and that meant I might need to lurk outside the house until one of them left.

When I'd got answers, then I'd come back and tell Phyllis about it. After that, I was going to contact Paul Grant because, whatever he'd said to me, at this moment he was the only cop I felt I trusted enough to talk to. Until I'd looked at that newspaper photograph, at least part of my mind had been clinging to the thought that neither of Phyllis's visitors had been a real policeman. Now that I knew one of them was, and the other was some kind of gangster, that comfort had vanished.

Finally, with everything off my hands, I'd get a good night's sleep and spend tomorrow literally minding my business.

Leaving Ben clean, satisfied and sleepy in his cot, I trailed into the kitchen. After I'd filled the kettle and switched it on, I delved into the fridge for something edible and ready. An apple and a lump of Cheddar cheese with dry corners seemed the only things that fitted requirements. I dunked the cheese into a jar of onion chutney and pushed a tea bag into a clean mug. That would do. Mr Spock arrived and indicated, by jumping on to the draining board and placing one paw significantly on my arm, that he needed milk. I poured a splash for each of us, mine into the mug and his into the chipped soup bowl. Then I swallowed the cheese and wandered into the sitting room with my apple and my tea just as the phone began to ring.

I froze and waited for the answering machine to pick up the call. It was Phyllis's voice which sounded tinnily from the speaker: '*Dido, I've been held up, I'll tell you about it when I get there but it might be another hour.*'

I made a dash for the phone, but she had hung up by the time I reached it; so I slumped on to the settee, took a mouthful of tea, burned my tongue, and began to think about questioning Lal.

CHAPTER FOURTEEN

Scene of Some Crimes

Whatever had held Phyllis up seemed unwilling to relax its grip. In the end, I had to leave Ernie combining baby-sitting with coffee-drinking and watching cartoons on one of the TV cable channels. The mid-afternoon traffic was moderate and for once the lights favoured me all the way up Archway. I covered the four or five miles that separated my chaotic flat from Lal Fisher's six-bed mansion in less than twenty minutes.

I was hesitating opposite her gate when I noticed what was waiting for me inside: the police patrol car standing on the drive-way, empty, one of its doors still open. I shot across the road and parked in the spot I'd used before, ignoring the voice that was saying to me, *All right, Dido: getting-out-of-here-and-minding-our-own-business would be a good move . . .* I was edging myself around the patrol car as I decided to try the concerned-friend ploy again and attempted without much difficulty to compose my face into an expression of honest alarm. Beyond that, I was going to play it by ear.

Halfway to the front door I noticed what the big silver car had been hiding from me: the police officer standing by the up-and-over garage door, which now showed a gap of about eighteen inches between its lower edge and the ground. He and I saw each other at the same moment. He raised one hand like a traffic policeman, opened his mouth and took a step forwards. I flung myself at him.

'What's happened? Is Lal all right? Where is she? What's

happened?' He hesitated. I took advantage and switched my tone to authoritative. 'Why are you here? Where's Mrs Fisher? I'm a friend of hers, she's expecting me.' I decided that was enough. As a concerned and mature friend of the family I might be tolerated, but not as an hysteric.

He still hesitated. 'I don't think . . .'

I planted my feet and said, 'Sergeant, please: *is Mrs Fisher all right? Where is she?*' At the same moment, I caught a lungful of a sickly, metallic smell, like roadside air on a windless summer day in central London; my eyes turned to the gap under the door, and I understood that inside the exhaust gas was as thick as soup.

'Constable Angus, madam. The lady who lives here phoned for help. She's not harmed, she's in the house with another constable. I think you should . . .'

There was no way I was going to let him finish that sentence. I interrupted, 'Then I'll go in and stay with her for a while. Is it her husband? Is it Andy? She'll need me.'

I must have looked stricken with anxiety. That was certainly how I felt. The constable made a decision. He preceded me and rang the doorbell. After a moment, the door swung open and an older policeman appeared. There was a low-voiced explanation.

I put one foot on the doorstep beside my constable and looked from one face to the other. 'We were supposed to be going shopping together this afternoon,' I said soberly. 'She's waiting for me. Where is she? Is Andy with her? Her husband, you know?'

The older man made the decision. 'She's in the kitchen,' he said. 'She's had a shock. I think she ought to go and lie down, but I can't get her to move. Perhaps you could talk to her.'

I said warmly, 'Of course I will. Poor Lal! Only . . . can't you tell me what's happened? I don't want to say the wrong thing.'

The constable didn't hesitate any longer. 'Apparently,' he said, 'she went to the garage, and found the engine of her car running and a person inside.'

A 'person'? If they hadn't been sure they had a corpse on

their hands, they wouldn't have left the victim. 'Is it Andy?'

'I wouldn't know. It is a male, about sixty years of age.'

'And was it Lal's own car?' I asked as I followed the constable in the direction of the kitchen, because I thought I could just about get away with that much. 'The gold-coloured Toyota?'

'That's right,' he said, and stood aside for me.

I replied, 'Oh dear,' with real feeling, and plunged inside.

She was sitting very upright at the kitchen table, looking straight ahead at nothing. Her eyes were dry, but something had drawn deep lines on either side of her mouth, and her carefully groomed blonde curls had collapsed into a shapeless mess, as though she had been dragging her fingers through them. Somebody, presumably the constable, had placed a cup of tea in front of her, but it was untouched. She didn't move or look at me.

I nodded to the constable in what I hoped was a reassuring and dismissive way and whispered, 'It's all right, I'll take care of her.' Then I rounded the table and put an arm around the stiff shoulders. 'Lal? It's Dido. Can I help you? Can I get you a drink?' She didn't move. I said, still softly, 'Is there somebody you'd like me to phone for you? Do you want me to ask Phyllis to come?'

I could feel her shiver, but she still didn't speak. I pulled a chair over close to hers and sat down and took her hands in mine. They were icy, so I chafed them. In the distance I could hear sirens. Help on the way. I nodded at the constable, who nodded back at me and headed down the hallway. The front door opened and shut.

'They'll be here in a moment,' I said. 'Help's coming.'

'No.'

I wasn't sure what I'd heard. I wasn't sure what to say. I tried, 'I can hear sirens. An ambulance. Is it Andy?'

'Dead.' She spoke more loudly now. 'Dead. When I found 'im. I 'eard the engine running when you was 'ere, but I never thought.' I repressed a gasp: because I'd heard it too, and I also hadn't thought, and if I'd just said something maybe . . . She was saying dully, 'When I went in, I knew, it was that thick in there.

I opened the door. Turned it off. 'E was still warm, but 'e'd gone.'

I couldn't help saying, 'Why?'

It made her look at me for the first time. 'What's that?'

I hesitated, but there was no point. I thought I understood, but I had to ask, 'Why did he do it?'

Little points of colour appeared surprisingly suddenly over her cheekbones. ''E never!'

'But . . .'

''E never. What are you saying?'

I shook my head. 'Lal, I'm not saying anything. It's just that if a person shuts himself into the garage and turns a car engine on . . .' I made the effort and managed to keep myself from adding, *the engine of your car, your 'missing' car, remember?*

She picked up the cup of cooling tea and drank it in one parched gulp. Then she banged it down. 'You're saying that's 'ow people kill themselves, right? Well, Andy wouldn't. Everything was just fine.' But I thought that a shadow fell suddenly across her face as she spoke the last sentence. The sirens arrived at the front of the house and died away.

Lal hauled herself to her feet. 'I better go up.'

I said, 'Are you feeling ill?'

'I'm all right. I just need to lie down. You can come if you like, for a bit, see me all right. I don't mind you.'

Who did she mind, then? Sooner or later she'd have to tell the police about finding him – it wouldn't go away. Sooner or later she was going to have to explain lots of things. Still, I kept my mouth shut and followed her up the wide oak staircase to the upper floor. On the landing, she hesitated and moved towards the door of a big bedroom at the front of the house. We stepped inside, into a kind of teenager's fantasy of Hollywood glamour. Obviously it was Lal's room, full of pink swags, cream shag carpet and mirrors. I tried not to stare too openly. Apart from a man's bathrobe hanging over the back of the chintz armchair, and a spartan-looking pair of hairbrushes on one of the chests of drawers, there were no signs of a male presence.

Lal flung herself down on top of the flowery quilted coverlet and closed her eyes in a decisive kind of way. I waited for a second, then sat in the bedside armchair, surreptitiously sliding the dead man's bathrobe on to the floor behind it as I settled. There was no sound in the room except the ticking of an old-fashioned ormolu clock on the dressing table. The noises of increasing activity in the front garden kept pushing against the cocoon of silence around us – the sound of engines, the arrival of a lot more people, voices.

'Dido?' It was a whisper.

I leaned forward. 'What?'

'Dido, you're on my side, aren't you?'

Side? I said judiciously, 'I'm not sure what you mean, but I'm a friend of Phyllis's – you do know that, don't you?'

I was watching her closely and saw what was almost a brief smile. 'I know. I 'ope so. You really own a bookshop?'

Light dawned. 'You mean, I really am not a police officer?' I almost laughed. 'When they come upstairs and chuck me out because I shouldn't be here, you'll see.'

This time she did smile, but she kept her eyes shut. 'Then do something for me. And Phyll? I don't know what's 'appened, cross my heart, because Andy didn't tell me about business stuff. You know? They thought – the bloody family all thought they should keep their women out of it! You're too young to under-stand, but Phyll knows, Frankie was the same. It may look like Andy did that, but I'm never going to believe it. My God, what a fucking mess!'

I heard the front door close downstairs. 'Where did your car come from, Lal?'

'Dunno. Honest. Frankie drove it away, like I told you. If Andy brought it back while I was down there with you, then I just don't want to think what . . .'

There were voices downstairs.

Her words became quieter, faster. 'I'm not going to tell them about Frankie or nothing. Listen, will you do something? Go into the little back bedroom – left outside 'ere, right-hand door. Make sure . . . make sure it looks all right. Quick, before they come up.'

I didn't dream of arguing. I left the door of her bedroom ajar, listened to two or three voices talking downstairs in the hall, sped diagonally across the thick carpet to the right-hand door on the landing and got myself through it. The room was nicely furnished in Lal's characteristic pink, and was clearly a spare bedroom. Somebody had drawn the quilted coverlet up over the pillows, but I thought that the bed had been slept in. I pulled the door almost shut behind me and moved closer, looking for what I was supposed to find, circling the foot of the bed.

A little bedside cabinet had been pulled to one side, and something was poking into the flounce of the rose-coloured valance, something out of place, a sharp corner . . . the corner of a box that had been pushed under the bed, invisible if you happened to look from the doorway. I knelt on the carpet, pulled up the frill and found an old cardboard box, yellow with age. Something you'd get from a supermarket – green lettering: *Hereford Farms Cox's Orange Pippins.* I hauled at it, but a flap was sticking up and caught in the bed spring. I doubled it over until I could look inside and see the wine-coloured covers of a book, an old-fashioned ledger. I levered the flap a little higher. There were others beneath it. *Damn it!*

Something shiny sprawled on top, something out of place, so I edged my hand in and hooked out a bunch of keys. Three, on a plain steel ring: two ordinary Yale-type door keys and a little one that might have fitted a suitcase or a briefcase; and a tag with a red-and-white enamel crest and the words *Arsenal FC.* I couldn't say I'd ever seen the keys before, though it was possible, but one useless piece of information that I seem to recall was that Frank Digby had supported Arsenal, the local football team. I dropped them back and pushed them well down into the corner of the box before I dragged the flap down. Then I realised: when he had left this house in Lal's car, Frank hadn't been going home. He had been meaning to bring the car straight back. Unless . . . Downstairs, the front door slammed. Unless his killer had taken them and the rest of his belongings from his pocket to delay identification, and brought them back here? And this box? Was this one of the boxes Frank had taken away?

I shoved hard and shifted it back a few inches so that the valance hung down straight. I couldn't risk making a noise by pushing the cabinet back against the bed, but I smoothed the coverlet. The bed seemed undisturbed if you weren't looking closely.

The voices were nearer. I slipped back to the door and put my eye to the crack. From there I could see the stairs: no one was in sight, but they were coming. I whizzed outside and was standing at the door of the bathroom when two uniformed police officers, a man and a woman, reached the head of the stairs and turned inquisitive faces in my direction.

I spoke before they could. 'She's a little better,' I said. 'She's lying down. Only I think a doctor should look at her.' As soon as I'd spoken, I knew that I'd burned my bridges behind me without having thought it through. What I needed now was a private talk with Lal. The sort of private talk that begins with the words, 'Tell me what all this is about right now before I yank every bleached-blonde hair out of your head . . .'

The woman said, 'Will you just show me where she is? I'll take over.'

I nodded politely and moved towards the door of the master bedroom on tiptoe. I peeked in, turned back and whispered, 'She's dozing.' I held my finger to my lips, opened the door, and was across at the bedside before she could follow me, bending over Lal. Her eyes sprang open.

I leaned down and brushed her cheek hypocritically with my lips and breathed, 'Frank's?'

She nodded almost imperceptibly.

I said, 'Everything's under control. And there's a police-woman here. She'll stay until you're feeling better. She's going to get a doctor to have a look at you.'

Lal closed her eyes and said, 'I don't want to talk to anybody.'

'I know you don't,' I agreed. 'I'll tell Phyllis what's happened. Try to go to sleep.'

When I straightened up, the WPC was looking at me with interest but not, as far as I could see, any suspicion. I asked, 'Will you look after her now? I didn't mean to be away from home for so long, and I'd better check that my baby-sitter is all right.'

She nodded and took my place in the armchair. I smiled and left the house, though not before the older constable who had let me in stopped me at the door and asked for my name and address. I was thinking straight enough to tell him the truth.

That was lucky, because as I was threading my way down the driveway, now entirely blocked by a second police car, an ambulance and a row of onlookers – mostly secondary-school pupils on their way home, from the look of them – I was just in time to watch the arrival of a big Rover and see Diane Lyon emerge unhurriedly. Our eyes met. For a second I thought of fleeing to the Citroën. So near and yet so far.

'Miss Hoare,' she said. Her voice was dry.

'Inspector Lyon,' I offered. 'Hello! I was just going.'

'In a minute,' she said. 'Just get into the car, please.'

CHAPTER FIFTEEN

Red Light

About halfway down the Archway Road I drove through a red
light without even noticing it until a van suddenly drew up
beside the Citroën, flashing its lights and honking. The driver,
a grey-faced skinhead, mouthed something at me. I bared my
teeth at him and snarled until he turned his face away and picked
up speed. Then caution kicked in and I pulled over into a
fifteen-minute waiting bay in front of a parade of small shops
and switched off the engine.

I'd come to a stop near a small grocery shop whose sign
offered 'European and Oriental Foods', and it occurred to me
that a cube of Cheddar cheese and an apple go only so far. Three
minutes later I climbed back behind the wheel with a little plastic
bottle of fresh orange juice and a deliciously greasy paper bag
holding two warm vegetable samosas: vitamins and comfort.
The samosas were fresh, and when the crisp pastry flaked down
the front of my jacket, I just picked up the pieces with the tip
of a finger and ate them. Wiping down with a tissue from my
permanent stock, I allowed myself a moment of introspection
and decided that I would survive a few more hours. In the
interests of full recuperation, I leaned forward to rest my fore-
head on the cold plastic rim of the steering wheel, closed my
eyes, and tried to review the complications.

Sitting in the back of DI Lyon's car in Verwood Avenue, I'd
had a chance to appreciate them.

She left me alone long enough for me to find out that the

childproof locks on the rear doors had been engaged, and so I had a choice of watching events patiently or climbing over the seat-back and trying to escape through the driver's door. I'd decided to wait and was rewarded by witnessing the arrival of two unmarked white vans that I knew from experience would belong to scene-of-crime officers, a second ambulance which turned around and left immediately, and another couple of unmarked cars whose occupants emerged briskly and joined the throngs around the garage. Cases of equipment were unloaded from the vans, and four men wearing white coveralls carried them into the garage. Then the main door was abruptly rolled down. Apparently the airing process was complete and the real business could begin in there.

At that point, Ms Lyon joined me. As interviews go, this one was informal. Awkward, of course. Though the delay had at least given me the chance to consider how much truth was required, and decide that facts rather than speculation were what I would offer. If asked. I gave her the facts: that I knew Lal Fisher was Frank's sister; that Phyllis and I had naturally decided to make contact and tell her about his death; that, also naturally, I'd been disturbed when she'd driven away in distress and had followed her home to make sure she was all right. A little less naturally, that I'd gone home myself for lunch and returned this afternoon because I'd started to worry about her.

It all sounded reasonable. Anyway, I thought so. Then I answered another of her questions with the assurance that I had never met or even seen Lal's husband, Andy; and she had hesitated, looking at me oddly, and replied with the information that he was the man that Phyllis and I had identified as 'Sergeant Andrew'. It didn't seem necessary to say that I already knew that, so I just said. 'Oh!' and tried to look baffled.

I don't know what else I might have added, except that one of the men in white overalls appeared from the house and headed in our direction, and she slid out of the car and opened the door for me. 'I'll call you,' she had said, turning away and going to meet him, and I climbed out and stretched, dropping my shoulder bag; a little flip of the wrist as it fell, and it skidded over the wet pavement towards Lyon and the new-comer and spilled out a few things like my wallet and hairbrush. I scrambled over, picking up my belongings and a couple of his phrases. He had said, 'The catalytic converter's smashed up, and we've found a glove print on the sticky tape . . .'

Lyon said something inaudible, and they both watched me retrieve my brush.

I gave her a little wave. Went to my Citroën. I'd switched on the engine and was ready to leave when I saw in my mirror that another car was arriving. This one was familiar, but I knew better than to hesitate. I found a gap in the passing traffic, turned the car around without any great haste, and was a few yards away when Paul Grant emerged, staring after me before he walked into the driveway. You might have thought that this was odd behaviour in a policeman who had just been suspended on disciplinary charges.

. . . *a glove print on the sticky tape.* Until now, I hadn't quite given up my idea that Andy Fisher had killed himself, running a hosepipe from the exhaust system into the car and then locking himself in and turning on the engine. I'd tried to imagine his motives, and connected them with Frank's death. *A glove print,* the man had said, and he'd run out in the middle of the examination to tell Lyon.

Something tapped at my window. I started upright and found myself face to face with a middle-aged man in the uniform of a traffic warden who was standing in the road, mouthing at me through the glass. I rolled the window down.

'All right, love?'

I said, 'I think so. I felt faint for a moment, but I'm better now.'

'Well, if you're sure, you'd better drive on. It's turned four, and this is a clearway now until six-thirty. You could take the next left and stop the car in the side street if you need to rest for a while.'

I told him he was kind and switched on my engine. The traffic behind me had stopped for the lights I had so recklessly run; I pulled out into the gap to drive sedately towards home.

About ninety seconds later, as I was turning into the Holloway Road, an answer slid into my head as gently as though it had always been there.

Why wear gloves to kill yourself? But if you were killing somebody else, you'd want to keep your prints off Lal Fisher's nice gold car as you slid her unconscious husband into the driver's seat and arranged a discreet little murder.

CHAPTER SIXTEEN

Histories

It was getting dark by the time I arrived at George Street, and light was pouring across the wet pavement from every window I owned. It looked like a party. The lights inside the shop were unexpected, but I could see that the grey square of my sign was still hanging on the door, and from one angle I glimpsed Ernie in the back room hunched over the computer screen. His face was intent. Reassured, I slipped past the shop, fitted my key into the door at the side of the building, and started to climb the stairs towards a babble of voices.

At the door of the sitting room I stopped. I'd arrived in the middle of a lecture. My father was laying out papers in piles, switching them around, and explaining hard. The others were talking too, Phyllis objecting to something Barnabas had just said while Ben expressed his own ideas forcefully. The papers were photocopies. Dozens of photocopies. I caught a dizzying prospect of newsprint, headlines and photographs. Apparently my father's day had been fruitful.

I swooped on Ben, lifted him out of the playpen and was greeted with a moist hug. The other two wound down. When it had become quiet, I said, 'Lal's husband is dead.'

'Andy's dead?' Phyllis said slowly. She had gone white. 'Him too?'

My father looked at her closely, then quickly at me. 'I think,' he said slowly, 'that a whisky is indicated, all round – with the probable exception of my grandson. If I may . . . ?'

I told him that he might, and we watched him retrieve the bottle of Bushmills that I kept for his benefit, find three small glasses in the left-hand cupboard of my sideboard, examine them sceptically for dust, and pour two ladylike shots and a larger one for himself. Then we sat and stared at one another.

'Well?'

I told him, keeping one eye on Phyllis, who was at the far end of the settee, her head bowed. She seemed to be interested in the play of light on the surface of the liquid in her glass.

At the end of my story, my father hesitated and then shook his head. 'Why the devil,' he asked sharply, 'should this man decide to kill himself just now?'

I took a sip of whisky and reached for my bombshell. 'He was murdered, too.'

Barnabas raised his eyebrows at me and waited. I told him what I'd overheard about the glove mark and what I believed that it meant.

'Why?' That was Phyllis speaking in a voice that was hoarse with strain. 'It must be connected, somehow. Or am I crazy?'

Then I told her that Lal's husband had been the tall detective sergeant with the lined face who had raided her flat. It wasn't exactly an answer to her question, but it was certainly relevant.

'That was *Andy Fisher*?' she said slowly. 'Yes . . . Well – well, maybe that explains it. Maybe he was the one who came back to give me the phone when they were leaving? Yes . . . and . . . and . . .' She shivered.

Barnabas and I had turned to her with one movement and waited. She looked at us and tried to smile. 'It's all so crazy. What I mean is – I went back to the flat today to get some clothes and things. Dido, did Ernie . . . ?'

I said that her message had reached me.

'While I was there, that young constable came back. They'd sent him to drive me back to the police station; they wanted to get my fingerprints to compare them and Frank's with what they'd found in the flat. They'd got something on a door handle that Andrew . . . Andy . . . touched. Dido already knows about that. When we were in the car he started asking me to make another statement about yesterday, and I told him there was nothing new I could say, really, but when we got there I answered the questions he asked and waited while they typed it up and then I signed it. It took a long time. Then there were the fingerprints. While I was waiting for the person who does them, the constable came back and said that they weren't needed any more, they'd identified Andrew's . . . his fingerprints from criminal records, and they didn't need anything else from me right now. He couldn't get rid of me fast enough.'

'What time was that?'

Phyllis shrugged. 'I didn't notice. Two or two-thirty, maybe?'

'The news about Andy Fisher must have just reached them at that point.' I calculated. 'It was about three when Inspector Lyon arrived at Verwood Avenue, and it felt as though she was in charge there in some kind of way. You know how it is when the boss walks in a bit late? People looked at her, people reported to her. Besides, she was visiting Superintendent Paige yesterday, and she was at Islington this morning when I went there. She pretended that she was looking into a complaint against Paul, but now they're both involved in some investigation that links Andy Fisher with Frank, and that must already have been set up by Scotland Yard before Frank's death.'

'Frank's death . . .' Barnabas hesitated and thought about it again.

'. . . was connected with that investigation,' I supplied. 'Caused by it, maybe?'

'Indeed.'

'And after we talked to them and worked out those computer-generated pictures of Andrew and Moore, somebody at the station must have sent them on to Scotland Yard, or some national database, and somebody there recognised Fisher. Moore too, probably. Barnabas, I saw Moore in the background of that photo that you left here for me. I wish I'd had a chance to ask her about Moore, if that's his real name.'

'It is,' my father asserted shortly. I stared at him and found him glaring back. 'And if you aren't more sensible than usual, he might also wind up proving my next point: this is an *extraordinarily* dangerous business in which neither one of you ladies should be involved for one second longer.'

I exploded, 'I did get your message! Barnabas, don't go on at me, it's *finished*! What do you mean, I should be sensible? I'm not *doing* anything! We aren't threatening anybody! I can't even work out what's been happening!' I stopped long enough to get my breath back. 'If anyone's in danger, I think it might be Lal. Barnabas, just what did you find out when you were at the newspaper library? Do you know what this is really all about? Who Moore is? I thought that he wasn't a real policeman until I noticed him in that picture you left. He must have been involved in Frank's trial. But Andrew – I mean Andy Fisher – wasn't a policeman, he was a criminal . . . Barnabas, why did you go to a music shop this afternoon?'

My father stared blankly, 'Music shop?'

I repeated Ernie's message, and my father's solemnity cracked for a moment.

'Tapes,' he said. 'Not music. There is a firm in Fleet Street which makes recordings of court proceedings. Fortunately I bumped into a young lady at the library who is a clerk in a solicitor's office, and she kindly explained. I thought that if I heard what actually happened at the trial it might throw light on what seem most peculiar gaps in the newspaper reports. I phoned from Colindale and made arrangements to listen to their recordings. I went down directly – apart from stopping off here for a word of warning about who we are dealing with and finding you were missing. I was expecting to be at Fleet Street for some hours, but the proceedings turned out to be shorter than I could have conceived. It was clearly intended to be a lengthy trial, the culmination of a vast police investigation. In fact it barely got started. Which in itself was enlightening, of course, though only in a rather limited sense.'

'Enlighten us, too,' I begged him. 'What happened?'

'Nothing, on the record, except for some opening formalities. In a nutshell, Frank and a second defendant called Barry White were charged with various offences which centred on something I'll explain later. There were formal pleas of not guilty; and then before the prosecution was due to open proceedings the jury were sent out of the court and the recording was suspended. When it started again, they both pleaded guilty to one offence each and were sentenced to two and three years respectively. The rest of the charges were dropped. The details are in the account from *The Times* – that pile there, I believe. Essentially, that was all that happened.'

'Two years?' I asked, doing the arithmetic.

'Frank got full remission,' Phyllis said harshly: 'and he'd been on remand for a while. He got out just after his operation.'

Barnabas surveyed his papers. 'It's here. I wish I could say "all" here, but hard facts are limited. One might almost think that the newspapermen couldn't make out what was going on either. It was strangely secretive. Unless I am merely being naive.'

'But you do know something.'

'*Something*,' he agreed cautiously. 'Do you recall the Hatton Carriers bullion robbery in the spring of 'eighty-seven?'

I shook my head and didn't bother reminding him that I'd been working in New York that year as a junior in one of the big publishing houses – sowing some wild oats just after I graduated.

'In that case,' my father said with an air of satisfaction, 'I might as well start at the beginning, more or less, which was twenty or thirty years earlier.' Barnabas's major weakness is his tendency to give illustrated lectures whenever possible: an old habit from his teaching days.

From the pile of photocopied sheets on the carpet at his feet, my father selected three and handed them over. I juggled them into the right order and found that, with a lot of overlap, they reproduced the four columns, six or seven inches high, which had appeared on the bottom of a page in one of the broadsheet newspapers. I was faced by a medium-sized headline which read 'End of the Old East End'; it was in fact a background piece by staff writers for the bullion robbery trial. The whole thing must have been over a thousand words long.

I looked at him. 'Do you have a summary?'

Barnabas sighed. 'In my salad days – the forties and fifties, I mean – Soho was full of little membership drinking clubs, some of which were centres for illegal gambling, prostitution, and all the various criminal activities that grew up around them. They flourished for several decades.'

'Sex, drugs and rock 'n' roll?' I suggested frivolously, leaning against the back of my chair.

'Drugs weren't so commonplace in those days,' Barnabas said shortly, 'and it was jazz, pop, swing or something, not rock and roll. Apart from that, yes. Also robbery, money-laundering, protection . . . One of them was the Black Cat Club.'

I opened my mouth, but he raised a hand and said, 'Let me finish. It was largely run by two extended families, originally from Hoxton: the Bruntons and the Whites. The senior figures were Jimmy Brunton and two brothers called Pete and Vinnie White.'

Phyllis stirred. 'I think Frank's father's name was "Jimmy". I thought he was dead.'

Barnabas looked at her. 'He is. He died of cancer in 'eighty-nine. The families had a variety of interests which they ran from offices above the club, and they did quite well for many years, in part because they had connections with the West End police.'

His voice had begun to take on the soothing rhythms of 'once upon a time a long, long time ago', and Ben, who likes stories, settled himself in my lap, leaned back against my chest with a thump, and put a thumb into his mouth to aid concentration.

'Friends?'

'And allies. Protection. The club could never have flourished so without making an investment in a few local policemen.

'Of course, in the end they went too far. In 'eighty-seven they planned and executed the ambush of an armoured car carrying something like twenty-five million pounds' worth of gold bullion through the City late one night. It was a rather odd business: the two families had been involved in intimidation and minor violence in connection with their normal business, but they'd certainly never been involved in anything like a major armed robbery before. Not, at least, as far as anyone knew. There was speculation – ' he gestured at the newspaper files '– that they had linked up with another gang. No names seem to have been mentioned.

'It went wrong. There were two police cars accompanying the armoured van. They stopped the one behind by driving a stolen newspaper van into it; then the driver of the lead car lost his head and stopped, instead of driving on full tilt and radioing for help, which I gather were the standing instructions. The next thing they knew there were men poking shotguns through their windows. Despite that, the driver reached for his radio; one of the robbers fired, and although the driver was only hit by a few stray pellets, his partner was killed. The guards in the armoured van then decided that discretion was the better part of valour and surrendered. The gang took the van and the undamaged police car, continued on their way, and promptly vanished.

'The dead policeman had been in his final weeks of service before retirement. The tabloids made it a human interest story. There weren't so many guns in London ten or twelve years ago and armed robbery was comparatively rarer than it is today. And there was gold: always a crowd-puller. It was a good news story. So a great deal of interest was taken in finding the perpetrators.'

'Unsuccessfully?' I guessed.

Barnabas nodded. 'The van was found burned out in a wood in Kent a couple of days later, and the patrol car was discovered a couple of miles away, equally burned out. The bullion was never recovered. The criminals, however, were eventually identified. According to the papers, somebody on the inside . . . "grassed". The Black Cat people were finally identified in 1991, and the club was closed down. Two of them – Barry White and Frankie Brunton – were arrested. Frank's father had died in his bed two years earlier, and Pete, Vinnie and a number of others just disappeared. Vinnie was traced to Brazil, but he died there in uncertain circumstances about three years ago. It was reported that he had been shot by an armed robber who was never caught. I make no comment. His brother, Pete, retired to Spain, where I assume he has been running a tourist pub and playing poker with his friends for the past decade. He'd be an old man now. Well, say about my age. There was no extradition treaty in those days.'

'But there is now,' I said, remembering something I'd read in the papers. 'Some new European Union treaty. The Fishers were in Spain too, until a few months ago. Lal told me there was some kind of family business in Marbella, a time-share racket probably, maybe with Pete White involved. Money-laundering, for a guess. The proceeds of the bullion theft? But why has all this blown up now?'

Barnabas shrugged. 'My researches are merely historical. Perhaps this new extradition treaty changed things? You should probably ask one of your police friends.'

'And perhaps they'll answer all my questions, and probably pigs do aerial acrobatics,' I retorted in my best Barnabas imitation.

He raised his eyebrows again and quite obviously decided not to bother commenting on this childish outburst. Ben thought the story-telling had stopped, and started to wriggle. I hugged him, and he settled again. For the moment. The telephone rang. Because I was encumbered, Phyllis answered it. She listened for a moment.

'I'll tell her.' She turned. 'Ernie says he's found something and can you come downstairs.'

'I suppose so.' I saw the anxiety in her face and laughed. 'I think I have an overdose of information. No, no, tell him of course I'm coming.'

'You give Ben to me and I'll see about his tea,' Phyllis said. She was very close to laughing too. That was something I hadn't seen for a while. I breathed a little easier.

CHAPTER SEVENTEEN

'★ ★ ★ ★ ★'

I switched off the lights in the front of the shop as we went through, leaving the shelves in darkness. A bit like the business itself this week, if I thought about it, which I was still trying not to do.

Ernie glanced at us from the computer. He looked smug. 'I found some more of it!'

Barnabas and I lined up behind his chair and stared over his head at the monitor.

'What,' Barnabas demanded quietly, 'is that?' The screen was full of the kind of gibberish I'd already seen. When Ernie explained that it was an encrypted file, my father's eyes lit up with a professional interest. He muttered, 'Did I ever tell you that towards the end of the war I was working on one of the earliest computers that ever existed, deciphering German codes? They called it "Colossus" – it was bigger than this machine, rather more the size of the room, in fact, and less powerful by a factor of two or three hundred. So! Encryption?'

Ernie digested the historical information with respect and then launched on his explanation. After a moment, I wandered over to where the post was lying unopened on top of the filing cabinet. I set the large envelopes that obviously held catalogues to one side; it was already too late in the day to expect to get any of the wonderful bargains that might have been lurking there unnoticed, and therefore I'd get around to reading them tomorrow. The rest consisted of a circular, warning the members of my booksellers' association about a couple of stolen books, and envelopes that turned out to hold two small cheques and one insignificant order. I dumped the lot, returned to the desk, and found Ernie keying and clicking his way through a series of windows to demonstrate his methodology.

Just as I started to listen again, he was saying, 'So there's two kinds of files, see? These ones, that's just accounts. And then there's these other ones. That's an encrypted file.'

'And to decrypt it?' Barnabas prompted him.

'See,' Ernie confided, 'it's just one of the standard programs, but we still need the password. See what you get?' He clicked the mouse, and the gibberish disappeared. 'Watch when I try to open this file. See?' He clicked the mouse and produced a small window and the words: *Enter password*. 'So we gotta type his password in there,' Ernie concluded. 'You got any ideas, Dido?'

I hadn't. But it was just possible that Phyllis did. 'What kind of thing would a password be? One word? How long?'

Ernie shrugged. 'Words, numbers, maybe even just a buncha letters. You wouldn' want to bother wiv' anything too long, so most people use their middle name or their date of birth.'

Date of birth?

I said confidently, 'Try a number: 141052.'

I watched him type the figures, which appeared on the screen as a string of six asterisks, and press the return key. The screen said that my guess was wrong.

'What was that?' my father demanded, and I told him about the combination of Frank's safe. He smiled slowly. 'Then the chances are indeed that he used something very similar here. People tend not to be very original. His own birth date seems most likely. That would be . . . ?'

I told him that I hadn't a clue.

'Then run along upstairs and send Phyllis down,' my father commanded. 'In the meantime' – he had turned back to Ernie – 'we could try his name, Phyllis's name . . .'

'Don't forget "Hatton"!'

'You gotta get it in the right order, with spaces and every-thing just right,' Ernie warned.

'And those might all be a bit too obvious. We'll have to keep trying,' Barnabas announced, looking around for the spare chair, with the obvious implication that he was there for the night.

I said, 'Ernie's been here for hours already. He probably needs to go home.'

My protégé flashed me a reproachful look.

'Ernie, if you'll just show me what to do . . .' my father was saying without listening to me.

I left them at it and went to relieve Phyllis. I'd decided that it would be more fun to feed Ben and give him his bath than to join the computer party. But I was also thinking of the pile of papers in my sitting room. Rows of asterisks seemed less interesting than getting to grips with the story of the Black Cat and its criminal management.

CHAPTER EIGHTEEN

Paperwork

'You look curiously like one of my students in the throes of an essay crisis,' my father observed. 'Should I assume that you are in the process of putting one and one together and making fourteen?'

I made a faint tick in the top right-hand corner of another photocopy, shifted it from the big pile on the right to the little one on the left, and put down my pen on the pad of paper that I'd dug out of a drawer in my bureau. 'I haven't got as far as fourteen yet,' I said. 'About one and a half.' Then I looked at him more closely. I'd just heard Barnabas and Phyllis climbing the stairs, and it struck me that he was leaning on the door frame, holding a handful of computer print-outs and looking pale. 'Are you all right? You didn't forget to take your aspirin?' My father takes a little aspirin daily, and has done ever since his heart attack a couple of years ago.

'I am all right,' he said gruffly, 'though food wouldn't come amiss, possibly followed by bed in view of my early start this morning. I sent Ernie home about half an hour ago, and I've been sitting at the keyboard typing silly things into a little rectangle. It appears that I am becoming a trifle impatient in my old age. I've brought a sample of the stuff away with me so I can sit down comfortably and stare at it.'

So they'd had no luck. I could hear Phyllis moving around in the living room; it sounded as if I was being tidied up.

'Have you locked up downstairs?'

Barnabas looked at me and said that as a matter of fact he had left the shop door wide open and the lights on, with a banner sign across the window reading 'Come in – all books free tonight'. I apologised and explained that I was feeling a bit tired myself.

'And you?' he asked. 'You have been reading the newspaper reports. Excellent. It might be interesting if we cross-indexed all the names and dates that are mentioned. Perhaps that might clarify the relevant facts. Or at least help us to decide which ones *are* relevant.'

I stretched my back and nodded. 'I've only been trying to get an idea of what really happened. The problem is just that everybody was lying, and the police weren't saying any more than they had to. We need more information about the investigation of the bullion robbery. I have the impression that they got absolutely nowhere for a long time, though there might be more details in other newspapers. By the time the trial started, most of the people involved had already vanished abroad, like Lal and her husband. She told me that they'd gone to Spain the previous year to run a time share. She made it sound like an ordinary business move, but I guess they could see there were going to be arrests. Presumably they came back to London a few months ago when Fisher decided there was no chance of being prosecuted any more.'

'Or because he knew perfectly well that whatever aborted the trial in 'ninety-two was still in effect. Have you discovered why that was such a damp squib?'

I had. In part, anyway. I'd found an editorial comment from the *Telegraph* expressing outrage that vital evidence had gone missing from the police station where it had been stored, and fulminating against police incompetence. I was fairly sure that some word stronger than mere 'incompetence' was needed to describe what had happened.

'And any traces of the mysterious Inspector Moore's name?'

'Absolutely,' I said grimly. 'He was only a sergeant, but in fact he was there: he was the panicky police driver whose partner was shot. His name doesn't come up anywhere else, but that's certainly him, going into the trial. I think he was going to be a witness.'

'How old would you say he is now?' Barnabas asked abruptly.

I thought back and hesitated. 'Fifty?'

'Obviously, he is no longer with the police.'

I looked at him. 'Oh. You mean he was dismissed?'

'Asked to retire,' my father said. 'Hadn't you noticed the hallowed custom of allowing police officers to take retirement on "health" grounds when they have done something wrong? And now I strongly suggest some food. You are looking tired. Phyllis is looking tired. I *am* most definitely tired. I could take all four of us out to a convenient family restaurant.' He sounded unusually unenthusiastic.

I said, 'One restaurant meal per week is the maximum that Ben is allowed, at his age, and anyway I've fed him and put him to bed. We could phone out for some Chinese . . .'

'Do,' Barnabas said a little surprisingly. 'Go and do it. While we wait, let me sit down at the table and look at this printout again. Perhaps I'll get a feel for it.'

We exchanged places. When I glanced back from the hallway I could see him scowling at the garbled shapes on the paper. I found Phyllis lying on the settee with her feet up and her eyes closed and asked her whether she liked sweet-and-sour. When I returned from discussing fried rice versus noodles, and telephoning our order, I found Barnabas still engrossed. Secretly I believed that the marvels of modern computer encryption had probably left my father's methods, developed half a century ago during the war, hopelessly outdated.

After a while, I became aware of a scratching noise behind me. Somebody was assaulting the kitchen window. I flung myself on it and raised it a foot, and Mr Spock stalked in between the bars, avoiding my eye. He walked stiff-legged on to the work counter, sat down, and pointedly began to dry the bedraggled fur on his back. He must have been shut out in the rain all day. Had I even fed him this morning? No, but surely Phyllis had. In a flurry of guilt I poured him some milk and opened an apologetic tin of yellow-fin tuna. He landed beside them with a thump, and got down to business.

When the doorbell rang, Barnabas came to a decision. He swept up the printout, added it to the piles of newspaper stories, and announced, 'We shall eat. Then you and Phyllis will go to bed, and I shall return home, take some bicarbonate, and see what I can make of all this by burning a little midnight oil.'

'Or get some rest yourself,' I reminded him over my shoulder as I headed towards the street door, pausing only long enough to dig into my shoulder bag, hanging on the hook by the door, and hope that I was going to find enough cash there to pay the delivery man. It would be nice if I could get on with my life. In the morning, I promised myself as I clattered down the stairs towards the scent of garlic and *hoi sin*, I would treat myself to a few luxuries like an overdue visit to the cash machine, like buying some milk and coffee beans, like asking Ben what he thought about life, like opening the shop and getting on with the business, like . . .

CHAPTER NINETEEN

Skeletons

I listened to the sound of my father's taxi heading off towards the main road and asked, 'How are you feeling?'

Phyllis had to cast around for the answer. She came up with, 'Dropping.'

I hesitated. 'What do you want to do?'

She grinned faintly. 'Go to bed. Or didn't you mean that?'

What I wanted was to talk about her plans for the future, but I sympathised. My problem was that, although it felt as though today had been going on forever, so many questions had been thrown up that I'd probably lie awake gnawing on them. I told her that I hadn't meant tonight, but tomorrow. And the next day.

'A lot's happened, hasn't it? All sorts of skeletons coming out? I still feel blank. It's just like everybody always says: you know he's dead, but you keep forgetting and thinking about things as though he isn't. But he's dead, and it *will* sink in.'

'And then?' I waited.

'I've been thinking. One reason why I went back to the flat, earlier: I wanted to call my brother in Perth. He thinks I should come home, and I guess he's right. I won't leave you in the lurch with Ben, Dido, and I won't go until Frank's buried, but I will use that air ticket as soon as I can.'

'Will you be all right?'

Phyllis laughed. 'You mean money? Well, that little bundle Frank had in the safe will help, and there's an old life assurance policy, believe it or not. He must have taken that out a good while back – I wouldn't have called him a good risk. Anyway, there's a will and some documents in the bank; Frank told me that a couple of months ago. But I never had any trouble finding a job.'

'You can sell the flat.'

'It isn't ours. We never paid any rent, but none of it belonged to us. It's all police property, even the furniture. So I can pack up my clothes and leave whenever I want to.'

'Even if they haven't found out who killed him?'

Phyllis said bluntly, 'I don't really care that much. What difference does it make now? I don't know if you can understand this, Dido, because you've never been able to leave things well alone all the time I've known you, and you always mean well, but I don't think it's up to me to find out what happened.'

I shook my head. She went on. 'See, I've lost somebody I was really fond of, but I can't change that. I suppose it didn't even make much difference, because his cancer was in remission for a while, but we both knew it had come back. More chemotherapy might have given him another year, but I don't think so. I was getting used to it, accepting what was going to happen. But like Frank said when we heard about the last test, well, he'd had a lot of fun. So I'll go home soon and get on with my life. I'm not likely to find anybody else, not at my age, and I don't know that I'd want to, but I have family there. Now Frank's gone, to my mind I should make a start as soon as possible, not sit around moping. Do you think I'm hard?'

I couldn't stop myself asking, 'Why was he hiding? He must have told you.'

'Only that he was in danger when he got out. He made some kind of deal with them at the trial, I'm pretty sure, but he wasn't allowed to talk about it. I don't know whether that's why he got the short sentence, or because of his health. Both, probably. Your father guessed about that. All I know is that Frank once told me he'd given them the names of some police officers that'd been involved in a robbery. He was going to testify at their trial when they were caught. There was something going on there, something bad, but he couldn't tell me about it.'

'Was it a bullion robbery?'

Phyllis shrugged. 'Frank never said. But that rang a bell when your dad mentioned it, so I may've heard something, some time. I do know it was something to do with Frank's family, including Lal's Andy. And those crooked policemen I mentioned. Frank wasn't involved in the robbery himself – he wasn't the kind of man who'd run around with a gun and hurt people. I always thought he'd only got involved because it was . . . I don't know – the family business. I couldn't really understand it, because he was a decent man. Or maybe I can. I'd say he was just the accountant: the man who kept the books and paid the wages, and any taxes he couldn't avoid, and the bills. And if you want my guess for what it's worth, I think he might have known what happened to some loot that they never found. So whatever's just happened to him started a long time ago and I can't do anything about it. Don't get me wrong: I'll feel better when it's out in the open, finished. I hope they catch the one who did it and put him where he belongs for the rest of his life, but I can't help them. It'll still happen if I go home. Dido, I really do need to go to bed, if you don't mind, because I think I'm babbling. I'm sorry about pushing you out of your own living room.'

I told her that I'd have a long hot bath and go to bed then myself. 'But,' I said, 'I can't help wondering if Lal is all right. Do you mind hanging on for a minute longer while I see if I can get her on the phone?'

'I'll say goodnight to her,' Phyllis said slowly, and I dialled the number from the scrap of paper I'd left under the telephone that morning and listened to it ring. I wasn't surprised that there was no answer; she wouldn't have wanted to stay there alone.

I couldn't think of anything else to try. Everything was standing still.

But I'd only got as far as the bathroom door when the phone rang in the sitting room. I reached it before Phyllis or the answering machine caught the call, and had just opened my mouth when the voice in my ear said, 'Dido, why were you phoning Mrs Fisher?'

'Good evening, Paul. How do you know that I tried to phone her?'

'Because we're monitoring calls to that number.'

I kicked myself mentally and said, 'Naturally. So – I gather that you really have been unsuspended? Congratulations.'

'You know I wasn't suspended.'

I admitted that I'd guessed. I'd had time by now to digest Colley's question about whether Paul had seen Fisher and Moore at the flat, and decide that the whole story of the suspension was an excuse to get him out of Islington. Unofficially, Paul had been moved because he had been asking questions about those two, and either somebody had thought he could do some good if he were seconded to Diane Lyon's team, or they believed he'd be safer out of sight if Moore knew who and where he was.

I took a deep breath. 'Well, where is she? Phyllis and I just wanted to have a word with her and ask if there's anything we can do.'

'She's all right,' Paul said shortly. 'She's in a private hospital for observation. We'll tell her you were asking. She can phone you if she wants to. And as far as you're concerned, I'm still suspended.'

As far as *I* was concerned? I said, 'Well, goodbye.' And waited for him to hang up.

'Dido . . . ?'

'Yes?'

'Have you eaten this evening?'

That wasn't what I'd expected. I told him I'd had a take-away.

'Well, I haven't. Can we talk about this situation like grown-ups? I think you might be able to help. Will you join me for dessert or just coffee or something?'

The word 'dumbfounded' popped into my mind, and I decided I was it. I made an effort and gasped, 'Where?'

'Wait a minute, let me think.' Wondering, I let him. 'Got it! I'm off duty in a minute. It should take me about twenty minutes to get over there, and I'll park in Upper Street on the east side, just north of you. So at . . . ten o'clock, let's say, you leave your place, turn right and right again, walk down to Upper Street, and turn north. You'll see the car, but don't stop. Walk straight on past it and keep going until you get to the Spanish restaurant on the west side of the road. Go in and take a table away from the window. You remember the place I mean?'

I did. We'd eaten there once or twice. I said, 'Why the cloak-and-dagger stuff?'

'In case somebody's hanging around you,' he said bluntly. 'You know why: I explained all that last night. I'll make sure nobody's following, because it wouldn't do either of us any good to be seen together.'

I told him that I was sure his reputation could only benefit from our public association, and hung up. I just had time to change my clothes, brush my hair, pick up something from downstairs that I'd decided I'd better hand over if I was going to keep my word to my father, and think up a list of questions I was going to ask.

CHAPTER TWENTY

Saraband

It was the slack time between the normal dinner hour and the closing of the local theatres and pubs. I settled behind a glass-topped table three-quarters of the way down the long, half-empty room, ordered a glass of fino, and focused on the door. Even before my drink had arrived, Paul came in with a briskness that made me think of an FBI raid: he just needed to be holding a big gun out in front of him to make the perfect dramatic entrance. He had reached the table, moved the second chair a fraction and settled in it before I had a chance to react. I would have said that his nerves were on edge, except that I realised he was carefully blocking my view of the door and the window and that meant that he was also preventing anyone who was passing the restaurant from seeing my face, or anything much except his anonymous back.

'What if the mob bursts through the door behind you with machineguns?' I asked sourly.

Paul grinned at me. 'You didn't notice that there's a mirror on the partition behind your head? I'll see them just in time for us to fling ourselves behind the upturned table and escape the hail of bullets.'

I goggled. He was looking tired but extremely happy.

'*Señor?*'

'Dos Equis,' Paul said briskly, and picked up the menu. He looked at me. 'Have you really eaten?'

Thinking about my recent diet and its vitamin deficiencies,

I told him that I could probably manage a small salad, and when the drinks came he ordered quickly, handed back the menus, and leaned forward.

I asked the obvious question. 'What's going on?'

'I'm not sure I should tell you yet. Keep it quiet, will you? Diane Lyon's asked me to apply for a job, that's all. It would mean promotion. But nothing's happening yet, and it may all depend on what comes off in the next few days.'

He took a gulp of his beer; I sipped my sherry in a ladylike manner, and we eyed one another cautiously.

'Good luck, but you didn't want me to come out and meet you to celebrate. Did you really think I might be followed?'

'Not really, though it seemed an outside possibility. I'm hoping that they've stopped even thinking about you and Mrs Digby.' I was opening my mouth to tell him about the silent phone calls, but he went on, 'Actually, I was sure you'd turn up if I told you it might be dangerous.'

Touché. 'You could just have come around,' I suggested, not sure whether to laugh. 'Paul . . .'

He was shaking his head. 'I got off on the wrong foot last night. I wanted to change the scenery and apologise. And I thought it might be better if Mrs Digby wasn't around. I hear that she's going to be staying with you for the time being?'

I nodded. 'On the settee. And you're right, there isn't a lot of privacy. Now tell me what you don't want her to hear. And while you're at it, tell me about Andy Fisher.'

He laughed out loud. 'Aren't I supposed to be quizzing *you*? All right, all right, what do you want to know?'

I looked at him in sheer disbelief. The arrival of my bowl of salad and his plate of meat and oily potatoes covered my silent astonishment. Whatever this new job was, the prospect had transformed his mood. I swallowed a black olive, got a grip on myself, and started to take advantage of it.

'How did Andy Fisher die?'

'Tests not finished –' he paused for a mouthful of roast suckling pork. I followed suit with a piece of tomato crowned by an anchovy '– but in a nutshell, somebody hit him on the back of the head, drove him into his own garage, settled him behind the wheel, rigged a piece of hosepipe from under the car to the interior, smashed the car's catalytic converter, and left the motor running. Superficially it looked like suicide.'

'What about the glove print?'

He stopped eating for a minute and looked at me.

'I was there, after talking to Diane Lyon, when somebody said something to her about a glove print.'

He shook his head at me with a slightly ironic grin. 'I don't know why you're pretending that I know anything you don't. The murderer wore gloves. There was a print on the tape he used to fix the hosepipe to the exhaust.'

'You can't identify glove prints . . .'

'Obviously. But there were no gloves in the car, or anywhere in the garage for that matter, so Fisher hadn't done that by himself. Anyway, we know there was somebody with him. But of course the pathologist would have thrown doubts on the suicide idea as soon as he reported the head injury. It just saved us a couple of hours.'

'So you knew right away that it was murder.' I remembered: 'Did you get anything from those security cameras on the house?'

Paul looked sour. 'The one over the garage was stuck at the wrong angle to do any good. The other one got a few frames of the car arriving, stopping while the door went up and then driving in.'

'What time did they arrive? Does the camera record times?'

Paul shrugged. 'The first thing that happened was when Fisher left the house this morning, just after nine-forty. Somebody was waiting to pick him up at the kerb. Nothing useful shows on the tape, though. The wife left, driving his car, about fifteen minutes later. At about a quarter past ten, a Toyota drove up with two people in it. They can't be identified. You can't even see whether the passenger is conscious or just being held up by the seat belt. They paused in the driveway while the garage door went up – it has a remote-control mechanism, damn it, so they didn't have to get out. They drove in and the door came down. Ten minutes later, somebody popped out on foot, stopped long enough to make sure the door was shut, and walked away without looking up. He was wearing a jacket with the hood pulled up, and he kept his face turned away, so he knew about the cameras.'

'Who do you suspect?'

This time the hesitation was even longer. I knew he was being evasive when he said, 'The spouse is always the first suspect.'

I let him see my opinion of that. I added, 'Anyway, she has an airtight alibi.'

I'd startled him. 'What's that?'

'I spoke to her on the phone just after nine-thirty, and she couldn't talk to me freely then. I'm pretty sure somebody was in earshot — presumably her husband, since that fits with the times. She was waiting on the Heath when Phyllis and I arrived just after ten-thirty. I looked at my watch when we first saw her, because we were a few minutes early, but she was already there. When she left us in the park, that was just about the time your hooded figure left the scene. I followed her home. It looked as though she was driving a car she was unfamiliar with — she said it was Andy's car — and it took her at least twenty minutes to get back to the house, probably longer, so it must have taken her that long to drive down to meet us, too. She was in my sight all the time, by the way. If you'll look at that part of the tape, you'll see that I stopped and rang the doorbell, and she finally let me in, but it took her quite a long time to realise that I wasn't going away and she might as well answer the door. I suppose you could ask why it took her so long to let me in, but she certainly wasn't the person who drove up in the Toyota.'

'It doesn't mean that she didn't have an accomplice. As you say, it took her a long time to decide to let you in. Maybe she's as guilty as hell and didn't want to encourage you to hang about.'

I thought over my first visit to Verwood Avenue. It had been full of strangeness. I decided not to say anything. Besides . . .

Paul said, 'What is it?'

'When I was still waiting for her to answer the door, I heard the car's engine. I didn't realise what it was, or maybe I could have . . . I keep thinking that if I'd just asked her about it . . .'

'Well, you didn't, and there was no reason for you to. Anyway, he must have been dead already. Well . . . thanks. I agree that Mrs Fisher isn't the actual murderer, if only because she would have to have been pretty lucky to overpower a big man like her husband, but there's still the chance that she had help. There are a lot of things about her that I don't understand.' He hesitated for a moment. 'Look, you'd better treat all this as confidential, but the hospital says that she'd been beaten up. That was probably the husband, and we were playing with the idea that she could have arranged for somebody to kill him.'

I said that I remembered seeing bruises on her wrist.

'According to the doctor, somebody gave her a battering a few days ago, mostly where it doesn't show.'

Thinking about it, I found myself struggling towards some kind of overall view. 'Has she actually told you Andy did it?'

'She hasn't told us anything. Says she doesn't know anything, didn't notice anything, can't imagine anything. She has a high-quality "poor-little-me" routine, as you might have noticed.'

I said slyly, 'So you'd call her uncooperative? Perhaps you'd like to batter her a bit too?'

He just snorted.

I put my fork down on my plate and picked up my glass, trying to decide how much to say.

'Paul, this is the way I read it: Lal Fisher was a career criminal's wife, daughter and sister. She's been keeping her mouth shut all her life. She doesn't like cops, and somehow I think that she'd absolutely hate Diane Lyon on sight. Her background . . . do you know her background?'

'Like her late husband's: East End old-time crooks.'

'Exactly. Old-fashioned, set in her ways . . .'

'Fair enough,' Paul agreed, 'but if she didn't kill him, why shouldn't she want to help us find his murderer? Especially since it's hard to imagine that the person who killed him didn't also kill Frank, and about the one thing she did consent to tell us was that she was very fond of her brother.'

I told him that Phyllis had corroborated that.

'So what's bugging her?'

I'd spent most of the day working on that problem and had reached some tentative answers. 'Three possibilities. One is that she's loyal to the old ties, and there's a conflict of interests: both Andy and Frank were killed by somebody she wouldn't want to betray to you.'

Paul shrugged. 'You *never* tell the coppers anything.'

'It's also possible, I suppose, that she might have done something illegal herself, though I've been getting the message that old-fashioned patriarchs like Andy and Frank wouldn't dream of letting their women be directly involved in crime. On the other hand, when I told her about Frank, the first thing she said was that it was *her fault*. I don't know whether she really meant anything.' I noticed Paul open his mouth to interrupt and think better of it. Instead, he looked sardonic. I ignored him. 'The final possibility, the one that I prefer, is that she's simply frightened. Look, I know why you said it must have been Fisher who beat her up, but what if it wasn't? Of course, there are some women her age who seem to think that husbands have the right. But if it was somebody else – somebody who terrifies her?'

Paul put his cutlery down slowly and shoved the plate away. He looked a little less happy now.

I took a deep breath. 'So your problem is, who and where are any of the people still alive who were involved in the Hatton Carriers bullion robbery?'

'How the . . . ?'

'I assumed you knew about it.'

I caught a flash of last night's bad temper. 'What has Mrs Digby told you, and why haven't you passed it on?'

The waiter was hovering. I raised my eyebrow at Paul, who controlled himself.

'I'm finished with the salad,' I said loudly, 'but I'd like another sherry, please.'

Paul nodded, ordered himself another beer, and held his tongue while the table was being cleared. When we were alone again, he said, 'Sorry.' We looked at each other across the table cautiously, each waiting for the other to speak. I was reminded suddenly of some complicated slow dance where you circle your partner, watching his steps, approaching and retreating again.

I lowered my voice. 'Damn it, Paul, Phyllis doesn't know anything. It was all in the newspapers at the time!'

'Barnabas?'

'Spent most of today in libraries, researching the story.'

Maybe I should speak to him.'

'Maybe you should listen to me! We saw that something went wrong at the beginning of the trial in 'ninety-two. It wouldn't be hard for *you* to find out all about it, if you don't know already. And the people who were directly involved in the hold-up had got out of the country before they were arrested. My first question is, how did they all manage to get away without being picked up? My second is, what happened after the trial started, when Frank and the other one suddenly pleaded guilty to a couple of minor charges, and everything else was dropped? Wouldn't you get a life sentence for an armed robbery where somebody's killed? My third question is why Frank Digby was released so soon, as though he hadn't really done anything serious, but at the same time given a new identity and police protection?'

Paul thought about that. 'All right, I don't see why you can't know. It's history. The people who got away – the White brothers, Andy Fisher, a few others – left the country because their friends on the force warned them they were about to be nabbed. Frank Brunton and Barry White, Vinnie's son, didn't get out in time, and in the end the two of them had to be either charged or released, so they were charged even though there were some investigating officers who wanted to let them go in the hope that they'd lead us either to the bullion or to whoever'd been involved in smuggling it abroad. Recovering it was a big priority; it was a lot of money, and the Met didn't look good.

'The day the trial began, as far as I can make out while they were actually swearing in the jury, somebody realised that most of the evidence that was supposed to be locked up in a West End police station had gone missing. Some joker had substituted bundles of old newspapers, properly packaged. At that point everybody seemed to panic. Brunton's solicitor may not have realised just how little the prosecution had been left with. Anyway, they offered Brunton a deal and he bought himself a short sentence by agreeing to help out; he had a lot of useful information in his head and in the books of that dodgy club they used to run. But I've been told that the thing that really got to him was being diagnosed with lung cancer while he was on remand. I guess he didn't want to die in jail. You can understand that. Barry White was sentenced to three years. He was supposed to have hanged himself in Lewes jail a couple of months later. They weren't sure it was suicide, but there was no evidence of anything else. These things happen in prisons. Oh – and a Sergeant Doug Moore took early retirement and moved abroad.'

'Protected?'

'Maybe, but the Crown Prosecution Service doesn't like it when policemen destroy evidence. More likely they decided they couldn't prove anything, and at least it was better than letting him stay in the force.'

'There's a lot of it about,' I sneered. He was silent. We do both read the newspapers.

'What happened about Frank's "co-operation"?' I asked with an effort.

'He was going to hand over the accounts of something called the Black Cat Club. They'd disappeared when the club closed down a year or two earlier, but it was obvious to us that until the last decade it had been used to launder money for half of London. They must have got rid of the bullion through the club's contacts, somehow. Brunton told them he had enough evidence stashed somewhere to settle half the unsolved crime in London for the past ten years. Then he got ill. There was an emergency operation which was successful, but I guess the word got out somewhere that it shouldn't have. By the time Diane Lyon's predecessor went to pick up the books, they'd gone missing. Brunton convinced them that he had no idea what had happened, so they stuck to the deal they'd made with him. In fact, they reckoned that only some member of Frank's lot that they didn't know about, or a policeman, could have known about the records, and either way that was just one more problem for us. They were hoping that they could use Frank to find the people involved. He was the only link left, and after a bit of discussion they decided to hang on to him and make him useful.'

I said, 'But you did find those accounts at the Fishers' place today, didn't you?' I watched his face darken, and for a moment I was glad we were sitting in a public place. I said, 'I didn't know what they were, or I would have told you. Lal told me *where* they were, and I caught a quick glimpse. I've only just realised *what* they were. You did find them?'

'Under a bed.' He spoke coldly.

'I think that Frank stayed in that room last Sunday night. Lal said he'd left some personal property with her before the trial, and it had been stored among their own things in Fisher's depot, and gone from there to the house without her husband knowing. She phoned Frank last week and asked him to come and take it away.' I doubled back and told him about the first message on the Digbys' tape. 'Then she left a second message for Frank yesterday, asking him to return her car – that's the Toyota Andy was killed in. Those must have been her spare keys in Frank's pocket. That was why we got in touch with her this morning: to find out what was wrong, what had happened. And tell her about Frank; she obviously didn't know he was dead.'

He was staring at his empty glass. After a moment, he stirred. 'There was damage to the bodywork of that Toyota.'

'What kind of damage?'

'Offside front wing.'

I said, 'Oh. You mean – was Frank hit by that car?'

'I don't mean that. It looks as though there was a collision with another vehicle. There's black paint in the scrapes.'

I worked at it. 'If Frank had an accident while he was driving the car, somebody might have reported it. You could find out where he went when he left Lal's house. You know he was missing for a whole day?'

'Only nobody has reported having any accident involving the Toyota.'

'Meaning—' I was thinking hard. 'Somebody might have run into it deliberately? Ambushed him?'

Paul looked at his beer and pushed the half-empty glass away. 'It's all bloody guesswork.'

'Wouldn't that mean . . . ?'

'Go on.'

'Lal says he borrowed her car because he was taking away whatever it was she'd been keeping for him. He didn't bother about those particular accounts books that I found in the bedroom, so they can't have been important. There was something with them that he did want. Other accounts? Something else?'

'So?'

'But somebody found out what he was doing and decided to take it away from him. That, or they wanted something else from him. Paul . . .'

He said, 'Well?' in the tone of somebody who knew that he had something on me.

I got hold of myself. This wasn't going very well. And yet I thought I knew something important. 'After they killed Frank, they came and searched his flat. Either he'd told them that something was there, or they reckoned it had to be. They took his computer.'

He stirred in his seat. I ignored him. I was on a roll.

'They must have found out, from him, that whatever he had with him – let's say they were records of some kind, other records – was duplicated on the computer hard drive. That's why they took it.'

'That doesn't do us much good. If you're right, that is. If it was me, I'd have had a bonfire somewhere by now.'

'They came back to the flat again.'

'Go on.'

I said, 'They were looking for his back-up disk, of course.' I dug into my bag and felt the hard square of the one that Phyllis and I had found in the little fire safe. I handed it over without looking at it. 'There are lots of encrypted files. You must have an IT person who can make something of them? I think you'd better get it to somebody fast, because the answers must be here.'

There was the other thing, the thing I'd been trying to tell him before he had distracted me by offering an unlikely amount of information. 'One more thing: yesterday afternoon, Phyllis was getting a lot of silent phone calls. That's why she left their flat and came to stay with me. They were made from a number that was "withheld", so we couldn't trace them. But obviously somebody is trying to frighten her.' I looked at him. 'That's the reason I believed you when you said we might be in danger. Whoever it is has probably worked out where Phyllis is staying. So I'd be grateful if you could take this away, because I'm going to tell everybody I've handed it to the police. Frankly, I'm considering putting up a notice on the window. If Barnabas finds out what's been happening . . .'

He was on his feet, holding the disk. 'I have to make some phone calls.'

I said, 'I know, but wait a minute, I've just thought of one more thing. I've been wondering what's just *happened*.'

He was already turning away from me, edgy. 'When?'

'That's what I don't know. Recently. Think about it, Paul: Moore has been "retired" abroad for a few years, Frank has been out of jail for as long, and the Fishers came back to England last year, since when Andy has apparently just been running this haulage business. It sounds as though everything was quiet for months. Or is there something I don't know?' I had a sudden idea, and asked him, 'Where did Moore go after he retired?'

Paul frowned and looked at the table top. I waited, but nothing came.

'Anyway, Phyllis didn't notice anything wrong. Then suddenly over the past week Lal panicked about the old accounts books, or maybe something else; Frank told Phyllis that he was going to have to be away on business, which I don't think ever happened before, and anyway she thought it was odd; he and Andy were both murdered; and Frank's flat was turned over by people who were up to their necks in that old hijacking. So it seems time to ask: do you know what happened recently, say in the past couple of weeks, that would have changed the whole situation for them?'

He looked at me. 'Do you want something else? Order it. Anything you like. Order one for me, too. I thought I was going home to bed, but I may have to put it off for a few hours. Order me something sweet, and a double black coffee.'

I said, 'I'm in trouble?'

He said, 'Not that you'd notice. It's starting to make some sense. I think maybe I'm going to owe you. Have a caramel pudding – they're good here. I'll be back in a minute.'

CHAPTER TWENTY-ONE

Message Delivered

———◆———

As I turned the corner, the bell in St Mary's spire a couple of hundred yards behind me clanged the hour, and I saw that the light in the sitting room was on. The heavy curtains had been drawn hours ago, but there was a thin line of brightness in the middle of the nearest window, and I shifted into a trot, wondering whether Ben had wakened. Or something worse. I got the door open, slid inside and put the chain on, listening. Not a sound from above, reassuring or otherwise.

In the doorway of the sitting room, I stopped. There was no sign of Ben, but Phyllis was wide awake, sitting upright on the settee with her eyes on the telephone. I looked at it, but there was no clue to her absorption.

'Phyllis . . . ?'

'Wait a minute. It will happen again in a minute.'

'What will?'

The telephone rang. She said, 'Don't!', but I reached the receiver, picked it up, and said, 'Yes?' Even before I'd spoken, I saw the light blinking on my answering machine. There had been other calls. '*Hello?*'

The line was open, but I couldn't hear anything at the other end. Suddenly I found myself dreading the idea that a voice might actually speak and decided to hang up.

The connection was broken before I could.

I looked from the receiver to Phyllis. 'How long has this been going on?'

The strain had reappeared on her face. 'He's back. It's the same one that was phoning our flat. He rings every fifteen minutes, doesn't say anything . . . You start to wait for the next one.'

I dialled the caller identification service number and was rewarded again with the electronic voice saying that my last caller had been using a number which could not be identified. Phyllis was right – it had to be the same person who had tried this trick at the flat in Power Street. Somehow he'd found my home number. Or was he trying to intimidate *me* now? I dialled the number of Paul's mobile and got no answer.

'I can't sleep,' Phyllis was saying. 'I keep waiting for the next.'

'Well-known torture technique,' I assured her brightly, hanging up, 'but you don't have to put up with it.' I got down on my hands and knees and stretched under the sideboard to unplug the phone. Anybody I might want to speak to could contact me on my mobile for the duration.

Phyllis watched and said, almost as an afterthought, 'Ben woke up a little while ago. I changed him, and he's asleep again. He was quite happy. He seems to be getting over the sniffles already.'

I tried a sniff myself, and realised I hadn't had time to think about colds. It might be prudent to set the security alarm and get some sleep. Try to. Even with the telephone silenced, I was imagining some thug with my phone number still dialling and dialling and listening to the ringing sound that he could hear even though we no longer could. Or standing outside in the street, looking up at the building . . .

I shook myself.

Phyllis was watching. 'Did you find out how Lal is?'

I sketched what Paul had told me about her sister-in-law's whereabouts and left it at that. It was too late to explain the rest. In the morning I would feel a bit more awake. And Barnabas . . . Barnabas would want to be brought up to date too. I yawned.

Phyllis said quietly, 'I'm going to turn out the light now. We're both tired.'

'I'm too tired to sleep. I think I'll go and have a bath and try to unwind. Are you all right?'

She said that she was. She said goodnight. The light went off as I was leaving the room.

I wandered into the bathroom and turned on the taps. There was a little gunge left in the bottom of my bubblebath. The label said 'Eucalyptus clears the senses and revives your system'. I hoped so. I filled the bottle with hot water and shook it up to try to get out the last molecule, since soothing and reviving were what I needed. When the tub was full and reasonably frothy, I turned off the taps and stood breathing in the scent and imagining that it was already making my eyelids heavy.

There was an unidentifiable noise. I thought for a moment that Ben was awake, talking to himself, but when I listened again I couldn't hear him. Outside, the evening air was full of sounds. It must be closing time; the pub on the corner was emptying, and some of its customers were walking in noisy groups along the side street towards the Essex Road. Traffic was still a constant grumble. After a while, I shook myself. I was asleep on my feet. I yawned and then started to pull my sweater over my head.

There were also sirens . . . several sirens out in the main road. When the quality of the sound changed, I realised they were turning into the side street. Then as quickly the noise was in front of the shop, bouncing between the walls of the narrow street. I yanked my sweater down and ran out into the hallway and through the door of the sitting room, where the blue light was flashing on the curtains.

Phyllis was sitting up. I said, 'Stay here. Look after Ben.' Then I was running down the stairs and fumbling clumsily at the chain, failing to disengage it. When it finally rattled against the frame, I opened the door and stepped out on to the pavement.

Two fire engines had stopped in the middle of the road just beyond the shopfront, and the crew were pouring out of them into the noise, which rolled and echoed along the road until somebody thought to switch the siren off. They were doing something at the far side. The nearest machine blocked my view, so I walked on to the end of the building and pressed myself back against the wall. Something had happened to a car in the residents' bay across the road. My car. There was a light inside that flickered and faded and then glowed in black clouds of smoke boiling up behind the closed windows. I heard glass crack. The firemen gathered around the Citroën with portable chemical extinguishers and I thought coldly, *Oh, it's petrol: they don't use water on that.* It probably didn't matter what they used, because the flames and the black, oily smoke were rising high above the roof now that the windows had broken.

A voice called, 'Get back now, miss!' I shrank away, and then turned towards the flat, seeing a new blue light flashing against the brick walls. A police car was turning into the road, and a crowd had started to gather to watch the fun. So for a moment I didn't even notice the second fire.

There is a small triangular paved space between the side wall of my building, just beside the door of the flat, and the rear wall of the shop on the corner which abuts my property at an angle. It is a space that nobody seems to own, which holds an abandoned dustbin and the bits of rubbish that blow or are tossed in. As I moved forward, I saw the fire. Somebody had dragged the old bin up against the wall of my house, and light was flickering inside it. For a moment it all went still, and I stood there seeing everything in very clear detail until one of the firemen behind me saw it too, and a couple of them pushed past. One of them kicked the bin over into the road and attacked the scattered fire with an extinguisher. I watched coldly.

The patrol car was blocking off the end of the street now. One of the men inside had gone to keep the onlookers back while the second moved towards the fire crew. I intercepted him and said, 'The fires were set deliberately. That's my car. This is my house.'

He settled his cap on his head, turning, and said, 'You live here? Can you give me your name? Do you know who might have done this? Anybody with a grudge? Don't you worry, we'll get to the bottom of it.'

That seemed unlikely. His face was in the shadow of his

peaked uniform cap, so I couldn't tell whether he was just being officious. I suspected so, but I pulled myself together and told him my name. I was thinking that it would be nice to know just who was warning whom, and about what. Never mind: a message had been sent. Not a very complicated message, just *I know where you live. Any time. Signed, DI Moore (Retired)*, and I'd got the point. I kept my back turned to my car as I talked to the constable because I couldn't bear to watch it burn.

CHAPTER TWENTY-TWO

Jam Tomorrow

———◆———

I lashed out hurriedly at the figure leaning over me, and some-body called, 'Dido?' Then I managed to focus on Phyllis stepping quickly backwards. A few drops of coffee jumped from the mug she'd been holding out. I groaned and dragged myself upright.

'Sorry. Sorry. I think I was having a nightmare.' I tried to focus on the window. Pale, clear sky. Sunshine out there some-where. 'What time is it?'

'Just on eight. So you did get to sleep after all.'

With what felt like a supreme effort of will, I avoided falling flat on my back again, took the mug in my trembling hands and whimpered, 'I must have . . . I feel dizzy.' I peered blearily in the direction of the empty cot.

'He's having breakfast,' she assured me. 'You'd better drink that and get up. Your father phoned a few minutes ago. He's on his way over – he sounds hopping mad.'

I sipped gingerly at the dark liquid, found that it was hot but tasteless, and decided that my body was threatening to stop working.

'You told him about last night?'

'I thought I'd better warn him before he got here. And the police just phoned to say they're on their way.'

My eyes, which had been threatening to close again, suddenly returned to my control, and the second sip tasted more like coffee. So provided I made no immediate demands on the mushy stuff that had been substituted for my brains during the night, it might be possible to begin the day.

I shifted my legs and discovered that I hadn't bothered to get undressed before falling into bed. 'I'd better have a bath.'

'You have about twenty minutes,' Phyllis warned from the doorway. We had both heard the sound of a spoon hitting the kitchen floor and knew that other things might soon follow it. 'Shall I make you something to eat?'

I thought about it and reckoned that I could manage some toast and jam for a quick energy boost. And some more coffee. Then I put both feet flat on the bedside mat and concentrated on standing up and moving in the direction of the bathroom.

Barnabas arrived first. I could hear the doorbell ringing a vigorous warning from where I lay holding my breath under the surface of the bath water, and by the time I had stuck my shampooed head under the mixer tap for a final rinse, he was in the hallway outside the closed door shouting, 'Are you all right? What happened?'

I said clearly, 'I'm all right.' By now that was almost accurate. There's nothing like having a lot of warm water all over you. 'Somebody decided to teach me a lesson last night, that's all.'

My father demonstrated that Phyllis had been correct about his mood, by growling, 'I hope they've succeeded where I myself have so clearly failed?' Halfway through his sentence, the doorbell rang again.

I said, 'That should be the police. Could you make sure it is them before you let them in, and keep them happy while I get dressed?'

I heard a snort and retreating footsteps; by the time I'd drained my second cup of coffee, which had been balancing on a corner of the tub, and pulled the plug, I could hear not just one but three familiar voices on the stairs. I wiped a smear of strawberry jam from among the crumbs on the plate that was balanced on another corner of the bath, licked it off my finger, and reached for the towel. When the voices had moved into the sitting room, I gave him a moment to settle them down and then wrapped myself in the bath-sheet and skidded across the hall into the bedroom where Ben, Phyllis and Mr Spock had already taken refuge. The day had only just begun, and I could tell already that it was going to be busy, unpleasant and probably full of recriminations.

I knew that there was a respectable navy trouser suit hanging somewhere in the overcrowded wardrobe. By some miracle, it turned out to be clean and fairly uncreased. I retrieved a pair of blue ankle boots from the tangle in the bottom of the wardrobe, stopped to fluff up my damp hair around my face, and caught a look from Phyllis, who was patiently leafing through *Goldilocks* one more time. I hissed, 'Diane Lyon's out there.'

Phyllis and Ben both looked at me. One of them said indulgently, 'You look very nice,' and the other one said, 'Um-mum,' and laughed. I straightened my back and marched off to face the music.

Lyon was sitting bolt upright on the wooden chair in front of my desk, looking even stiffer than Barnabas. I checked out Paul, slumped back against the cushions on the settee. He had a look around the eyes which suggested that he might not have got to bed, but he roused himself and gave me a stare which he obviously intended to be meaningful, leaving the obscure impression that he wanted me to do something. Be tactful, probably. He might be regretting having been so forthcoming last night. I settled into the second armchair, from which I could watch the faces of both detectives, and said demurely that I hoped I hadn't kept them waiting.

Inspector Lyon inclined her head ambiguously. 'We're here about what happened last night. Mr Grant tells me it had something to do with the case we're working on. What happened?'

'Well, I got home at about eleven-thirty . . .'

'Were you driving? On foot? Was anybody with you?' she interrupted sharply.

I flinched and told her that I'd been on foot, and alone. I added in response to more interruptions that I'd noticed nothing unusual about my car, parked across the road, and that I had seen nobody hanging around as I reached my front door. While I was talking to her I kept half an eye on Paul; apparently I was saying the right things, including not explaining that I'd been on my way back from our meeting. Lyon asked more questions and I outlined the events of the following half-hour to the point where I had abandoned the whole mess and retreated upstairs behind locked doors and my intruder alarm. 'I suppose I'd better do something about the car,' I finished unhappily.

'It's just gone,' Lyon said. 'I sent a police transporter. They say it appears to have been arson, but we'll need to see if we can find anything else.'

I sat up straighter. 'I'd better tell my insurance company it's a write-off.'

'Refer them to me if necessary,' she said. 'Now: can you explain why this happened? Assuming it wasn't casual vandalism, that is?'

'Are you suggesting it might be a *coincidence* that somebody set fire to my car last night, to say nothing of trying to toast my side wall?'

Barnabas stirred abruptly and we all looked at him. He said, 'Occam's Razor.' We all stared at him until he explained impatiently, 'I refer to the well-known principle that the simplest explanation is probably the correct one. "Entities must not be unnecessarily multiplied" is the usual translation. A number of attempts have been made – for precisely what reason I can only guess – to intimidate my daughter and Mrs Digby. The simple explanation is that this is the latest one.'

Diane Lyon very nearly smiled. 'I'm aware of the actions of the men calling themselves Moore and Andrew, of course, and of their identities. DI Grant tells me you've been doing some investigating, Professor, and that you also understand the situation. What I don't see is any motive for this. Have you heard any more since Tuesday morning, either from them or any accomplices they might have?'

Accomplices? I pulled myself together and said firmly, 'Silent phone calls. The first ones went to the Digbys' flat. I have the tapes from their answering machine here – you can hear them, if you like. Yesterday we began to get the same thing here. Somebody rings up, doesn't speak, hangs up after a moment.

That went on for a couple of hours. We unplugged the phone after a while, and there's been nothing since.'

Lyon nodded thoughtfully. 'They know about you, Miss Hoare, and presumably they've discovered that Mrs Digby is staying here. How did they find you?'

I marshalled my thoughts. 'When I was driving back from the Digbys' place on Tuesday morning, I thought for a while that a car was following me; in fact, I even took a roundabout route home, but I told myself I was imagining it. Only now . . .'

Barnabas said, 'What is it?'

I decided to say exactly what had just popped into my head. '*They* know that Phyllis is here, Barnabas. The police: I told Superintendent Colley at Islington, and Phyllis gave Superintendent Paige's people this address. Moore was a policeman, and he's supposed to be retired, but he showed me a warrant card. How did he get a warrant card? Is he getting help from someone in the force?'

'What else?' Paul asked. He was more alert than he looked.

I threw him a dirty look. 'I just remembered that I told Lal Fisher I own a bookshop in Islington. I thought that she might prefer to come here to have a chat about Frank, if she felt safer knowing who I really am. And I told her that Phyllis is staying with me.'

Paul and Lyon exchanged a look which Barnabas interrupted dryly: 'There is another possibility, of course. You told me that you gave Moore and Andrew – Fisher – your name. It might not have been entirely beyond their resources to have consulted the telephone directory. If they rang this number, and Mrs Digby answered, Moore would then know her current whereabouts. Occam?'

'All right,' Lyon said sharply. 'They're trying to frighten you. In that case, what do they want? The computer files? I'm aware, Miss Hoare, that you've handed that evidence over to DI Grant. It's a pity you didn't do it a little sooner.'

'Handed it over?' Barnabas said loudly. 'Dido!'

I looked at him and scowled. 'I gave him Frank's zip disk. Are you suggesting that I shouldn't have?'

Just for once, I'd caught him. Surprise, confusion and a comical disappointment chased across my father's face. He said coldly that of course he hadn't meant any such thing, and we left it at that. At any rate, until I could tell him privately that I hadn't surrendered Ernie's back-up disk. I hid my smirk by saying quickly, 'There is one more thing. Lal told me she contacted Frank originally to ask him to pick up some of his belongings that she'd been keeping: he borrowed her car to take them away. It seemed to me she was telling the truth about that, anyway. The point is, she kept referring to "them" – some boxes, plural. Frank Digby left one behind at Verwood Avenue; I know you found it. Maybe the others are what they're looking for, and they assume Phyllis knows where Frank left them. I presume there was nothing like that in the Toyota when you found it yesterday? Do you people actually know anything about those missing boxes, or where Frank took them?'

Lyon said abruptly, 'She's in the other room, I think,' and was on her feet and marching towards the hallway before I could do anything more than wonder whether I should try to interfere. The three of us who were left behind listened shamelessly to the voices in the bedroom. I thought I already knew what Phyllis would be saying: she didn't have any answers, either.

'I'll try to persuade her to call a press conference,' Paul muttered. 'It's about time anyway. We can ask for witnesses – anybody who saw anything up at the house yesterday, anybody who knows about one or more missing boxes, if that's what they were. If we publicise our interest, it might at least persuade them that you and Mrs Digby are just innocent bystanders.' He looked at me ironically.

'From the way Lal was talking, I'm pretty sure that she knows more about them than she admits.'

Paul nodded, shrugged. 'We'll have to convince her to let us in on it.'

Lyon was on her way back, having abandoned the interrogation as a bad job. She stopped in the doorway, inspected us all closely, and finally focused on me.

'I have to get on. Miss Hoare, is there anything else at all that you can tell me?'

I said that, as far as I was aware, I didn't know anything more. She seemed to accept that and shifted her focus to Paul. 'I'm going over to Devonshire Place myself. I think it's my turn to talk to Mrs Fisher: maybe she'll be a little calmer this morning. In the meantime, I'd like you to join the team going to the depot. You know what you're looking for – explain to Henderson. I'll radio him to wait for you outside the big school just south of Tottenham Hale. I hope it won't take too long, but I want you to go through the company's offices with a toothcomb, and the storage facilities too if you judge that it's necessary. Apparently the boxes were up there for a long time until they were removed to Verwood Avenue, and perhaps they've gone back again. In any case, we need to know what's going on up there and whether it's kosher.'

They were raiding Black Cat Haulage – and about time! – though I couldn't imagine that Frank would have taken anything back there of his own accord. I also couldn't imagine why it would have taken him a whole twenty-four hours to hide the stuff anywhere that was so near by and obvious, before they found him. He had been missing all day Monday, and it couldn't have taken him that long to drop off a couple of boxes somewhere, then buy a plane ticket and mail it.

'What about them?' Paul was asking.

I didn't understand until Lyon scowled at me. 'That's right, we'd better leave somebody with you. I'll ask my driver to come up and be introduced. He'd better keep an eye on things in case your arsonist comes back. The back of the building's secure? Then I'll phone Islington and ask them if they can send somebody over to relieve him as soon as possible. It might be a couple of . . .'

A trilling sound interrupted. I looked around for my mobile and then realised that the sound was coming from Lyon's. She pulled it out of her bag and flipped it open. 'Lyon.' We politely pretended deafness, but we all saw her expression change. After a moment, she said, 'Thanks,' and switched off. When she looked at Paul, her face was emotionless. 'That was the clinic. Mrs Fisher has left.'

Paul was on his feet. 'What happened?'

'She seems to have walked out during the ten minutes or so when the shifts were changing over. Discharged herself. Scarpered. Whatever! I'm going over to have a word with the WPC who was supposed to be watching her, and see if I can get anything out of the medical staff. I'll send the constable up.'

She had stalked out and down the stairs before any of us could move. We heard her voice in the street, the slamming of a car door, and an engine starting. The street door shut quietly, and there were footsteps on the stairs. A slightly startled face peered around the edge of the door.

Paul said, 'This is Constable Hart.'

The constable edged in: a square, dark man with dark eyes who looked from one to the other of us a little uncertainly, I thought – for a policeman. Paul said, 'You're keeping an eye on things here until Islington can send over some protection, then get yourself back to the Yard – unless you've had other orders from the boss by then. Don't go until you're relieved, if it takes all day. Right?' He looked at me. 'I have to go.'

The constable said, 'Sir,' and looked cautiously around my toy-crowded, book-jammed living room.

I said 'Good luck' to Paul's back, and started to ask, 'Will you ring me when . . . ?', but he had gone.

The three of us were left staring at one another.

Barnabas said, 'Goodness. "The clinic?" "Devonshire Place?" Does Scotland Yard always place grieving but suspect widows in the most expensive private hospital in London?'

Constable Hart seemed unsure whether we expected him to answer that. I laughed. I wouldn't have put it past Lal to have insisted.

Barnabas swept on, 'I'm sure we would all appreciate a cup of coffee. I wonder if . . . ?'

I said, 'I will.' Waiting for the water to boil while I ground a few coffee beans would just suit me.

In theory I was supposed to relax now in the happy knowledge that it was all over bar the tidying up, which could be left to the police because they certainly had more desire to find Moore than I did as well as a considerably better chance of doing it safely. In theory, I should be relieved. In practice a little voice in my head kept chanting, *No, no, this doesn't make sense.* I looked down and discovered that I had ground the coffee beans into a damp brown sludge. I was still standing there with the coffee grinder in one hand when Phyllis appeared in the doorway.

'Ben's dropping off now. What was that? Did something happen?'

'Lal's missing from the hospital. It sounds as though she walked out on them. Phyllis – where would she have gone?'

Phyllis frowned. 'I don't know her well enough to say. She can't go home . . . A friend?'

That would be the obvious answer, but I wondered. They had been away from England for a long time, and there'd been something about Lal's behaviour in that big, empty, pink house that had left me thinking of her as a self-absorbed, lonely woman. Were there still any friends in England who were close enough that she could go to them if she needed to hide? . . . Or family? A bell rang. I dug around in my memory and pulled something out.

'Phyllis, didn't she say she has an adult son?'

'Yes. He lives in London, I think.'

She was right about that. Hampstead. Something about a 'nice 'ouse in 'Ampstead'. I looked carefully at Phyllis and asked her what was so amusing.

'I heard he was a solicitor,' she spluttered. 'Frank used to say that was just about the funniest . . .' She stopped and turned away and fell silent. I gave her a hug. The kettle switched itself off for the second time. I finished putting the coffee beans away in the fridge and began to dribble water into the filter, thinking furiously.

CHAPTER TWENTY-THREE

Fishing Trip

I stepped outside with dignity and listened to the heavy door of the clinic closing behind me with an expensive clunk. From the steps I had a clear view along Devonshire Place, and I checked automatically for the sight of a traffic warden approaching my little rental car. Then I reminded myelf that there must be lots of time left on the meter. I'd fed in enough coins to cover an hour's visit, and had only been inside for about a quarter of that before I ran out of credibility.

For speed, I had taken a taxi and my driving licence and credit card to the nearest hire firm and rented a little red Fiesta to get over to the private hospital where Lal had spent the night. Here, I borrowed Phyllis's name and presented myself at the reception desk, asking for news of my sister-in-law's health. Naturally, the receptionist had denied any knowledge of her, but I'd stood my ground. Diane Lyon obviously hadn't intended to let me know where Lal was, but Barnabas was right: the reference had been perfectly clear. When I remained politely unbudging, the receptionist had passed me on to the administrator's office. That was where the problem had come up. I had been demanding to see Lal Fisher, but the woman behind the desk had eventually narrowed her eyes at me and begun to wonder aloud why I was referring to Mrs Elaine Fisher by the wrong name. 'But we *all* use her nickname,' I had protested quickly, trying to look amused. 'She *hates* "Elaine".' I thought I'd covered myelf, but I obviously wasn't going to get away with it. I knew as surely as if I'd seen her there that Diane Lyon had already come and gone, leaving strict instructions and a trail of hurt feelings behind her. I'd said I would be in touch, trying to give the impression that I personally would hold them legally responsible if my relative, their distracted patient, came to any harm, and left before anybody had time to check up on me.

I was still considering the last thing the administrator had said as I left: 'When you do find Mrs Fisher, will you remind her that we still have her handbag and her coat?'

I stood on the top step, as Lal must have done a couple of hours before, and tried to think myself into her stilettos. She had presumably taken her chance while her guard had been looking the other way, and had vanished, coatless and without even her bag, which meant that she was adrift and penniless on a freezing February morning. I looked left and right for inspiration, and it came from the middle of the road, where a stream of taxis, both empty and full, brought illumination: shelter and transport. She wouldn't go home to a murder site that was presumably under surveillance, and I was more sure than ever that she'd taken refuge with the son; but how do you go about locating a solici-tor called 'Fisher' who lives in Hampstead – a large, heavily populated area with vaguely defined borders that expands if you are listening to a greedy estate agent's sales pitch – when you don't even know his initials?

The picture of an old-fashioned cut-throat razor slid unbidden into my mind. Occam's, that is. *You could start by finding yourself a telephone directory*. Thank you, Barnabas.

I trotted down the street to the car, checked my wristwatch, and illegally pushed another couple of coins into the meter after making sure that nobody was watching. My immediate destina-tion was the big hotel on Russell Square where I had been happily buying and selling books only last Monday, and I doubted that I'd find parking space any closer than this on a weekday.

The bar at that hotel is a wonderful room full of wood, leather, mirrors, potted plants and chandeliers, an imitation gentleman's club with waiters who cultivate the appropriate manner. I've spent a lot of happy hours there with my fellow booksellers in various stages of drunkenness. Within fifteen minutes I was comfortable in a leather armchair behind a table that held a double vodka, a small bottle of tonic water, and two telephone directories. Fuel and research materials. I dug out my pen and notebook and started looking for the Fishers.

The residential directory listed eight with various initials living within the Hampstead postcode area, and five more who were close enough outside it that they almost certainly would claim to 'live in Hampstead'. I subtracted the four that were flats. On the whole, I thought Lal's phrase about the 'nice house' eliminated those. I scribbled down the initials, addresses and phone numbers of the rest; if the younger Mr Fisher had an unlisted phone, I was beaten, but if not . . . A trawling of the solicitors in the business directory revealed no 'Fisher' practising in Hampstead, no firm by that name anywhere in London. I wasn't really surprised: at thirty, he was probably working in a big firm and not necessarily as a partner. I took a gulp of vodka, pulled out my mobile and dialled the 'B. Fisher' at the top of the list. Two rings and the phone was answered. I opened my mouth, but a thin, old voice was already saying, '*This is Mrs Bernard Fisher. I am sorry that I cannot answer my telephone at this time—*'. I hung up without leaving a message, crossed the number off the list, and tried the next, which was answered by an au pair whose eastern European English was just good enough to tell me that her employer ran a restaurant, 'very good, in Golders Green'. By then, I'd worked out an angle. By the sixth call I'd almost accepted that it was an unlisted phone after all.

T. J. Fisher's telephone was answered by a woman's voice, and I went into my newly polished routine. 'I am *terribly* sorry to bother you at home,' I said (sincerely), 'but Mr Fisher asked me to phone him here about an urgent legal matter he's handling for us, only I was supposed to ring a couple of hours ago. He isn't still there, is he? Or could you give me his number at work?'

'Zero, one, seven, one . . .' the voice began promptly, sounding only mildly surprised.

I said, 'Sorry, just a minute.' Then I took a deep breath and babbled, 'Sorry, my pen seems to have run out. I've got another one now: go ahead.' I wrote the number she gave me in the space opposite the 'T.J.' just in case, thanked her and switched off. The Fishers' street, I seemed to recall, was somewhere on the western edges of the Heath, between the village and Finchley Road. My *A to Z* had gone up in smoke inside my car, but I could get a new one at the newspaper stand in the lobby. I gave the hovering waiter my best smile and a two-pound tip and left my drink unfinished.

CHAPTER TWENTY-FOUR

A Window of Opportunity

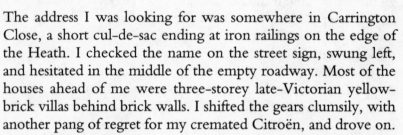

The address I was looking for was somewhere in Carrington Close, a short cul-de-sac ending at iron railings on the edge of the Heath. I checked the name on the street sign, swung left, and hesitated in the middle of the empty roadway. Most of the houses ahead of me were three-storey late-Victorian yellow-brick villas behind brick walls. I shifted the gears clumsily, with another pang of regret for my cremated Citroën, and drove on.

Halfway down on the right I came across an unexpected enclave of postwar houses, smaller than the old villas, built in a plain, contemporary style of white-painted brick and sealed natural wood with picture windows, linked by double garages at the sides. I cruised past, marking the Fishers' number in the middle of the row. At the railings I did a quick three-point turn and drove back.

Lal had been right: these were nice houses. Maybe a little too identical for my taste, but nice. A small red car sat by the Fishers' blue-painted front door. It seemed too old to be at home in this expensive road, but perhaps the young solicitor had gone off to business in his, presumably, more respectable vehicle, leaving the little Fiat for the wife who had spoken to me on the phone. That meant she was still here, since residents in this kind of street don't normally bother walking down to the shops. As the car was waiting in the driveway, Mrs Fisher might be on her way out even now. I had to decide whether I was going to intercept her and ask for news of Lal, or wait for her to leave and then try to get at Lal herself while she was alone. If she was here. I reminded myself that I was just guessing.

I was still hesitating when the front door snapped open. The person who appeared was a thin, dark-haired girl in a long black coat. As I watched, she hesitated in the doorway, half turning back. Was she speaking to someone inside the house? She slammed the door and walked to the car. I sat very still while she fastened her seat belt and backed into the road. She drove off fast.

The more I thought about it, the more sure I felt that she had stopped to say something as she was shutting the door. Also, she had left the door of the empty garage open wide. That was asking for trouble if the house was empty, even if she was only going down to the main road for a packet of cigarettes and intended to be back soon.

I'd better move.

For the second time I started to open my door only to be stopped. Someone had appeared down at the corner. Sack. Postman. I watched him reach the first of the modern houses, swerve up the path, vanish, reappear, cut across the lawn and step over the low clipped hedge, then come down next door's path. Neither I nor Lal wanted a witness: I'd wait. He was cutting across the driveway in front of the Fishers' garage now, pushing something through their letter slot and then hesitating. He had something else, something larger than an envelope in his hand, and the mail slot was too small for it. He reached out to the bell, then stooped and placed a packet on the doorstep before he turned away. I dismissed him and concentrated.

The front of the house was broken by the main door, which was flanked by several small windows, and the big picture window with casement sections at each end. A Venetian blind with its slats closed tight blocked the whole expanse of glass, but I could see a bottle of washing-up liquid sitting on the sill between the glass and the blind, suggesting that the room behind the blind was a kitchen. I was still looking at it when a slat twitched. I held my breath. After a moment, the front door opened a crack. A hand slid out. The packet vanished. The door slammed.

I left the car unlocked and walked quickly up the drive. The one thing that would cause a problem now was if a neighbour saw me skulking. In broad daylight, in a street like this, that's asking for trouble. I straightened my shoulders. Honesty. Confidence. The stains of engine oil that I noted on the floor of the empty garage confirmed that two cars were normally kept there. I was hoping to see a little internal door into the house, but as far as I could tell without breaking my step, I was out of luck, and I didn't want to waste time. Either car could return at any moment.

The door of the house was inset just beyond the corner of the garage, beside a small frosted window which presumably lit a lavatory or cloakroom. I tripped over to the door and just touched the bellpush. To anyone watching me it would look as though I'd rung. I pretended to wait for an answer while I planned my moves. Assuming it was Lal I'd glimpsed, she might notice me at any second, and I couldn't be sure what she'd do. I pretended to ring again and looked more closely at the left-hand section of the big window. Something odd: either the frame had warped or the casement section was open a crack. Casually I turned my back on the door and mimed hesitation. I took two equally casual steps forward so I could scan the rows of windows on the two big Victorian houses opposite. If anybody was at home over there, I couldn't actually see them looking out.

Sometimes, when you're trusting to luck, it's better not to hesitate. Still trying to look as though I had every right to be doing whatever crazy thing I did, I stepped casually towards the wall. I was right about the side being open. I shoved my fingers into the crack, tugged, and located the stay that held it. When I pushed my hand up hard, I was almost startled to feel something shift. I jabbed. A metallic clatter made me wince, but I held on. *What is she going to do – call the police and have you arrested?* A big pottery planter, one of a pair filled with Christmas roses that were long past their best, gave me a step up. I pulled the casement wide, reluctantly put the knee of my clean navy trousers on to the ledge, and pushed head first under the blind, keeping my fingers mentally crossed.

I landed wrist deep in a sink full of dirty dishes.

Lal was standing in the doorway, watching me. Our stares locked. Then she moved forward, grabbing one of the kitchen chairs by its back and swinging it across the floor.

She said, 'Jesus, Dido, you are a funny girl. Climb down out of that sink and let's get the window shut. Listen, do you have any money on you? I need to borrow a couple of 'undred. I've got to get out of London.'

CHAPTER TWENTY-FIVE

Still Running

Perching on the unmade bed in the guest room, using a towel to press as much dishwater as possible out of the cuffs of my jacket, I watched Lal's face reflected in the dressing-table mirror.

The blinds on this window were shut tight, and she had turned on the lights and settled in front of the mirror to put on her make-up and tease her hair into its elaborate curls. I'd watched her examine the little hairbrush dubiously before she used it, and read the label on some liquid foundation, sighing humorously. Her expression said that these things had all been borrowed and were emergency supplies, not up to her personal standards. But her movements were brisk.

''Ow did you find me?' she asked suddenly. 'Did Phyll—? No, I don't think she knew anything about Jim and Rebecca.'

I explained just how I'd happened to learn about her escape from the clinic, and passed on the message about her coat and bag. She shrugged. Then I explained exactly my reasoning.

She was also watching me in the glass. 'You didn't tell anybody else?' I shook my head. She put the brush down, still without turning to face me, and asked, 'Why not?'

I couldn't read her expression. She was right: why not? I felt a spark of annoyance. 'The only thing that interests me is making sure that Phyllis is all right. Because I don't know exactly who I can trust. Because I thought you'd rather talk to me than the police, and there are things I think you know and I need to understand. All right, you're right, I probably ought to have saved myself the hassle by contacting my friend in the CID – I think he's all right, even if I'm not so sure about the rest of them. Because . . .' That was probably enough, but I added, '. . . one of the detectives involved in this investigation told me you might have hired somebody to kill your husband. Did Andy beat you up?'

That made her turn around to face me directly. 'Andy! *Hell*, Dido, Andy was a *decent* geezer.' Her face was not friendly.

I met her glare for glare and asked, 'Then who did?'

'What are you talking about?'

I leaned back, propped on my hands, and tried to look masterful. 'I asked you who hit you if it wasn't Andy? Not Frank?'

'Just what . . . ?'

I interrupted: 'The hospital told the police you'd been beaten up. I noticed the bruises on your wrist myself, when I was at your place yesterday.' She pulled the sleeve of the dressing gown over what was left of the yellowing marks, but I wouldn't let her get away with that. 'Who did it? If it wasn't Andy, then was it Frank?'

She went back to her hair, snarling, 'Hell, Dido! I thought you said you knew Frankie!'

I kept my mouth shut to let the atmosphere cool. Lal spent the time teasing a lock of hair into a curl over her right temple. After a while she said, 'No, it was somebody you don't want to know.'

'A friend of Andy's? A man called Moore? The retired policeman – that one?'

She twisted around on the bench, and this time she looked wary. 'How d'you know Doug Moore?'

I told her the truth: the story of how her decent geezer and the crooked cop had turned up together to ransack the Digbys' flat. Halfway through she turned back to her mirror, so I threw in last night's fires for good measure. When I'd finished it was so quiet in the room that I could hear the clicking of the second hand on the quartz clock.

Eventually Lal sighed. 'Dido, I told you I need to get out of 'ere. Will you help me?'

I pretended to think about it. 'Just tell me two things: tell me the truth about why you phoned Frank last week. What did you want? Why was it so urgent? And then tell me what Moore is after.'

'Dido, Phyll and you just don't wanna know.'

I exploded. 'Lal, Frank was murdered – in case you've forgotten. Phyllis has been threatened. The police are scuttling around wondering what's going on and whether any of their own people are mixed up in it, and there's a police guard in my home right now because I've been petrol-bombed by some scum who are well past their sell-by date!' My voice was rising and it was easier to go on than stop. 'My business is going to pot, I'm worried for my baby and my father who is an old man, as well as for Phyllis and me . . .' I was starting to shout, so I made myself take a deep breath or two.

Lal's face was cracking into something that was almost a grin. Then she was on her feet, letting the dressing gown slide to the floor. She was in her slip, and I could see another of the big yellowing patches on her left shoulder. Out of a nearly empty wardrobe she grabbed a hanger with the blue dress she'd been wearing yesterday. In something like three seconds she faced me, fully clothed.

'Let's see if there's some way to get this sorted. Leave it to the women to do the work, eh? But you gotta 'elp me get outa 'ere. One thing is, if you can find me so can somebody else, know what I mean? I don't want these kids in the mess.' She stopped suddenly and shook her head. 'Not just that. You know my son's a lawyer? Funny thing is, this whole thing, me turning up 'ere, bothers 'im. Well, 'e's upset about his dad, really. So 'e says I'm being stupid, I should 'elp the police with their enquiries – you get the picture? That's what 'e'd do if he was me . . . It's funny, when Jim was a kid Andy used to whack 'im every time 'e done something off-colour. Andy wanted Jim straight, and I guess Jim is – and it's too late to change things now.' She made a wry face. 'Funny, eh? So I'm better out of 'ere until things work out, for everybody's sake.'

'Where can you go?'

'I'll think of something.'

I said very clearly, 'Who killed your husband? Was it Moore?'

'No! You know, Doug's an 'ard bastard, but most of the time Andy and 'im got on. Andy knew Doug Moore a long time. All right, I wasn't over the moon when Doug turned up in Marbella last summer and they put this plan together about coming back, but it was working out. Did they say it was Doug?'

I shook my head, trying to remember. 'As a matter of fact, the killer was caught on one of your security cameras, though he didn't show his face. My friend said it didn't look like Moore, but they can't be sure. Tell me about last summer. You said Moore "turned up"? Where? Why?'

'Dido, it'd be better if we left right now, 'cause it strikes me if you worked out where I am, somebody else will soon, coppers or worse. I made Rebecca promise to go to the machine and get me fifty quid, but if you can 'elp out I won't even wait for 'er to get back. We better talk to Phyll and I better tell you some things first. Not now, though. Can we 'op it?'

That sounded good. I dropped the towel on to the bed and followed her out of the room. Even in her stilettos, she out-paced me along the corridor and down the stairs. There was a big walk-in cupboard by the front door. Lal plunged inside and came back buttoning herself into a plain beige raincoat that was a little tight around the hips. She tugged a black-and-white spotted scarf out of the sleeve and tied it over her head to hide the blonde curls.

'I'll go out first.' I paused to recognise that Lal seemed to be infecting me with her sense of danger – probably not a bad thing. 'If it's clear, I'll give you a wave, and you come on. But if I see anybody hanging around, I'll get straight into the car and drive away, and you'd better stay inside and lock all the doors. If it's the police who've turned up, you keep quiet until they go away and I'll come back for you as soon as they give up. If it's somebody else, I'll stop the car down at the corner and . . . wait . . . I know, phone the police and tell them – this house is number sixty-three, isn't it? I'll tell them there's a prowler in the back garden next door. That should get a patrol car here, sharpish. Then as soon as everything's quiet again, I'll come back for you. Clear?'

'Crystal,' Lal agreed promptly.

But a minute later we were both safely in the red car with all the doors locked, rolling sedately down to the stop sign at the corner. Apparently, we were still on the run. The street behind us showed no life except for a very old lady tottering along the pavement behind a very small white dog.

Lal said slowly, 'I should of left a note saying I'm all right. I better phone, leave a message on the machine that I'm with a friend and I'll be in touch. Don't want that poor little cow thinking something's 'appened.'

I handed her my mobile, let up a bit on the accelerator, and made the turn into Finchley Road. 'Do it now. Then I'm going to phone Phyllis and find out whether she can meet us. I have an idea about where you can stay.'

Lal stopped poking at the buttons of my phone and asked cautiously, 'Where's that?'

'What about Phyllis's flat? There's no reason for anybody to look there. If you just remember not to answer either the phone or the doorbell, you should be fine.'

She shrugged. I decided to take that for agreement, waited for her to leave her message, and took back my phone. We were coming into the one-way traffic system at Swiss Cottage now, creeping through a series of lights. I just caught the last of the green at the bottom of the hill and slipped into the filter lane by the library, ready to turn east.

'Now,' I decided to say, 'can we begin at the beginning? Lal, do you know anything about the Hatton Carriers bullion robbery?'

She shook her head slowly. I wasn't sure whether it was

disbelief or resignation. All she said was, 'Bloody 'ell, Dido, you are a funny little thing.'

I gritted my teeth, beat down the temptation to deliver my passenger to the nearest police station, and drove on to find reinforcements.

CHAPTER TWENTY-SIX

Where We Are

I stopped the Fiesta on a yellow line before we got to Chalk Farm.

'Where's this?' Lal asked.

I explained, 'I'll phone from here. I want Phyllis to come out and meet us without letting anybody know what's going on. That may be tricky.' But safer, until somebody could persuade Lal that she'd be better off in protective custody; and right now I wasn't even sure myself whether that was true. I added quickly, 'I'd like you to talk to my father. He knows a lot about the bullion robbery, and I think he'd like to ask you about it.' Or, at any rate, he'd be seriously annoyed not to be given the chance.

'Policeman?' Lal asked casually, looking at me out of the corner of her eye.

'Retired professor of English from Oxford University,' I said briefly.

Lal blinked but didn't comment. I rang the phone in the flat. Phyllis answered and hissed, 'Where are you?'

'Are you alone, or is there a policeman at your elbow?'

'No, he's in the bathroom. Wait – he's washing his hands.'

'Sheesh!' I lowered my voice. 'All right, then, just listen. Can you and Barnabas get out of there and come over to your flat to meet me? I'll be there in fifteen or twenty minutes, and I have somebody with me who wants to talk to you. Bring your keys with you; you'll see us parked in front of your block in a red Ford Fiesta.'

'I can do that,' Phyllis said with barely a hesitation, 'but you might want to phone downstairs for yourself. Your father's in the shop. He said something about somebody having to run a business, and marched off half an hour ago. Ernie just got here.'

I rang off and punched the shop's number. The phone was picked up at the second ring, and a plummy voice announced, 'Dido Hoare, Antiquarian Books and Prints. This is Ernest Weekes speaking. How may I help you?'

I choked, 'It's me. Is everything all right?'

The voice became recognisable. 'Hey, Dido! Are you okay? The Professor told me what happened last night. I wish I'd of been here! Listen, you want me to move in for a coupla days? I know you got the plod upstairs, but you can't count on them, and you know I won't let you down.'

I found myelf considering his offer seriously. 'Ernie, I don't like having you miss classes when the exams are so near, but if you could stay around at least until we have a chance to talk it over, that would be good. Can you put Barnabas on the line?'

'Gone,' Ernie announced. 'He left a message for you, though. He says to tell you he's gone down to the *Guardian* to talk to a guy who's investigating police corruption. He says this guy knows what happened about the trial. Have you got that? He took a taxi again. He says he'll get back asap.'

I thought about it as soon as I'd worked out what the word 'asap' meant. Good. There had to be some answers somewhere, in somebody's head if not in the files, and I still didn't know how much of the picture Lal actually had. Much less what she was ready to share. 'If he gets back before I do,' I said, 'give him the same message: that I'm talking to somebody who knows about the same thing, and I should be back soon. Ernie . . . I don't suppose we've had any customers?'

'That lady who lives down the road and always comes in and buys stuff to read,' Ernie said. 'Two quid. We was talking. She says your books are getting too expensive.' I found this news particularly shattering, because as far as I could remember Mrs Acker had never actually said that much to *me* in the five or six years she'd been coming in. I dragged my attention back to Ernie, who was still talking. 'Look, Dido, I been working on that disk we backed up. We still need the password, and I been looking everywhere on the disk and I can't see it. I guess maybe I should stop and wrap some parcels or something?'

I wanted to scream dramatically but pulled myself together because after all . . . Something clicked. I looked over at Lal, who was listening openly, and said to her, 'Can you think of a word or number that Frank might have used for a password in his computer? Maybe something important and private to both of you when you were growing up?'

Lal stared. 'I don't know anything about those sort of things.'

But I was already counting on my fingers. Six. That would be good enough. I said to Ernie, 'Try "Elaine". E–L–A–I–N–E.' I switched off, because I was getting tired of Frank Digby's little games.

It took me more like thirty minutes to pull up into what was starting to feel like my personal parking space outside the flats, but there was no sign of Phyllis, either in the street or at the window upstairs. I leaned back and tried not to worry. When I glanced at Lal, I found her eyes closed.

'Are you all right?'

She shrugged. 'I could murder a cup of tea. How long do you think . . . ?'

But something moved in the rear-view mirror, fifty yards behind the car, and I watched Phyllis and the pushchair come into sight around the corner. Ben was wriggling a vigorous protest about not being allowed to walk, and Phyllis was slowing down, scanning the street ahead. I waited until I could see that nobody was following them and went to help fold the pushchair and manoeuvre it into the boot. They settled into the rear seat with Ben held tight on Phyllis's lap, reminding me that one of the seventy urgent things I had to do was buy a new child car seat, not to mention a new car to fit it into.

Phyllis broke the silence awkwardly. 'Well, Lal, I'm sorry. Are you all right? Is there anything I can do?' Her voice was stiff.

I glanced sideways for a second and saw the red-tipped

fingers smoothing and smoothing the cloth of the borrowed coat. Lal mumbled. She raised her voice and said, 'I don't know, Phyll. I got to ask you – do you think that Andy 'ad anything to do with that . . . with killing Frankie?'

I held my breath. In the driving mirror I could see Phyllis's face. She considered the question seriously. After a while she said, 'I wondered. Andy was one of the men who came to the flat Tuesday morning, so I think he must have been one of them the night before, too. If he was, then he must have known about Frank, and he might have had something to do with it. But then I think: isn't it more likely that the same person killed both of them? I don't understand it.'

Lal let out a kind of strangled snort. 'Makes two of us. Andy, Frankie – they was mates, all the time we was kids at home. I don't like to think of them falling out, not that bad. No, I can't swallow it.'

'What about the other one?' Phyllis asked hoarsely. 'Moore.'

Lal tucked a hand under her seat belt as though she needed to stop it flailing about. 'Bastard! I'd like to say yes. All right, Dido, you asked: yes, 'e was the one that bashed me up. But Andy and 'im done a lot of business together for a long time. And in case you wonder, no, I didn't tell Andy.'

I said, 'Why?' and held my breath.

'Why bash me? Or why didn't I tell Andy?'

I watched her face when I said, 'Both.'

Her lips tightened. 'I told 'im I didn't know where Frankie'd got to, and 'e lost his rag. And I didn't tell Andy because I was scared of what Andy'd do. Doug – I don't say 'e isn't the type to kill some poor sod that gets in 'is way, 'e 'as a lousy temper, but you know it wasn't as though Andy could just walk away from things . . .' She faded into silence.

Phyllis asked, 'What are we going to do?'

My turn. 'Did you bring your keys? Will you let Lal stay in your flat for a day or so?'

'If she wants,' Phyllis said quickly. 'If you want, Lal. But why? You can't hide there for long. The place is a mess, and there isn't much food or anything. Sooner or later you're going to have to deal with the police. Matter of fact, that flat belongs to them. They're going to want me out.'

'Just a day or two,' Lal said defensively. 'I need some peace and quiet to sort myself out without them bothering me all the time asking things. I want to work out some things in peace, so I don't mess up.'

'So do I,' I said bitterly, suddenly remembering I had forgotten to phone the insurance company, which probably made seventy-one urgent things. 'So does Phyllis. Can't we put our heads together and at least try to work on it? Lal, you *must* have a lot of the answers.'

Lal said explosively, 'All right! I'll tell you two what I can and that's not much. Anyway, there's nobody left to be 'urt, now, is there, if it all comes out? But you gotta 'elp me, Dido. I told you – I don't 'ave a penny, I need to borrow some cash. Because until we know what's going on, and get it sorted, I keep thinking I might need to make a run for it, get out of London, so unless you can climb into the 'ouse through some window so I can get my things, you're going to 'ave to find me some money.'

Phyllis said abruptly. 'Frank had some. That'll be all right. What do you mean about climbing through windows?'

Lal said, 'I'll tell you about that. Couldn't believe my eyes. Look, we oughtta get outa sight. Right?'

CHAPTER TWENTY-SEVEN

Lal's

Phyllis unlocked the door and pushed it open. The air was stale and cold, and Lal shivered as she looked around the dark hallway. She said apologetically, 'I really feel the cold 'ere, nowadays. You know, I'm going back to Spain when this is over. I got friends there. We play bridge twice a week, you know? That kinda thing. I been thinking of taking golf lessons. Learn proper Spanish even. Really settle. I never really liked that place up Verwood Avenue. Not the sort of neighbours that talk to you, know what I mean? Maybe I'll just go straight back to Marbella.'

Without comment, Phyllis stepped over to the wall and turned up the thermostat.

We crowded into the kitchen, where a tap dripping slowly into the sink and the humming fridge gave the room some life. Lal and I sat down at the little table while Phyllis put the kettle on and Ben decided to find out what was hiding in the cupboards. Funny – they all seemed content, and yet I was flooded with a sense of urgency. Somebody had to move things on before more people got hurt.

I dragged myself together. 'Lal, we've got to know exactly why you phoned Frank and asked for help. Is it true, what you told me about the boxes? I saw one, the one I think you wanted me to find when we were upstairs yesterday – what was in the others?'

Again, she said, 'All right. Only I better tell you about that gold robbery first, since you're asking: yes – that's where things went wrong in the first place. Yes, Andy was in on that, they all was: friends, family . . . not Frankie. Frankie wouldn't 'ave nothing to do with it. I remember 'e said we was getting into new country, and some of the natives there was rubbish. But Jimmy said yes. Our dad, I mean, the one my Jim's named for. Jimmy was an old man, 'e wanted one last, big hit, and then some peace an' quiet for a change. And there was other people who wanted to 'ave a go because it was a once-in-a-lifetime chance. So they done it one night, and it worked out all right, and in case you think this is all about buried gold or something, I can tell you that was out of England on the way to Spain before they even found the armoured van they grabbed.'

I said, 'Wait a minute: is that what Black Cat Haulage was really all about – smuggling stolen goods out of the country?'

Lal shot me a funny look. 'Well,' she conceded, 'it wasn't the first time. So, they 'ad a near-miss with Customs on the Spanish border, but I guess somebody got a bung. From Spain it went on over to India by plane. Crazy about gold, them Pakis.' I held my tongue and waited. 'It got paid for in Switzerland with what they call "bearer bonds" – that's something like cash – and Frankie flew over to Geneva to get them. You with me? The idea 'e'd thought up, 'e was going to take that lot over some place in the West Indies, I forget the name, set up what they call a "trust", and everybody'd all get paid from it, four times a year, just like a pension or something, enough dosh for the rest of our lives. I don't understand all that, but Frankie told us they didn't 'ave a snowball's chance in 'ell of working out what'd 'appened, and if they did there was no way they'd get their 'ands on the money, because the law is different there from 'ere.'

I half understood what she was talking about. 'What went wrong?'

'One of them, Vinnie White, 'eard the Flying Squad was on to them. Vinnie said somebody grassed. 'E thought it was Doug, but later, when Frankie got arrested and got off so light, Vinnie changed 'is tune. We'd been in Spain for a bit, by then, and we just didn't come back – Pete turned up one day, Pete White, and said better not risk it. The rest all just cleared out right away, and when Frankie got back from Switzerland with the bonds, 'e was on his own. Oh – there was some poor sod, one of the cousins, who got stuck because 'is old lady was sick, and Frankie and 'im was picked up. Frankie saw what was up, so 'e 'id the stuff with some old papers from the club, the Black Cat, in a coupla boxes and got it all down to Andy's depot. There was some accounts for our old club in Soho, and there was a big envelope with the bonds. Frankie shoved it all in with our furniture we stored for when we came home; then before 'e told Andy about it, they picked 'im up. And that was that.'

'You mean the bonds were stuck in England?'

'Well, we didn't know that,' Lal said sharply. 'See, there was nobody 'ere that Frank could tell, because somebody'd already grassed them up and the 'ole lot of them was busy scarpering to a coupla places like Spain and South America where they couldn't be got out; the minute they turned up in England they'd be nabbed. So they were stuck.'

Phyllis arrived at the table with teapot, cups and a carton of milk, ignoring the clatter of her saucepans as Ben decided to see what they were for. She looked drawn. I tried to keep an eye on her, Lal and Ben simultaneously, and I said, 'Clear so far. More or less what my father worked out from the newspaper files. So only the two of them went to trial, and that went wrong right away when some evidence went missing, and Frank got a short sentence and was out in months.'

Lal was watching Phyllis uneasily. 'Some people said it was Frankie who was the nark, and that was why 'e got out so quick. That, or 'e'd bought 'is way out with the bonds. But Andy always said Frankie never. If 'e'd given them bonds up 'e'd of got ten per cent reward, Andy said, and pro'bly the lawyers could 'ave bargained for 'im not even to go on trial.'

Phyllis said harshly, 'He was getting four hundred a month from his pension, the disability benefit, and this place. There was never anything else.'

Lal glanced at her again and said, 'I know that, girl; wait a minute, I'm almost finished.'

Ben got the door of the cupboard under the sink open and started to investigate some detergent bottles. Phyllis and I started to move but Lal pounced, picked him out of the mess, and sat down again with him, startled and pink-faced, on her lap.

I crossed my fingers under the table and said, 'What happened last autumn? Why did you suddenly decide to come home after all? And how did you know about the stuff that Frank left at the depot, if Andy didn't?'

Lal looked at me as though I was being slow. 'Frankie told me when I come over for their wedding. Said somebody besides 'im better know where it was, just in case something 'appened.'

'You didn't tell Andy?'

'I was going to,' Lal said after a second's hesitation, 'but then I saw what'd happen. There was nobody Andy'd trust to send out the bonds. So 'e'd of come back for them, and they would of nabbed 'im. Those boxes was safe enough till Frankie got out. That's what I thought. We were doing okay as it was. Frankie agreed: keep my mouth shut, best thing. Only Andy was getting fed up. He said Marbella is full of tossers these days, 'e never liked it that much, and the business – the time share – was doing all right with the Spanish management company. Andy kept saying 'e wanted to come back.'

'And then?' Phyllis prompted her, as though we'd arranged it between us to take turns.

'Then they found Pete dead in his swimming pool. Used to live just down the coast from us. Supposed to've drowned, but Andy started to wonder, and then 'e 'eard the Spanish police was saying somebody 'eld 'im under. Then Doug turned up from Palma just after, and said 'e'd run out of money and 'e was coming to get his cut from Frankie. 'E asked Andy to come back with 'im. Not much argument there. See, everybody there was talking about this new law – they can arrest you in Spain anyway, not like the old days. But Doug said the fuss 'ad died down, and anyway there was no evidence against Andy now. The stuff they put together for the trial was gone. It was Doug that lost that evidence, you know? Got it out of the station just before they sent for it – that was why Frankie and Barry's trial went wrong.'

I wasn't surprised, but the question remained: 'Moore was the one who stole the trial evidence? But why?'

Lal snorted. ''E was driving one of the police cars that was escorting the gold van, but nobody saw him do nothing that night, and the Met couldn't prove nothing so they just got rid of 'im. So we come back a few months ago.'

My head was starting to swirl. One thing was clear: when Lal decided to confide in you she gave you your money's worth. It felt as though she was pouring out all the secrets of a lifetime. I grappled with it. 'Wait. Moore came back to England for the bonds?'

Lal nodded.

'Why would he get a share of the loot? Do you think that Frank might have refused?'

I thought I'd cracked it until Lal shrugged. 'It didn't 'appen. Doug couldn't find Frankie. Frankie'd dropped right out of sight when 'e come out of prison.'

'But you knew where he was,' Phyllis said softly.

'Doug Moore didn't know I did. Anyways, I *didn't* really because I made Frankie give me your phone number but not the address. I knew it wouldn'ta been safe. Andy knew I'd been in touch, but 'e didn't tell Doug that. Only, Doug 'ad the idea I must know where my own brother was, an' 'e kept nagging.'

'And in the end he tried hitting you to persuade you?' Lal looked at me silently, and I still hadn't got the last bit of information I needed to make sense of it. I was being slow. 'Why did Moore get a share? For hiding the evidence?'

Lal seemed to find that funny. 'Doug was mixed up with our lot for years. Bent as an 'airpin. Then that bullion caper was 'is idea. 'E was on guard of them shipments for a while, so 'e worked it all out: 'ow 'e could find out the route of the next one and tell us, 'ow 'e could warn us just before they was leaving, where our lot could get at them. It was even Doug who laid on some extra 'elp that time, a coupla geezers 'e knew, and 'e got them the guns. Didn't you know that?'

I did now.

Ben gave a wriggle and slid to the floor. He was looking thoughtful. I knew the look and began to wonder about taking him home.

'Where *is* he – Moore? Do you have an address?'

I knew Lal was being evasive when she shrugged. 'Stopping in some mate's council flat. Why? You don't want to find 'im.'

I may have shown her what I was thinking, because when I said that, on the contrary, I did want to find him, or at least have him found, before he decided to burn anything more of mine, she turned pink. I added for good measure that if Andy hadn't believed him to be dangerous, then Andy was wrong. I was picturing a little bundle of bearer bonds worth a few millions, wondering where they were now and what a man like Moore would do to get his hands on so much money. How many people would he kill for them?

It was Phyllis who returned to that last question. 'When you phoned Frank last week, what did you want?'

Lal looked at her. 'Phyll, I was scared. Doug asked me, and when I said I didn't know where Frankie was, 'e . . . you know. And I didn't dare tell Andy, because 'e wasn't so young, and I knew if anybody got 'urt it'd be Andy, not Doug. So I told Frankie to come and get that stuff 'e left, because it was in the 'ouse, it come up with our things last November, and Doug or Andy was going to see it sooner or later and all 'ell'd break loose, because they'd know I knew. Maybe I wasn't thinking straight, but I just wanted Frankie to take it away. Only Andy come in just after Frankie turned up on Sunday. Frankie said 'e was just visiting me, and they even went out for a few drinks, and come back together *singing*, and Frankie told me 'e'd stay the night to give 'imself another chance in the morning, and then when Andy went up to the depot after breakfast I let Frankie take my car, and we got the stuff out just like I said. 'E left that last box, it was only old stuff from years back, couldn't manage every-thing in one load, and 'e just found all the boxes of evidence that Doug sneaked away before the trial – said 'e didn't know how the fuck that got there, but it did. I guess that was Doug. It wasn't nothing to do with Frankie, but he said better lose it before Andy and me got dropped in it. Frankie was really pissed off when 'e saw that stuff there. But the bonds was where 'e left them, stuffed down under them books from the old club. We loaded my car, and Frankie said 'e'd be back in a few hours. And that was the last time I seen 'im.'

The voice trickled into silence, and then she was crying again in that quiet, frozen way I'd seen before. Maybe she had taught herself to cry like that so they wouldn't notice her.

My mobile broke the silence. I answered.

'Dido?' It was Barnabas, sounding preoccupied.

I confessed my identity.

'Dido – Phyllis and Ben aren't here . . .'

'It's all right,' I said. 'We're all on our way back. Is something wrong?'

'Not if you're on your way,' my father said. 'That's all I wanted.' I certainly wasn't imagining the odd sound in his voice. 'I'm downstairs. Call into the shop on your way in.'

'Five minutes,' I said, on the grounds that instant agreement would probably save time in the long run.

Phyllis said, 'I'll just show Lal where to find the clean sheets, then I'll walk back. If you can get Ben home without me?'

I told her I'd strap him into the pushchair and jam that into the back between the seats. It wasn't far. 'You'll be all right?'

Of course she would, she said.

CHAPTER TWENTY-EIGHT

Wrong Tack

I'd parked illegally in a space across the street, unloaded Ben, stopped just long enough to retrieve the black-and-white scarf that I'd noticed on the floor in front of the passenger seat where Lal must have dropped it, and headed for home. Looking through the glass as I passed the door of the shop, I caught sight of Ernie prowling excitedly around the back room. It was only a brief glimpse through the connecting door, but something had certainly happened. We detoured inside to investigate.

'Who or what,' Barnabas greeted me unexpectedly from the chair at the computer, 'is "Elaine"?'

'Lal Fisher's real name. It worked?'

'Magic!' Ernie crowed.

Barnabas disengaged his attention from the computer screen, leaned back and examined my face. 'So – you found her? Or was this just a guess?' He noticed my hesitation. 'What? What?'

I evaded his question by the time-honoured method of asking one of my own. 'Ernie said you'd gone out. This man at the *Guardian* – did you find out anything useful from him? And what's in those encrypted files?'

'I've only just made a start,' my father admitted, 'but so far we have a string of financial records for the years 1985 to 1991, listing sums of money, sources and recipients, including some very imaginative methods of payment. The late Mr Digby is obviously their author – Ernie assures me that they are "proper" accounts, correctly drawn up. There are accounts for Black Cat Haulage, a time share operation in the south of Spain, and other little businesses here and there. There are interesting records of on-going payments to a person identified as "M." – Mr Moore, I presume – between 1984 and 1991, which I should think Miss Lyon might find enlightening, if not unexpected. But I have only just got here to find Ernie with this wealth of information, and I've scarcely even had time to scan it. If we can dispense with the details temporarily – what have you done with Mrs Fisher?'

I looked at him hard and said, 'She went from the hospital to her son's house in Hampstead, and I managed to catch up with her there. She doesn't trust policemen. Frank and Andy's people always had the police in their pockets, and she's afraid that Moore can find her through his contacts in the Met. She's frightened of him.' When I was sure I had his undivided attention, I let him see me glance at Ernie. It was unfair to involve him in hiding Lal's present whereabouts from Diane Lyon, even if I had committed myself to doing that.

Barnabas nodded fractionally. 'She may have good cause. I have to tell you that the young man at the newspaper has a very different angle on this whole business. To him, this is primarily a scandalous saga of incompetence not to mention blatant corruption in the Metropolitan Police which has been ignored, hushed up and denied by the upper ranks for several decades. He informs me that they have been making a new attempt recently to tackle . . . can I smell something?'

I said, 'I need to change Ben, but I need to talk to you too. Is our policeman still upstairs?'

'There is very little privacy up there,' Barnabas admitted. 'I had always assumed that when I commenced a life of criminal deception I would do so in slightly larger premises, with the police conveniently elsewhere. I suppose you have a suggestion?'

I told him that nothing came to mind at once except perhaps bathing and feeding my child and then seeing whether he wanted a nap. Barnabas hesitated, then abandoned the files to

Ernie. 'Perhaps,' he suggested, 'if Mrs Digby were to take over from you . . . ?'

I said that she would be coming back soon and that he would be able to enjoy spending some time with his grandson until her arrival freed us to take a walk around the corner. It was the best I could think of for the moment.

Upstairs, on the settee, hidden behind the sports pages of the *Evening Standard*, yet another uniformed figure sprawled. As the three of us arrived abruptly he scrambled to his feet looking flustered and said, 'PC Peters, Mrs Hoare. I hope I'm not in your way?'

I made polite noises which didn't include enlightening him about my marital status, discovered that he was going to be with us until he was relieved at six o'clock, and told him to stay put. Then Barnabas, Ben and I retreated into the bathroom and shut the door. Barnabas seated himself on the edge of the bath and sank into his private thoughts. Ben and I did what was necessary.

'The next step,' Barnabas said abruptly, 'is to amalgamate the information we've got from various sources. Compare and collate names, dates and facts from all that you and Mrs Digby and I know and those new computer files reveal.'

I was unenthusiastic. Maybe the whole business was starting to get to me. Maybe I felt too pressured to have enough patience for my father's proper research methods. Ben and I set about washing our hands, and I said tetchily that I thought we had a pretty full picture without going into all that. The encrypted files gave facts and figures and would presumably form a basis for Doug Moore's prosecution, when and if they caught him. 'It's all down to Diane Lyon locating Moore. It's clear from what Lal said that he's a thug. He was after the bearer bonds Frank had. He killed Frank to get them.'

'So you think he has them now?' Barnabas asked slowly.

I said briskly that it seemed most likely he and Andy had taken them away from Frank, and that the two of them had quarrelled over the spoils. That I couldn't care less about who had done what to whom ten years ago. That it was a police job. A thought struck me. 'Why aren't you saying this to me, rather than the other way round? You usually moan about my not minding my own business.'

'You are *quite* wrong about this,' Barnabas said abruptly; then his expression changed, and I knew he was sorry he had spoken. But he didn't need to go on because I'd started to feel uneasy even while I was laying it out. If Moore had got his hands on the bonds, having killed two people for them, why was he still hanging around London setting fire to my car when he should have flown to — where had Lal said? Palma? — at top speed with the loot? Reluctantly I accepted the facts: I'd got into a mental rut about Moore and it had stopped my thinking clearly. Maybe I'd needed to believe my own version because it ended so comfortably.

The doorbell gave a blip; I handed Ben over to my father's supervision and headed for the stairs, bumping into Peters coming the other way. It was only Phyllis. I introduced the two of them, then grabbed her arm and bundled her into the kitchen, where Barnabas was strapping Ben into his high chair and wondering aloud whether there was any food in the house.

I shut the kitchen door and leaned on it to hiss, 'Is she all right? Did she say anything?'

Barnabas was looking from one of us to the other. He said, 'Where?'

Phyllis whispered, 'Our . . . my place. She's all right. I said I'd bring her some money. She's got this idea about being able to get away if she has to. I don't think she'll stay there on her own for long. I don't know whether we should let her go, Dido.'

I didn't think we were going to be able to stop her. Not short of tying her to a chair. I wondered uneasily what Diane Lyon was doing at this moment and whether the raid on the depot had come up with anything. If we could reassure Lal that Moore was in custody . . .

I needed to make a phone call and said so.

Phyllis nodded. 'Meantime, I'll find something for Ben's lunch, if you like.'

'Then I'll go downstairs. I'm going to give Ernie a chance

to go round the corner for ten minutes – he must be hungry. He'd better have some money, too . . . I may have to go to the bank.'

'I think there's enough cash in the house,' Phyllis said. Her tone was dry. She had put some water on to boil; now she slipped away and returned from the bedroom with the little bundle of notes, Frank's emergency hoard. I accepted a couple of them and was heading for the stairs as the phone rang in the sitting room. When I picked it up, a familiar voice said gruffly, 'Dido?'

I struggled with the sense that something had gone wrong again. 'Paul, I was just going to phone you. Did you find anything?'

'I'll tell you another time. Look: I've just been told that you have Mrs Fisher there. Is that true?'

'No, of course it isn't! What do you mean, you were "told"? Who says so?'

'Somebody up at Number Three Division was talking about it. Palmers Green told Lyon. She's angry.'

I leaned against the sideboard and instructed myself not to overreact. 'How could I possibly be hiding Mrs Fisher here? Do you think this constable of yours is blind?' I threw the man a glance and made sure that he was listening. 'Maybe I've bribed him to join our conspiracy?'

There was a moment of silence before he asked, 'Who is it?'

'Peters. Constable Peters.'

Another fraction of silence. When the voice came back, it was conciliatory. 'I wasn't thinking. Peters is a good man, he'll take care of you. I wonder how the word got started?'

I said that I couldn't care less. 'But I do have some real information for you. You know that computer disk of Frank Digby's I gave you? Have you passed it on to somebody? It's full of encrypted files, and I know what the password is: tell them to try his sister's name – Elaine.'

The voice was satisfactorily startled: 'Are you guessing? How do you know? Did Mrs Digby . . . ?'

'Sheer brilliant guesswork,' I said quickly. 'As soon as I

realised that "Lal" was a nickname, I made the connection.'

'Miraculous,' he said a little shortly. 'I'll pass it on. Dido . . . ?'

'Yes?'

'Listen, I'll get back to you inside half an hour.'

'Ring my mobile. I don't know whether I'll be upstairs or in the shop, but I don't want this phone waking Ben up just as he drops off.'

Paul's voice, as he was saying goodbye, told me that his attention was already elsewhere. I sent my child a mental apology for using him as an excuse and went on to deal with the next problem.

CHAPTER TWENTY-NINE

Cold Reality

———◆———

Watching Ernie's familiar back, all big puffa jacket, combat trousers and boots, reach the end of the street and turn the corner, I felt a pang of doubt and realised that I'd been feeling safer merely because he was on the spot. I almost ran after him and asked him to come back, but I pulled myself together, slunk back into the shop and locked up. Then I went into the office, where cold reality hit me over the head.

We hadn't seen a serious customer in the shop since last Saturday, probably because we'd been closed most of the time. Ernie and Barnabas had been busy chasing coded files which had absolutely nothing to do with me or a bookshop or even books – except, I admitted sourly, accounts ledgers that were two hundred years too modern to be of any interest to an antiquarian book dealer. A stack of folding wooden shelf units and a pile of cardboard boxes blocked the way to the packing table and reminded me that I'd stopped halfway through unpacking the books I'd brought back from the fair. At the moment, it felt about as likely that I was going to get around to replacing the rest of them on the shelves as that I'd break into a tap-dance. Not that there was any room here to tap-dance, anyway.

In a pile out of reach on the packing table sat five unopened parcels of various sizes, presumably delivered some time during the past two or three days without my having noticed them, and all of them hopefully containing books which I had ordered from postal catalogues just before my life collapsed. I could feel self-pity welling up. Beside them was today's second post, which Ernie or Barnabas had thoughtfully sorted into two piles: catalogues in the one (which I should already have opened and read through), and envelopes in the other one, presumably containing things like offers and orders and, with a little luck, cheques from contented customers. Business. Nobody was doing it, nobody was going to do it if I didn't and, damn it, I didn't even *want* anybody else to be doing it!

I kicked a cardboard box and fought through to grab the mail, balanced the computer keyboard on top of the monitor to free up some space on the desk, and told myself that I wasn't going to be thinking about anything but books for the next hour. Really. I unwrapped a little pile of tasty catalogues: natural history, modern firsts, travel and illustrated, Weiner, Pollak, nineteenth-century, Quaritch's twentieth-century literature. I found a pen, sat down, and opened the first of them: Alberti, Aragon, Azorin, Bassani, Beckett . . .

I was deciding that I couldn't quite afford the 1605 Francis Bacon that a dealer in Somerset was offering while I started to divide the contents of the smaller envelopes into piles for payment, reply, and a visit to the bank with the paying-in book, when a rattle at the street door made me look up. Ernie was back, flourishing a fat little carrier bag at me. It looked like kebab and chips this time. I ignored the rumble in my own stomach, grabbed my jacket, checked that I had both sets of keys and the little bundle of folded bank-notes, and rushed towards the door. I had accomplished something, and Paul hadn't phoned back yet, and it was time to find out what Lal was doing over there on her own. Lal was the key. I didn't trust her, but I had the money to deliver as my excuse to check up.

Pulling up outside the flats reminded me that only yesterday my lovely blue Citroën had sat in exactly the same space that was now occupied by this red midget. I dragged my mind away from useless regrets. The windows of Phyllis's unit showed no sign of life, no lights. At least Lal was being discreet. The rows of cars parked on either side of the street all seemed to be empty. Good. I slid out on to the pavement and remembered how to use the locking system. Maybe I'd have remote-control central locking on my new car, when I got one – it would be useful for loading and unloading heavy boxes. I walked up the path to the entrance and let myself in with Phyllis's key. The stairs were deserted all the way up and the glass shades still hadn't been replaced. No sound was coming from the Digbys' place. It could have been empty. *Doubly good*, I told myelf. *Nobody can possibly guess that she's here.* I rang the bell which, as I'd anticipated, was not answered. Then I opened up with the second key, stood in the doorway and called softly, 'It's all right, don't worry. It's just Dido . . . Lal?'

The note was sitting on the hall table, and the reason the place was so peaceful was that it actually was empty. Lal must have found the small scrap of blue notepaper in some drawer. It had been crumpled up, as though for a moment she had been in two minds about leaving it. I held it flat to the light from the landing behind me and made out words written with a ballpoint pen in a clumsy, square script: 'Sorry Phyll and thanks for the help Got to go I got the Tenner you lent me, I'll let you have it back soon.' It wasn't exactly a surprise, but I wondered anyway how far she thought she could get on ten pounds.

Unless somebody had come and taken her away.

I shut the door behind me and went exploring.

The living room was not as we had left it. Somebody had searched the place once more, shifting the cushions around, pulling out the drawers, leaving the sideboard doors open, scattering a stack of magazines and dumping the books from a shelf into a heap on the floor. I made a circuit through the other rooms and found the same story. Things were worst in Frank's office – naturally – where the drawers had been left half open and various papers and files were back on the carpet again. In the untidy bedroom, some of the drawers were also open, with clothes stirred around inside them, and the wardrobe door was ajar. Even the mattress was crooked on the base. The coverlet was rumpled, as though somebody had been lying on top of it, and I could still see the imprint of a head on the pillow.

I sat down on the edge of the bed and thought about it. This wasn't the kind of search that had been done the other night, and Moore must realise by now that the bonds weren't here, so I'd put my money on Lal herself. Only where had she gone after she had turned the place over, and why?

I pulled myself together and followed a burst of music back on to the landing. It was coming from one of the doors on the other side of the stairs. Somebody was at home. Presumably if Lal had not gone of her own accord, they would have heard a fuss? I double-locked Phyllis's flat and went over to ring the bell. The door was opened by a tall, skinny twenty-year-old whose sweat-shirt, split jeans and glasses shouted 'student'. Presumably one of those very students who were always borrowing tea bags or cups of milk. To judge by the rich herbal smell drifting out, they were in to smoking something other than tea bags today.

I gestured at the Digbys' door. 'Hi! Phyllis asked me to come and pick up her friend who's staying here, but she doesn't seem to be in the flat after all. You haven't seen or . . . heard anything from across the landing, have you?'

He grinned down at me and inspected the scenery. 'Hi! Um . . . yeah, there was this blonde woman coming out of there just when I was coming home. I'm John, by the way.'

'And I'm Dido. Did you notice the time, John?'

My new friend thought it had been about two o'clock. I learned that Lal had been on her own, wearing a green coat and carrying a handbag. The coat sounded like Phyllis's best, which made me wonder what else she might have lost. At any rate, Lal's departure seemed voluntary. I thanked John and left for home, half fuming, half relieved, entirely fed up with Lal Fisher.

Back in the shop, I sent Ernie upstairs with instructions to let Phyllis, though not our resident policeman, know what had happened and then stay there and have a cup of tea or something. I wanted the office to myself for a bit. I wanted to think. Failing that, I could at least sit in peace and do some mindless and useful work, like listing the cheques to pay in at the bank. It was too late to get there today, but I could have them ready for the morning. And there was still one catalogue I hadn't even opened. I settled at the desk and looked for the paying-in book.

When the light grew too dim to read by, I came to, switched on the desk lamp and, by reflex, looked at my watch. Nearly five. The rectangle of sky visible through the little pane of glass over the door to the yard was dark. The wind was rising, and there was an icy draught blowing in from somewhere. I pulled my jacket over my shoulders and decided to finish quickly and go upstairs.

I was entering a couple of new invoices in the ledger when my attention was caught by headlights sweeping through the darkened shop. Looking down the aisle to the front door, I watched the big silver car that I'd last seen in the Fishers' driveway slide to a halt across the road just in front of my modest hire car. I froze. The driver's door opened and Paul Grant started across. I reached my own door and got it open just as he arrived and bowled into the shop.

'Dido, we need to talk.' He clearly meant urgently.

All right: I agreed with that. I pointed. 'What's that thing doing here?'

He shifted. 'What? Oh, the car. That's one of the things I have to explain. Who's upstairs? Is the constable still there?' I nodded. 'Then we'd better stay here. Let's get out of sight.'

Oh yes, something had gone wrong. Good! I thought I could see a little truth-telling ahead.

Once in the office, he tipped a stack of cardboard boxes off the visitor's chair, turned it around and planted himself on it, leaned forward, crossed his arms over the back, and showed alarming signs of falling asleep in that position. I was about to protest when he blinked and asked, 'You don't have any coffee down here, do you?'

'Just instant. I don't think there's any milk, though.'

'It'll do. Sugar. Please. I don't think I've had any sleep since Tuesday.'

I repressed the observation that this made two of us and went to fill the kettle at the little sink and rinse out two slightly used mugs.

'It'll take a couple of minutes. Paul, what's up?'

He repeated stupidly, 'What's up? . . . Sorry. Can't help it.

Wait: where is Mrs Fisher? Have you got her? Don't play games with me, the silly cow may really be in danger.'

I just stopped myself shouting at him. 'I haven't got her, but I'll tell you where she was, if you'll tell me what's happened. We've already agreed that she can't be upstairs, remember? You can go up and ask your constable if you like. Now, just say what this is all about. What's happened since you phoned me?'

'Isn't that thing ever going to boil? All right. We went up to the depot and had a look around, and we found two things. There was a patch in the corner round the back of the yard where somebody'd had a bonfire. The usual little bits were left: scraps of charred paper, bits of old cardboard, paper clips, fasteners – that kind of thing. We picked up what we could, started to look. Police documents . . . court documents . . . has to be the missing evidence from that Old Bailey case. Then we found . . .'

He faded out. I said loudly, 'Go on.'

'We found a corner in the loading bay where there were traces of blood and flakes of dark paint from a car. Same paint as on Mrs Fisher's car. Did I say her Toyota was damaged? When we found it in the garage with Fisher's body inside, the offside wing had been damaged by another car – black paint. Did I tell you that? Somebody took Brunton and the Toyota up to the depot. Must have happened on Monday after six o'clock, when they'd shut for the night. Covered by a mobile security outfit, so they don't keep a night-watchman. Must have needed a couple of them to do it. Fisher had to be involved – it was his place. Talked to Brunton and beat him up, put what was left of him into another car and took him away, dead or alive then, and dumped the body a couple of hours later, maybe. With me?'

I was, though with difficulty. I was also trying not to think of Frank's face as it was when I'd seen him lying in the morgue. I think I've probably seen a couple of violent deaths too many.

The kettle switched itself off at last, so I dumped double spoonfuls of coffee granules into two mugs, filled them, and added sugar to make them palatable. On second thoughts, I added another sugar to one, stirred it, and handed it over.

'Paul?'

'Mmnn?'

'Were there any signs of something else there, burned along with the court evidence, maybe by mistake?'

'Such as?'

'Lal Fisher says that the money they got for the gold bullion was converted into bearer bonds in Switzerland. Frank brought those back to England in 'ninety-one, just before he was arrested; he had time to hide them in the Fishers' household goods that were stored at the depot. They were sent to the new house this winter, along with the Fishers' other things. I don't imagine Andy knew anything about it, and Lal thought she just had Frank's boxes of old papers. The problem was, Moore must have dumped the missing prosecution evidence at the depot too, it probably seemed the safest place, and they were taken to the house along with Frank's stuff. So Lal was trapped between Moore and her family when Moore turned up asking about the bonds, getting too close. She panicked and asked Frank for help. Frank took most of the stuff away on Monday. So – were the bonds burned by mistake with the rest of the stuff? Because Moore and Andrew obviously never found them.'

Paul said, 'Oh, damn it!', and we both watched the mug slip from his fingers. The coffee splashed violently over our feet. 'Where have you got that bloody woman?'

I couldn't milk the situation any longer. I sipped my own coffee experimentally, decided I wouldn't drink it, and told all. 'Lal took a taxi from the hospital to her son's house. She'd mentioned him to me, so that's where I went looking for her. She was afraid to stay there – she doesn't trust you people and she had to hide from Moore. We loaned her Phyllis's flat. When I went back a little while ago, she'd gone. She left this.' I pulled the scribbled note out of my pocket and handed it to Paul, who read it with suddenly wakeful, red-rimmed eyes.

'So she's out there somewhere? . . . Do you have *any* idea where?'

I told him I didn't because I really didn't know for sure. Personally, I'd finished climbing through other people's windows, though if I'd been DI Paul Grant I would certainly have considered sneaking back to Verwood Avenue to check out the house. Maybe they already had. My attention returned to the car parked across the road.

'Why are you driving Andy Fisher's car?'

His look was bleak. 'Bait. Lyon's idea. She's sent me here to tell you what's going to happen. My instructions are to leave the Fishers' car outside your door. Try to make it look as though she is here – Dido, if you're lying about this you'd better tell me now. We assume that Moore is still keeping an eye on this place, and if he sees the car he'll think she's gone to ground with you and Mrs Digby. With any luck at all, he'll turn up to get her. You know she probably has those bonds herself, don't you? No, there was no sign of anything like that in the fire. Anyway, Lyon's using Mrs Fisher for bait, and she's got cars staked out all around you. We can't put our people into this street because it's quiet, they'd be too conspicuous here. We've parked plain cars and vans in the streets running past the ends of yours, just this side of the junctions with Upper Street and the Essex Road. You're in a box with our people at all the exits. All right, so we didn't know about the bonds, but we realised that Moore and Fisher were after something like that, after what happened at the Digby flat. And nobody but your lady friend could possibly have them now. I'd say that Digby gave them to her before he was killed. Unless he went to dump them some place that she knew about. It's the only explanation.'

I could feel a slow anger rising. 'So, my family is supposed to sit here quietly as bait for the murderer, so that you can find out whether you'll manage to catch him this time? Well, *what* a bright idea!'

Paul yawned. Suddenly I hated every inch of him.

'Dido, look, you have me down here and Peters upstairs, and he'll be replaced at the end of his shift with one of Lyon's own team. They're armed.' I blinked and wondered whether I was supposed to find that news comforting. It wasn't. 'I'll stay here until you're safe. We're going to send in a couple of taxis to get you and the others out at the end of Peters' shift. I want you to go upstairs and pack everything you'll need for a couple of nights. You've got less than an hour to get ready, so you'd better move. We'll put you up at a hotel well away from here.'

'And wait for the rat to walk into your trap? What about Lal?'

'We'll cross that one when we get there,' Paul said. 'Will you go up and tell them to get ready, please? *Please?* I'll stay down here. I don't want to show my face in the street unless I have to.'

I said, 'I'll bring down some milk when I come back.' I was so angry I could hardly breathe.

CHAPTER THIRTY

Moving Out

————◆◆◆————

Obviously Barnabas had decided that our guard was harmless, because when I appeared in the doorway of my sitting room I found him settled at my desk, while the constable shared the settee with Ernie. Peters was scanning the opening credits of *Neighbours* on the television. Ernie was sitting well away from him looking self-conscious. Engrossed in his reading, my father ignored them both. He had sorted his photocopies into piles and laid them out in circles on the desk and the floor around it, turning that area into a faint imitation of his own living room, where books and papers normally fill most flat surfaces. He had found some sheets of lined paper in one of the drawers, and I could see that he was making notes in the form of lists. There were several sheets of longer notes in his own handwriting, to which he was referring.

All three of them glanced up.

Out of sheer habit, I started to manoeuvre – and then remembered that there was no point any more. 'Paul Grant is downstairs,' I said shortly. 'Diane Lyon's come up with the truly bright idea of luring Moore here and arresting him, and they're evacuating us at six o'clock. They're putting us into some hotel for a while. Where's Phyllis?'

My question was answered by the sound of splashing from the bathroom: presumably she and Ben were keeping each other amused.

'They are not putting me into a hotel,' Barnabas observed

calmly. 'I suppose I had better go home. Dido, we might talk? I have a list of . . .' His eyes moved briefly to the constable's face, but our guard was politely pretending to focus on the teenage anguish that filled the screen, and my father visibly made up his mind that there was no longer any point in secrecy. He went straight on: '. . . all the names of the people involved in the bullion hijacking and the subsequent investigation. I want you to look at it and help me to remember what we have been told about their current whereabouts. There has been an astonishing level of mortality among the group. I suppose that might be an occupational hazard, but it does seem excessive in a group of retired criminals. I have started to wonder a little.'

But I was dealing with four or five other problems and couldn't begin to imagine having the time to speculate about the historical fate of a bunch of minor crooks. I said rapidly, 'I have to talk to Phyllis. We'll need to pack for the three of us for at least two days. Ernie, I'm going to give you the money for the time you've done this week, and I don't think I'm going to need you at the weekend. I'm not sure when I'll get back here to open the place. I'll phone you when that happens.' I could feel my temper rising again and decided to shut up now. Turning on my heel, I headed towards the back of the flat, checking my wrist-watch as I went. If we were going to be ready by six, we'd have our work cut out.

Three minutes later, I obeyed Phyllis's pleas and left her to deal with the domestic side of our departure. Pouring out enough dry cat food and drinking water to support both Mr Spock and a pride of lions for a month, I grabbed the remains of a carton of milk from the fridge and ran downstairs balancing it on the pile of scribbled notes that Barnabas thrust at me as I left. The shop was in darkness, only the light in the cracks of the office door showing that someone was inside. I let myelf in and navigated down the aisle in the dark, to find that Paul had moved to the comfort of my desk chair and was face down in the cata-logues, snoring slightly.

I refilled the kettle, plugged it in, switched it on, and was considering kicking one sprawling leg when he woke up with a start.

'Dido? What time is it? Are you ready?'

'About a quarter to. They're packing. Well, Constable Peters is only watching television. We'll have to drop my father and Ernie off somewhere safe when we leave here. The rest of us are with you.'

There was something in my voice that made him blink and sit up straighter. 'What's wrong?'

'Paul, you're still asleep! How long is it going to be before this mess is sorted out and I can get back here? You do realise, don't you, that I'm going to make a stink about that woman deliberately putting me and my family in danger?'

He groaned. Then he laughed. 'What woman is that? I can tell you that the Commissioner would say it's the pot calling the kettle black. Let's start with *you* conspiring to pervert the course of justice, conspiring to conceal evidence, conspiring to conceal the whereabouts of a major witness – if we're being charitable about her – and obstructing the police in the execution of their duties at the scene of a murder . . .'

'It's unprofessional!' I yelled.

'It's taking a bloody long time to boil,' he muttered. 'Did you switch it on?'

We both looked at the kettle, which sat stubbornly silent on top of the filing cabinet. I went over and felt the side. Warm. 'It's old,' I said stiffly. 'It takes a while to heat up.'

Paul said, 'She doesn't have the funding to run this kind of operation round the clock for more than about two days. If it hasn't worked by then, he's probably gone anyway. You'll be back here by Saturday morning, so you'd better hope we can find our happy couple before then and discover which of them is the villain. Or maybe they're in cahoots?'

I said that Moore was the one who had beaten her up, and he said vaguely that maybe she liked that kind of thing because some women do, and a kind of sizzle started coming from the kettle.

He was looking at the papers I'd dumped on the desk.
'What's this?'

'Barnabas's notes,' I said coldly. 'He's been researching old
newspaper accounts of the bullion raid. In fact, he went off today
and researched one of the reporters who wrote them. I'm
supposed to be reading that lot and seeing what I can make of
it while we're twiddling our thumbs in a hotel bedroom.'

'Are you?' he said. His voice was vague. He had picked
up one sheet with 'Fatalities' printed across the top in
Barnabas's decisive capitals, and had apparently just found something there that made him frown when we heard a rap on the
glass of the street door. Paul looked up. He said slowly, 'It's
early.'

I switched off the lights as a precaution and opened the door
to look down the length of the aisle. The figure outside was
vaguely familiar. When he moved back so that the streetlight
shone on the top of his head, I recognised him, although he
wasn't in uniform.

'It's all right – I know him. He's stationed at Palmers Green.
He's on Frank's case.' Something must have happened, because
the constable seemed to be off duty. The idea of a sudden break-
through came to me, the hope that maybe after all we could stay
here and get on with our lives, and I rushed towards the street
door. My hand was on the knob as Paul called from behind me,
'Wait a minute! Let me get it.'

I ignored him and opened up. The young, red-headed
constable – Mathews – smiled at me as he stepped inside.

'Miss Hoare? I was hoping I'd catch you. I've been sent to
ask if you'd mind answering a couple more questions. Won't
take a minute – if you don't mind?'

There was a movement behind me. The constable heard it
too. Then he must have caught sight of Paul in the shadows
behind the central row of bookcases.

Paul said, 'You're stationed up at Palmers Green, aren't you?
DI Grant, Islington CID. What is this?'

'Sir,' Mathews said. He moved a step closer and held a hand
out towards me. 'Miss Hoare, do you see what I have here?' In

the darkness, it was just a lump. He flashed a look over my shoulder. 'Detective, you may not be able to see it from where you're standing, but I have a handgun and I'm pointing it at the lady. Miss, you'll be all right. There's somebody outside in the car who just wants to talk to you. Detective, I'm sorry, you're going to have to come along.'

I looked sideways through my display window. Across the street at the kerb, facing north, with its headlights off and its engine running, I saw the angular lines of a high, black, off-road vehicle with tinted glass windows. It had apparently materialised from thin air just ahead of the late Andy Fisher's silver car. The light from the streetlamp glinted on the patch of bare metal on the front nearside wing, and I knew exactly what I was seeing.

'Just go outside,' Mathews said.

I stepped out as calmly as though nothing was real. Paul came close behind. I heard the shop door bang.

The light from one of the upstairs windows threw a rectangle on the road at the edge of the light from the streetlamp. The two made a pool of brightness on the wet pavement. I glanced up at the window. Behind me, Mathews' polite voice said, 'You don't want to call out. Nobody's going to be hurt, we just want to find Mrs Fisher. If she's staying here with you and Mrs Digby, we want to talk to her. We have an offer to make.'

I bit my tongue. Paul said, 'What kind of offer?'

Mathews ignored the question. 'So I'd like you to walk over now and ring your doorbell. Whoever comes to the door, be careful what you say. Don't try to warn anybody, just say that Mrs Fisher is to come down for a minute.'

I thought of Ernie and the police constable upstairs, a few feet away. Ernie and Peters, and Paul had said Peters was a good man. I faltered. My mind was working with all the speed of a bug in molasses.

Mathews said suddenly, 'What's wrong?'

'We're looking for her too. You must know she's not here.' Paul's voice was harsh.

Mathews kept his eyes on me and said, 'Do I? Who *is* up there?'

I faltered, 'My family. A couple of my employees . . .'

'A police guard?' the constable suggested abruptly.

I wasn't sure what I ought to say, but Paul said, 'Yes.'

We stood silently in the middle of the empty road. I watched Mathews smile oddly and glance over at the black vehicle.

'I thought so,' he said tonelessly after a moment. 'Walk over and open the driver's door, Miss Hoare, and get behind the wheel. It's left-hand drive, so you want this side. Wait a minute!' I waited, frozen, as he came around to me. He pushed something into my hand. I held two flattened rings awkwardly without looking at them. Metal. Warm from being in his pocket.

'Now,' Mathews said gently, and I reached like a puppet for the door handle.

CHAPTER THIRTY-ONE

Illusion

I sat very straight in the driver's seat and wondered what was wrong with me because although – obeying Mathews' quiet instructions – I had just handcuffed my right wrist to the top section of the steering wheel, part of me was blankly refusing to believe that any of this was happening.

The handcuff made it impossible for me to turn around. Or maybe I just couldn't risk a straight look. I reached across clumsily with my free hand to adjust the rear-view mirror so it reflected the back seat. There was enough light for me to see Moore's face. He was sitting on the far side of the car. If he had been directly behind me, I might not have been able to stand it.

I could feel something shaking. Mathews had supervised Paul's entry to the seat immediately behind mine, and the two of them were doing something. I couldn't see Paul's face, and something was pulling at the back of my seat. When Mathews slammed the door and walked around the back of the car, Paul remained invisible.

Moore said loudly, 'Don't bother, you won't do it. I had somebody handcuffed down there a couple of days ago, know what I mean? There's no way you'll get out of it. Cramped? You're taller than Frankie was. But I'm happier with you doubled up out of sight. Miss Hoare?'

I couldn't answer.

'Miss Hoare, can you drive an automatic car?'

I jerked my head.

'Good, because we'll be going a little ways. Can you reach the key?'

I tried, and found that the steering wheel was frozen, with the engine off, and the handcuffs kept me from reaching the ignition. I pushed forward a finger, fruitlessly. He grunted.

The passenger door slammed, and Mathews was beside me, fastening his seat belt. I could see his hand holding the gun loosely on his lap. He left it there and reached across to the ignition to switch it on. He replaced his hand on the gun. After a second, Moore said, 'Go on, then, carefully. No, we'll have the headlights on. Just don't draw attention. My colleague will show you where the switch is.'

Silently, Mathews touched a lever and the dipped headlights shone down the deserted road. I found the automatic shift and slid the lever into drive, and the car seemed to slide of its own accord into the middle of the road. Behind me, Paul was still.

At the junction with the next street I braked and waited, not even glancing left and right. Somewhere close, in both directions, police vehicles were supposed to be waiting for us. Waiting for Moore. Only now Moore had hostages. It seemed likely that nobody had thought of that possibility. Obviously they hadn't noticed him driving into George Street, so why would they notice him as we drove out? In the present situation I hoped they didn't. Of course, if Paul had been sitting upright so that they could see him, their stupid trap might have worked, and . . . I suspected that being shot would hurt more than anything that had ever happened.

I whispered, 'Which way?'

'We'll go out the way we came in. You know, Miss Hoare: straight across and into the council estate – the way you showed us the other morning, coming back from Frankie's place.' Hoare's voice was patronising. 'There are police vans down at the end of this road. No need to bother them.'

Something jerked at the back of the seat. Paul had woken up. I checked that the road was empty and drove forward, making a slight dog-leg, and rolled us into the narrow passage between two of the blocks of flats. I slowly skirted an overturned dustbin and asked, 'Where are we going?' My voice sounded odd.

'We're going to look for Lal. I'm sorry she wasn't there after all. So now you'll have to help us out a bit longer. She'll be back at the house, if I know the girl, with the lights off, packing up her nice things and some things that belong to me. We'll go and talk to her. When we get through the back gate here, you go along to Upper Street and turn right. Keep going straight up Holloway and Archway. Drive nicely. Mathews will set you right if you have any problems. Do you understand?'

I wanted to speak, but it didn't matter what I said. I tried to focus on driving nicely instead. That helped. I was still moving in a nightmare, but it helped.

We drove north. I drove. Moore had specified the main road, and we were caught in streams of heavy traffic. It felt to me like the middle of the night, and yet normal people were just going home from work and the last pale daylight still brightened the sky beyond the buildings to the left. I saw what the handcuffs were about. Nobody was going to jump out at a red light.

Waiting to edge on to the big roundabout at Highbury Corner I had time to look around me. Two feet away, behind the wheel of the neighbouring car, a woman was talking into a mobile phone. If I opened my window I could almost touch the hand that was holding it to her ear, but she wasn't looking at me.

'Watch it,' Mathews said softly, and I woke up and found that twenty feet of empty road had opened up ahead as the traffic edged forwards. I caught up.

'What are you going to do if Mrs Fisher is at home?' Paul asked suddenly. His voice was muffled.

The question remained unanswered. It was a good one, though. As though a valve had opened somewhere, I found that my mind was working again. Lal knew that Moore and Mathews had killed her brother. Or was that Moore and Andy? My mind hopped over the problem of Mathews, of where he came into it, because it was all too difficult. Anyway, Lal knew. *We* knew that they had killed Frank. Moore had just admitted it. Why had he admitted it?

I realised suddenly that I'd never really believed I was going to die, ever. It was time I grew up.

Just drive.

From somewhere low behind me, Paul was talking again in a flat, reasonable voice. 'We're pretty sure she doesn't have them.'

He got Moore's attention. 'Have what?'

'The bearer bonds,' Paul said conversationally. 'Not unless your mate had them at Verwood Avenue when you killed him, but we damned well didn't find anything there.'

I heard a dull sound. Paul was silent. It took me a moment to work out that Moore had casually hit him. There was a red light at the next junction, and I stopped for it. Maybe next time, if I rammed the car in front, they wouldn't bother to kill us before they ran away. Probably they'd just jump out. I thought that was our best chance.

'Shut the fuck up,' Moore said suddenly. 'Me kill Andy? What are you trying to pull, sonny? Me and Andy Fisher had our differences, but if I was going to kill him I'd've got around to it years ago. We were in business together for a long time. So his wife's a stupid old tart, so what? We came back to England for the bonds – that's just business.'

'If you didn't kill him,' Paul said, 'who did?' His voice was tight. Whatever Moore had done, it hurt.

Suddenly Mathews said, 'It's jammed solid up ahead. Isn't there some way of getting around? This is going to take all night.'

'Make a left,' Moore said after a moment. 'We'll try going through Kentish Town.'

I was driving up the middle of the road at the time, so I tried cutting sharply across the inner lane. And got away with it. Disheartened, I ignored the honking behind me and shot away into a quiet road lined with tall Victorian terraces.

'Watch it,' Moore warned. But it didn't sound as though he cared. I flashed a glance at him in the mirror. He had turned away from Paul and was staring tensely at the back of Mathews' head.

I was lost. The men were silent. Cutting through residential roads, without instructions, I tried to keep the car heading roughly northwards because I couldn't think of anything better to do. *Just be ready*, I thought. After a while, as the ground began to rise towards the heights of Highgate, there was the slope to help me; at each junction, I turned uphill. At some point I found myself in a road where the traffic was heavy again, a through route, and when the roadway narrowed and steepened, and the walls of a hospital rose to the right, I recognised the place.

A left turn took us into the main route through Highgate Village. Verwood Avenue was a mile or two ahead and time was running out now.

'You,' Moore said suddenly. 'What's the name again?'

'Grant,' Paul grunted. 'Islington CID.'

'You turned up at Frankie's flat the other morning, Grant. I remember you. You on the murder team?'

Paul said, 'Not then. I was told of a robbery at the flat, that's all. We hadn't tied that in with the body up at Trent Park.'

'Not then?' Moore prodded. 'Right. But you're in it now. And they think I killed Andy Fisher?'

Paul was silent for a moment. Then he said, 'If not you, then who was it? Mrs Fisher? Who else knew about the bonds? Was it about the bonds, or something different?'

'You ask a lot of questions,' Moore said slowly. 'Maybe you still think it goes with being a cop?' For a moment he sounded almost amused. 'Better not push it.'

I could feel a kind of rhythmic jerking behind me and guessed that Paul was trying to do something to free himself. Perhaps to cover any noise he was making he said, 'I'm still asking you who else but you could have killed Andy Fisher.'

I was driving on autopilot, because it had just struck me that there was something that I knew, or had started to know, or that Barnabas had said. Niggling. Or something I'd seen? Without stopping to think about it I heard myself say, 'And the others? What about the others?'

'What others?' Moore asked after a moment. He sounded surprised that I'd spoken.

It was coming back to me. 'That man who was convicted with Frank, who was found hanged in prison. I don't remember the name. Was he murdered? And wasn't there somebody called Vinnie who was shot in South America? And Lal said somebody was drowned in a swimming pool last year in Spain. There were others, too, weren't there? I can't remember all of them.'

From somewhere near my right elbow I heard Paul mutter, 'Shut up, Dido.'

I said loudly, 'It all started with the bullion raid, didn't it? And you never even saw the money from that, any of you?' I glanced in the mirror and saw Moore shifting in his seat. I wanted to giggle. He was looking out of the side window, and his lips were moving, so maybe I could try to distract him. Spook him. It looked as though it was down to me to get us out of this mess. I said softly, 'That whole business was jinxed, I guess.'

Moore said, 'You make your own luck, Miss Hoare, don't forget. Turn right at the next lights and take the second left.'

We drove silently along residential streets lined with big detached houses, turned left at a vast suburban church, and finally came to a T-junction.

'Left again.'

I obeyed, and said, really wondering about it all now, 'So many deaths. That started with the hijacking, didn't it? You made a mistake, and your partner was shot. What was his name?'

But it came to me even before I finished asking: I'd seen the dead policeman's name, it had been there at the head of Barnabas's 'Fatalities'. The feeling of confusion came back with a rush because there was something here that I didn't understand.

'Turn off the headlights,' Moore said, 'and swing straight into the next gate.'

I fumbled at the switch, the car became dark, and we were coming at the Fishers' house from the other direction. I turned late and shallow in the darkness, and hit the kerb with the front wheel, but the big off-roader just jounced over it and swerved up the driveway.

At my side, Mathews was releasing his seat belt. He was turning towards me, and my heart banged because his gun was coming up, but he went on twisting around until Moore shot him in the face with a noise that filled the car like a bomb exploding, and in the roar of that second I lost control and the car leapt ahead and hit the front steps and stalled and I couldn't hear anything at all now except the ringing silence in my ears.

CHAPTER THIRTY-TWO

You Make Your Own Luck

It was cold. Moore had left the passenger door open, and I could feel a raw wind gusting into the car. If I leaned forward I could just see Constable Mathews' legs on the ground where Moore had dumped the body, between the car and the house. At least his face was invisible from this angle.

Something touched my right arm. I jumped and whimpered; and because I heard the sound I realised that my deafness had been temporary. The relief made me shake.

'Dido?' A hand grasped my elbow hard. 'All right? Listen to me! *Listen!*'

I tried to speak, failed, breathed, said hoarsely, 'All right.'

'Listen: can you switch the engine on? Put the drive into neutral. Try it with your free hand. Reach through underneath the steering column.'

Instinctively I looked up at the front door. Moore had opened that with two violent kicks that had burst the lock and splintered the frame, then pushed inside, leaving it ajar. Lights were on somewhere in there. Moore and I had both been right that Lal would go home.

'Try!' Paul urged. His voice rose. 'You have to get us out of here right now.'

I pressed myself forward on to the wheel, which had frozen again when the engine stalled, moved my free arm painfully through the restricted space under the steering column, and tried to bend my wrist up and back. I could feel the metal of a dangling key brush the back of my hand. I heard myself whimper again and tried pulling back an inch, twisting harder. After a moment I gave up.

'I can't even touch it. You . . . ?'

'No way. Damn! I can barely reach your arm from this position.' He was silent for a moment. I went on staring at the doorway, which remained empty. 'I take it you don't have your mobile in your pocket?'

'It's back on the desk.'

He was silent again.

Stupidly, I started to apologise, but he interrupted: 'All right, listen to me. There's something you'd better know. You may be able to make use of it. He won't be as worried about you as he is about me. You might . . . try to make a deal with him. Remember he said he'd handcuffed Frankie here, to this bloody seat frame?'

For a moment I wondered what he was talking about.

'Dido, there's something underneath here in front of me, just beyond the frame. Underneath your seat. I've been trying to find out what it is without letting him notice. I've got something – it's made of stiff paper, with a sort of bellows end and what feels like a tape tie. There are papers inside. It could be the bonds. If Digby had the envelope on him when they stopped the car, maybe he managed to shove it underneath while he still . . . before anything happened to him. All right, I'm guessing, maybe Lal really does have them. But I think it's the bonds. Dido, you might have a chance to bargain. If you need to, offer him the bonds. Understand me? You'll just have to do your best, do you understand?'

Paul thought he was going to kill us.

The knowledge should have paralysed me. Instead, I felt a crazy relief just because this made it all simple. In the whole world, there was nothing I had to do except try not to be killed. Don't think of Mathews' face. Or . . . do, perhaps. Remember, because it made everything simple.

Inside the house, another light came on. Then others appeared upstairs – in the windows of the master bedroom.

'Why? Mathews – how?'

'Damn it, Dido, I told you to shut up.' He sounded more exhausted than angry. 'The name clicked five minutes before you remembered it. I've just seen it myself on those papers you brought downstairs. You really should have looked at them. The sergeant who was killed during the bullion hijack was Mathews. This one's father, I think. Moore's partner. Lyon had just started to wonder if Moore had arranged for his partner to be killed during the raid, because Mathews probably knew all about Moore's involvement, so he was dangerous. This Mathews must have been a teenager at the time. I wonder whether he guessed even then that his father's own partner had double-crossed . . . ? What was that?'

The lights in the upstairs windows had gone out, and another one came on to the left of them.

'Maybe the son was planning this ever since, brooding about all his father's old cronies sitting in their villas out of reach of the law, laughing. I wonder where this Mathews has been taking his annual holidays just recently? Somebody's certainly been killing the old gang off over the last couple of years – that clicked at Scotland Yard weeks ago when the Spanish authorities notified them about Pete White. That's why the files were reopened and Lyon was told to find grounds for Moore's extradition, get the whole business sorted out once and for all.'

I understood that Paul was talking, was saying these things, to keep me from panicking; even knowing that, I found that it worked. 'You mean *he* did it? He must have been the third man who raided the Digbys' flat! It was *Mathews* who was killing them all?'

'Except for Frankie, where he obviously had Moore's help. I'd say it was Mathews on the security video yesterday. He's the right build. I wonder if he made the mistake of keeping those gloves . . . ? Do you want to try again?'

I'd been watching the front door, but I pressed myself forward hard against the wheel and brushed against the keys with one knuckle. My bent wrist cramped agonisingly and I had to force it level to stop the pain.

'It's too much of a coincidence,' I objected as soon as I could speak, 'that Mathews should be working at the local police station just when Moore and the Fishers turned up again in his patch.'

Paul said, 'Don't you understand? Mathews got a transfer up here six months ago. He must have heard that the Fishers had moved into the area. Then he probably made contact with Moore. He must have hinted he was on the make and wanted to be useful. Son of his old friend? They didn't realise he'd guessed what Moore had done. Then he proved himself by helping Moore to kill Frank Brunton and getting rid of the body. Maybe Andy Fisher really did refuse to help Moore there.'

The light remained on upstairs, but there was a movement in the entrance hall, and then Lal seemed to burst out. She was barefoot and coatless, and her hair had fallen over her face, though not far enough to hide the blood that was seeping from a cut on the bridge of her nose. Moore was behind her. He bounced her hard against the side of the car, and then shoved her through the passenger door. When she was huddled beside me, silent, he slammed the door and climbed in behind. The gun was still in his hand. He said, 'We been sitting here too long. Drive.'

I slumped forward with my head against the wheel and whimpered, 'I can't reach the key.'

When he rose and leaned over me, I couldn't help shrinking. I kept my head turned away. The engine started. He said again, 'Drive. Turn us around. Make a right in the road.'

Now that the ignition was on, the frozen steering wheel would turn. I backed, telling myself to keep breathing. Slow, deep. In. Out. Again. I turned the big Jeep like vehicle in a circle and drove carefully through the gate, calmly now.

It was cold.

When we reached Colney Hatch Lane, Moore barked, 'Left here.'

'Where are we going?' I asked. My voice had got loud again.

Beside me, Lal caught her breath.

'You're not going much farther,' Moore said. 'Just follow directions and you two'll be free in a minute. As soon as I drop off at my place and pick up my passport, I won't need you any more. Lal will drive. Lal is coming with me. We're old mates. Andy wouldn't want me to leave her here for you to arrest her, would he, Lal?'

Nobody said anything. The arc-lights above the road bridge and the all-night supermarket loomed ahead. I was watching Lal out of the corner of my eye. She had straightened in her seat, and I saw that she was doing her silent crying again. This time I believed it, but it made me want to hit her, only Moore had already hit her and the hand nearest to her was shackled to the steering wheel.

The voice behind me said, 'You see that little right-turn lane in the middle of the road just ahead, before the lights? We're going to turn in by the repair shop there – see it?'

I nodded, signalled and pulled in very carefully. Cold. We had turned into a suburban street of respectable Edwardian terraces with little gardens in front of them, low brick walls, privet hedges, cars parked along both kerbs.

'Left at the next junction,' Moore said flatly. 'Then at the next one after, you're bearing right. Drive in along the side of the pub and keep going until you can get into a parking area on our left.'

I felt my seat jerk as Paul moved and knew that he was trying desperately to find a way to break the handcuffs or the frame they were attached to. I let up on the accelerator. We rolled gently along the narrow road, leaving room for a van that was coming in the opposite direction. The second junction was confusing, because the road markings made it look as though our road bent hard left. Then I saw the pub and shot into a narrow service road which led to three low council blocks. Opposite them, I saw the dark row of small trees with the unlit parking area behind them. Beyond a high fence at the far side ran the North Circular, bright and noisy with its high sodium lights and six lanes of traffic.

'Take the last entrance,' Moore said. 'Drive in, go right down to the end. That's it. See those brick storage sheds in the corner? Stop in front of them and turn the headlights off. Keep the engine running.'

I navigated, half blind, between the dark rows of parked cars and stopped just in front of a brick wall, sitting with my foot on the brake. Moore leaned over and did something, and I saw Paul sit up stiffly, rubbing his right wrist. 'I'm dropping you two off here,' Moore said. 'Miss Hoare . . .'

He stopped what he had been going to say. Then he giggled. After a moment, he said, 'I've cocked up. Know what, Lal? Mr Mathews handcuffed the lady to the steering wheel, and the key's still in his pocket. I guess you're our driver for the evening, Dido. Lal and I will just sit comfortably in the back seat, chatting about old times, and you can drive us all the way to Harwich to catch our boat, all right? You drive very well, I'll say that for you. Lal, you be good for a minute. Grant, you're leaving us here.' In the mirror, I saw him raise the gun slightly and hold it on Paul as he leaned over and did something behind my seat. Then he slid out of his own door and circled to the front of the car, always facing us. When he was in front of the bonnet he stopped and raised the gun. Through the windscreen, I could see the blackness inside the barrel that he was pointing at my face. He beckoned. Feeling sick, I listened to Paul open his door. I kept my eyes on Moore as Paul entered my field of vision. He stopped just out of the other man's reach. Then the gun turned away, pointing at the ground. The knot in my stomach didn't loosen. There was a movement at my elbow, and I knew that Lal was sitting up, watching them. Moore said something that was lost in the mutter of the engine. Paul didn't stir. Moore spoke again and shifted his weight on to his heel, turning, and Lal screamed, *Do something! He's going to kill us all!'*

Moore stepped backwards, the gun rising again as I jabbed my foot down on the accelerator and twisted the steering wheel hard, and the car jumped at him just as he fired. I saw the flash but didn't hear it because at that same instant we hit him and the brick wall together with a hollow, metallic crash. The engine stalled for the final time. There was no sound at all except for the whimpering from the seat beside me. Both men had gone.

When I finally got my door open, there was a body lying

on the ground just below me: Paul — eyes shut, face distorted, blood welling out from somewhere near his neck. I couldn't tell whether he was conscious. Or even alive. A little puddle of blackness started to spread very slowly out from beneath the car.

Beside me, Lal was fumbling for the door handle, trying to speak. I made out, 'Stop it, you've got to stop the bleeding or 'e'll die . . .'

How could I stop all that blood? When I hit the wall, the steering wheel had frozen again, but I wriggled out, trying to avoid the blood that was slowly pooling below my feet, and failing. I hung on to the wheel with my imprisoned hand and let my weight carry me down. Then I pulled Lal's lost black-and-white scarf out of my pocket and bunched it clumsily, one-handed, and kneeling in Moore's blood I looked, in the dim light, until I found the torn place in Paul's shoulder and pushed the bundle of cloth down against it with all my weight.

On the other side of the car the door opened. I thought that she was running away. Then over at the entrance to the nearest flats I heard her shrieking. Another voice shouted. Something. I knelt and pressed hard against the blood and closed my eyes, waiting for the sirens. After a while, they came.

CHAPTER THIRTY-THREE

On Balance

The room was dim but not dark, and so it must be morning. A cloudy morning. I turned my head and discovered that I could make out a few white dots drifting past the window. Snow. Stupid snow. I turned back and looked at the clock. The hands were just on eleven. I was fairly certain that there was something I was supposed to be doing, but just for the moment I couldn't think what or why. Saturday . . . it was Saturday, and I could hear that church bell fussing about some wedding or other. That must have been what woke me. It was Saturday, but the shop wasn't going to be opened up, not by me. I lifted my head to check the cot and saw that it was empty. Ben and Phyllis had probably started breakfast hours ago.

I decided to stay in bed for the rest of the day. I was tired, and outside this quiet room there were all kinds of darkness that I had no desire to face.

Something stirred and the door creaked. I watched it move and heard the steps on the carpet, so I was ready for the weight that landed abruptly on the foot of my bed. Mr Spock plodded heavily towards the pillow and examined my face with care. I whispered, 'I'm all right. Don't wake me. Settle down.' I waited for him to retreat and make himself a nest in the bend of my knees. Then I could get back to the business of sleeping.

When the phone rang in the other room, I opened my eyes and lay wondering whether I ought to answer it until I heard the movements in the hallway. The ringing broke off. I could hear Phyllis's voice. After a few moments, her steps returned and there was a whisper at the door. 'Dido?'

'I'm awake. What is it?'

'Your father.'

I closed my eyes. 'Is he all right? Tell him I'll phone him in a little while.'

The bedroom door swung wider. 'He says he's coming over in about an hour and to be ready because he's booked a table for twelve-thirty at that restaurant he likes, and do you want him to bring anything when he comes?'

I couldn't find the energy to argue, so I mumbled, 'No – thanks,' and closed my eyes again.

A moment later, a heavier weight landed on the bed; when I opened my eyes, Ben was scrambling vigorously over the duvet. He looked glad to see me. I sat up and grabbed him for a hug. Phyllis sat down watchfully on the edge of the mattress, and Mr Spock departed.

I said, 'I'm too tired to get up.'

'As a trained nurse,' Phyllis remarked slowly, 'I'd have to say that it's not a brilliant idea, you lying there being sorry for yourself. In my experience, you'd better get moving around doing ordinary things. You'll feel better if you go out and have something to eat. Why don't you have a bath and get dressed?'

'Maybe you should phone Barnabas and tell him I can't.'

'Of course you can,' Phyllis retorted. Then she offended me by laughing. 'Your father says he has a few questions he needs to ask you. Can you think of any way to keep him out of here? You might as well let him buy us all a spaghetti while you talk to him.'

I stopped feeling offended, heard myself giggle, and said, 'Phyllis, I killed a man. It wasn't an accident, I meant to do it. It makes me sick.'

She looked at me. 'You had to.'

'How do you know?'

'Lal told me.'

Lal – bloody Lal. I couldn't make up my mind whether I hated the very name or . . . Probably.

'Where is she? How is she?'

'Back in the flat for a couple of days. Said her daughter-in-law was asking too many questions, and she wants to be quiet. I told her she can tidy up the mess she left. She was cleaning out the kitchen cupboards when I saw her.'

'Really?'

'She's pretty practical.'

'More than you?'

'Me?' Phyllis said, and laughed.

I said hoarsely, 'I killed a man. Mathews and Moore killed Frank, Mathews killed Andy Fisher and God knows how many of the others, Moore killed him; but Moore's just as dead as the rest of them and I did that. You don't have to say that he deserved it, or that I had to – I know I had to, and it ought to help, it does help, but it doesn't wipe it out – what I did.'

'Then there isn't much I can say,' Phyllis agreed. 'Dead is dead, I know that . . . He underestimated you, didn't he? I don't know how you managed – I've seen people just waiting to go into the operating theatre who were shaking so hard they couldn't move, but you managed to save three innocent lives. He must have thought you were just a poor helpless woman. A lady, even.'

I wasn't sure, but I suspected that she was laughing at me ever so politely.

The doorbell rang, and the three of us looked at one another.

'That *can't* be Barnabas yet.'

'I'll get it,' Phyllis said. I listened to her going down the stairs and opening the street door. There was the sound of greetings, then questions, and a quiet conversation. It was a little while before I heard the door shut and her footsteps returning. In the meantime, Ben had decided to crawl into bed with me, and we propped ourselves up side by side against the pillows and prepared to face whatever it was.

It was flowers. Phyllis sidled into the room, eclipsed by a double arm-load of white and yellow roses with baby's breath and rampant greenery.

'That was Constable Peters,' she said, smiling. 'First time I've ever seen a police car delivering flowers. I'll put them in water, if I can think of something big enough to hold them.'

As far as I could remember, the only vase in the flat was the Waterford crystal that had belonged to my mother. It was a reasonable size, unlike this bouquet.

'The bucket?' I suggested. 'The new floor bucket? That's dark green, it might look all right. What is it? Did they have a whip-round at the police station or something?'

'There's a card,' Phyllis said. She obviously knew something. She extracted a long envelope from the greenery and handed it to me, and I undid the flap and slid out a lined filing card with the words 'North Middlesex Hospital' rubber-stamped across the top. The writing below was painful, having been done left-handed, but businesslike. It read: *I owe you. I won't forget. Paul.*

He *did* owe me. Facts are facts. I'd done the best I could, but now I was angry again. To put it plainly, something unforgivable had happened because I'd been set up by Diane Lyon, who should have known better, and betrayed by somebody I'd thought was my friend because – let's face it – because they had offered him promotion, hadn't they?

But I knew it was time to put the memory of my own helplessness, and of what I'd done, away in a box and stop looking at it for a while.

Time to get up.